Emma's
MARRIAGE SECRET

To: Jessica ~

May the words we write
bring glory to God!

Margo Hansen

:)

MARGO HANSEN

Emma's
MARRIAGE SECRET

✦ A NEWLY WEDS SERIES ✦

TATE PUBLISHING
AND ENTERPRISES, LLC

Published by Tate Publishing & Enterprises, LLC
127 E. Trade Center Terrace | Mustang, Oklahoma 73064 USA
1.888.361.9473 | www.tatepublishing.com

Tate Publishing is committed to excellence in the publishing industry. The company reflects the philosophy established by the founders, based on Psalm 68:11,
"The Lord gave the word and great was the company of those who published it."

Book design copyright © 2012 by Tate Publishing, LLC. All rights reserved.
Cover design by Kenna Davis
Interior design by Nathan Harmony
Edited by Amanda Bumgarner

Published in the United States of America

ISBN: 978-1-62024-109-7
Fiction / Christian / Romance
12.05.18

To Luke and Megan
Alexis, Rylee, Traven, and Zean

To Travis and Brooke
Jazlyn and Nyah

To Casey

And to Bruce
All my love

Acknowledgments

When I begin a story, I'm never quite sure where it is going to take me. This Newly family has often reminded me of my own family, and for that reason I will acknowledge the following:

Always my *Lord and Savior, Jesus Christ,* comes first. It is by His grace that any work of mine is accomplished and to His glory goes the praise.

To *Bruce:* Because you are my wonderful husband and a fantastic father, and without you this couldn't be possible. I love you.

To *Nancy, Joel, Miles, Murry,* and *Brent,* my siblings: Growing up with you was so much fun! Though I haven't based any of my characters on you, I do see some resemblances to you in them at times. Thank you for always being there when I need you.

To my brothers-in-law and sisters-in-law: *Randy, Ellen, Lynda, Lydia, Bonnie, Ted & Cindy,* and *Judi:* You complete our families and enrich us with your personalities, your talents, and your generous spirits.

To all my *nieces* and *nephews,* their *husbands* and *wives,* and all the *great-nieces* and *great-nephews*: What a family tree we've grown! If you see your name in one of my books, remember that I had it before you did!

And to *Tate Publishing:* my thanks once again for helping make a few dreams come true.

Sand Creek

Russ and Sky Newly

TYLER(M. JADYNE CRANDALL)

LUCY (M. BUCK RILEY)

DORCAS(M. CAVAN NOLAN)

EMMA

REX

ABEL

Hank and Randi Riley

BUCK(M. LUCY NEWLY)

DUGAN(M. MELODY WELLS)

MALLORY(M. MICHAEL TRENT)

JETHRO

PARKER

RODNEY

ROSS

Jonas and Bridget Nolan

ROONEY

BERNADETTE

Evan and Ella Trent

MICHAEL(M. MALLORY RILEY)

GABRIEL(M. LEIGH SHELDON)

ESTHER (M. DEXTER RIGGS)

MARTHA

JOHN

Duke and Angelina Tunelle

REBECCA(M. PERCY SCOTT)

ROBIN(M. PETER SCOTT)

RALPH(M. PHILIPPA GRAY)

RAY(M. CORA MACARDLE)

ROBERT

Harry and Gretchen Nolan

ANNIE(M. MONTY DAVIES)

CAVAN(M. DORCAS NEWLY)

Jasper and Martha Riggs

PERCY SCOTT(M. REBECCA TUNELLE)

PETER SCOTT(M. ROBIN TUNELLE)

DEXTER(M. ESTHER TRENT)

BERNARD(M. PEARL MADDOX)

CLAYTON

RHODA

PENNY

George and Janet Spencer

MALACHI

Gerald and Bertha Nessel

Taylor and Violet Gray

PHILIPPA(M. RALPH TUNELLE)

Bert and Gertie Davies

MONTY(M. ANNIE NOLAN)

Clyde and Belle Moore

Ray and Nola Hill

Grandville

Tyler and Jadyne Newly

EDMUND

Buck and Lucy Riley

Ralph and Philippa Tunelle

Malcolm and Hermine Tucker

PAUL

MARK

JESSE

Michael and Mallory Trent

MARCY

MARTIN

Bernard and Pearl Riggs

THOMAS

Ray and Cora Tunelle

MINERVA

Palmer and Hazel Granville

SIDNEY CRANDALL

Way Station

Gabriel and Leigh Trent	Dugan and Melody Riley
ADELE	JASON
	JANELLE

Chapter 1

Sand Creek

"So as the school year comes to an end, I want to thank each one of you for your attention and hard work. Just don't forget everything you've learned over the summer, okay? You are dismissed."

Emma Newly couldn't help the laugh that escaped from her lips at the sight of twenty-one eager children racing for the door. The clumping of shoes on the wooden floor together with the giggles and squeals of joy as the children made their escape was over in seconds. They were gone! Emma breathed a sigh of relief and felt the first stirrings of freedom seep in through the still open doorway.

School was over.

Quickly she gathered her belongings. The boxes of books and supplies stacked around her desk were ready to be put away in safekeeping during the vacation. She paused. Would she be the one to open them again in the fall to prepare for a new school year? A frown passed over her face. She had enjoyed teaching these last two years, but she was nineteen now. Wasn't there anything more exciting to do with her life?

She allowed herself a last appraisal of the one-room schoolhouse with its wooden desks, the raised platform for her own desk, the small stove that was too hot to sit close to but not hot enough to be away from. She turned to the hooks and shelves in the back, making sure that no belongings had been left behind by the departing children.

"What's taking you so long, Emma? I want to get home."

Abel, Emma's younger brother, barely stuck his head in the doorway as if he were afraid to walk in all the way and be imprisoned by the classroom again.

"Coming, Abel! I'm just doing a last-minute check before the school board puts away the supplies." Emma hurried to the door after her brother. She climbed into the wagon he had waiting, and they were off before she had time to get herself settled.

"You *are* in a hurry!" She laughed.

Abel grinned. "The farther away from that building I get, the better I feel." He glanced over at his sister's face. "Don't get me wrong, Emma. You're a great teacher and everything. It's just that, well, do you know what it's like to call your own sister 'Miss Newly' all the time?"

Emma's face sobered. "Has it been that hard for you, Abel?"

"Naw." He shrugged his shoulders, and Emma noticed how broad they were getting. At fifteen, he was already the size of their father. "The other guys give me a hard time now and then, but I'm okay. Are you teaching next year?"

"I don't know. I'd like to do something different, but what else is there for me to do in Sand Creek?"

"Aren't you never gettin' married?"

"Ever," Emma corrected, and then she laughed. "Whom would I marry?"

"Well, Penny Riggs says her brother Clay likes you."

Emma was startled. "Clayton Riggs?" Her mind pictured the good-looking boy she had grown up with. *Boy.* That's how she thought of him even though he was a year older than her. She still thought of him as a boy, not a man. She smiled uneasily at Abel.

"He needs to find someone who wants to be a farmer's wife and live on his father's farm. That's not what I want."

"There's always Rob Tunelle, then," her brother suggested.

"Martha Trent is sweet on Rob."

"Then what about—?"

"Abel." Emma stopped her brother. "You don't have to try to find me a husband. I'm not interested in getting married yet." Emma sighed. "Not for a long time yet." She looked ahead down the dirt road and then beyond to the hills in the distance. "I want to go places and see things. I want to see more than just Sand Creek before I settle down, don't you?"

She turned back to Abel again. "There's got to be some excitement to life, something more than just the everyday stuff."

"You want to go away?" Abel searched his sister's face with a worried expression on his own.

"Just for a while, Abel. I just want to see what else there is. But don't worry, I probably won't have a chance to go anywhere for a long time yet." They were coming up to the buildings that made up the town of Sand Creek. "Hey, we better stop at the post office for the mail. Mother's hoping to hear from Dad."

"Dad could tell you about other places, Emma. I bet he's been just about everywhere when he does his detective work." His face brightened. "Why don't you become a detective like Dad? You already know everything to do; he's been teaching you, hasn't he?"

Emma laughed. "Now that would be perfect! The trouble is the Pinkertons probably wouldn't hire a woman detective, little brother."

They stopped on the main street of Sand Creek, and Emma waited in the wagon while Abel ran in to pick up their mail. She studied the small town around her with critical eyes. No one would view Sand Creek as a thriving community. It was small, but it satisfied the needs of the people it serviced. Besides the post office there was a telegraph office, Nolan's hotel and mercantile, the church, the barbershop, the blacksmith, the doctor's office, and most recently, a dentist office.

Emma's eyes narrowed. Sand Creek wasn't much, but she loved it. Sometimes she wondered at her wanderlust when she had so much right here. But Sand Creek was a dead-end. It was pretty certain the railroad would never come to their small town. They would always have to travel to Freesburg to catch a train to get anywhere.

"Uh…good afternoon, Emma."

The hesitancy in the voice made Emma aware that she had been staring into space. She focused on the young man standing beside the wagon and felt a nervous twinge pass through her as she recalled her brother's recent remarks.

"Oh, good afternoon, Clay. How are you?"

"I'm fine, Emma, just fine. How about you?"

"I'm fine." She waited. Never in her life had Emma been nervous talking to any of the schoolboys she grew up with. She'd get Abel for this!

"How are your folks?" Clay Riggs continued. Emma noticed he was fiddling with the brim of his hat as he looked up at her. His overalls were well worn and dusty as if he had just come from plowing the fields, and the skin on his arms and face was already browned by long days in the sun.

"They're fine too. My dad's away on a case right now." Emma sought for something else to say.

"A case? Oh, he still does some of that detective work, doesn't he?" He dug his boot toe in the dirt beneath his feet. "My pa says it's foolish to go messin' in other people's affairs."

Emma's mouth tightened.

"I mean, it was different before your dad was married, like when he and Hank Riley helped our moms get here from the East. But after a man's married, he should settle down and stay at home." Clay didn't notice the rigid set of Emma's shoulders. "Anyway, Emma, I was kind of hopin'—" he cleared his throat "—you might allow me to call tomorrow evening." He glanced up at her again.

Emma stared straight ahead while she endeavored to control her temper. How dare he speak of her father in that way!

"Emma?" Clay tried to get her attention.

Emma heard a scrape of boots on the boardwalk and then her brother's voice, "Hi, Clay. What are you doing in town?" Abel handed Emma some envelopes as he climbed into the wagon beside her.

"Hey, Abel. Uh…Emma, I'll see you tomorrow, then?" Clay still questioned her.

Abel looked curiously at his sister's silent features and recognized the look she had on her face.

"Say, Clay, Emma's going to be pretty busy tomorrow, so you better not plan on anything. We'll be seeing you." Abel slapped the reins on the horse and left Clay Riggs staring after them, dust clouding his still figure.

They drove in silence for a while. Then Emma quietly said, "Thanks, Abel." She breathed a deep sigh.

"For goodness' sakes, Emma! What did he say that made you so mad? You haven't looked like that since you caught Ross Riley trying to smoke behind the schoolhouse."

Emma's face flushed. Her temper was well known to be displayed as what the Newly family members called "Emma's look." Her parents had schooled her often in her growing-up years on taking control of her temper and giving her feelings over to the Lord, but Emma still battled her emotions daily.

"He said some awful things about Dad, Abel. He said Dad was a fool for still working for his old boss after he got married. Well, I'll tell you, no young man is going to come calling on me if he thinks my dad is a fool!"

"Okay! Okay! You don't have to yell at me. I'm not the one who said anything."

"Sorry, Abel." Emma rubbed a hand over her forehead. "Let's forget about Clay Riggs and enjoy this beautiful spring day." She looked over the wooded countryside, the plowed fields, and the gurgling creek they were following. She closed her eyes and took a deep breath of the spring-scented air. "Mmmm! I feel better now." She opened her eyes and almost immediately grabbed Abel's arm.

"Stop!" she commanded in a whisper.

Abel pulled on the reins. "Why?" He too spoke quietly and looked in the direction his sister was pointing.

A deer was standing just inside the forest next to the road.

"Mother's been wanting some fresh meat. What do you think?" Emma asked excitedly.

"I've got the gun under the seat. I'll get him."

"Oh no you don't, Abel Newly! It's my turn and you know it."

"You're wearin' a dress, for Pete's sake!"

"I'll manage. You coming?" Emma reached for the gun and checked it over carefully. She quietly climbed out of the wagon, and then bending over she gathered her brown skirt up between her legs and tucked it into her waistband, making a baggy sort of pants out of it.

Strips of white petticoat and pantaloons peeked out of the folds of the gathered garment, and black button boots showed off her shapely ankles and stocking-covered calves. She winked at her astonished brother then quietly crossed the creek and edged closer to the animal. Abel followed, displaying the same wilderness skill that his sister had.

The buck was eating peacefully, yet aware of the approach of the two hunters as evidenced by his raised ears, which he twitched back and forth. As of yet, he hadn't raised his white tail, which would mean he was about to bolt. The sound of the wagon had not disturbed him, so apparently he fed by the roadside often, which would make it quite convenient, thought Emma, for loading him into their wagon.

Emma stopped a short distance from the animal and took careful aim. Abel remained motionless behind her; Emma could barely hear his shallow breathing in the still forest. Suddenly there was a noise to their right. The deer's tail shot up, and he leaped away from them, but Emma followed his movement with the rifle and shot. The deer dropped to the ground.

"Good shot, Emma! I thought he was going to get away when he took off like that. What scared him anyway? I didn't make any noise." Abel moved around her toward the fallen animal.

"I don't know. It came from over—oh!"

Emma still held the rifle, and instinct made her raise it. She stared at the furry creature she saw standing a short distance from her.

"Put thet confounded thing away! You plannin' to shoot me next?"

Emma held the gun steady though her eyes widened and her mouth dropped open. She heard Abel come up behind her and together they stared at the strange man.

"Who are you, mister?" Abel asked, and Emma heard the false bravado in his shaky voice.

"You gonna point thet thing somewhere else, or do I have to take it away from you?"

Emma lowered the gun but kept it ready. "My brother asked who you are, sir," she said. She mentally chastised herself for the tremble she heard in her own voice. My, he had given her a fright!

"Well, now. Why should I tell two youngsters my business?" The fur-clad man approached, and as Emma got a better look at him, she gripped the rifle tighter.

He was old. His face was covered with a gray beard, long and grizzled. His uncut hair stuck out in all directions from under a coonskin cap, and when he spoke again, Emma saw stained teeth. She shuddered.

"Why'd you youngins shoot that buck? I was followin' him until I found a spot to camp, then I was gonna take him down and have me some venison steaks for supper."

"You are trespassing on private land, sir."

"Whooee!"

Emma jumped at the man's yell. He spit and rubbed his mouth with the back of his hand. "Was a time this was all open land and a fella could come down from them hills without seein' another soul. I 'spect next you'll be fencin' everythin' in."

"Are you a trapper?" Abel asked in awe, noting the variety of furs covering the man's body.

"I'm from the hills—not that it's any business of yours." He took another step toward them, and his bushy eyebrows shot up at the sight of Emma's skirt tucked into her waistband.

"Thet what females are wearin' now?" he asked in surprise.

Emma blushed furiously, but she refused to be intimidated.

"Well, we better get that buck split open so I can get me my steaks."

"That's *our* deer, mister!" Abel spoke hotly as the man walked toward the fallen animal. Emma put her hand on Abel's arm, stopping him from saying more. They watched in silence as the man reached into his belt and drew out a huge knife. He spun it in his hands a few times then threw it with perfect accuracy into the neck of the deer, allowing its blood to flow out.

With skill, he gutted the animal clean, skinned off a section, and cut off a large portion of meat, which he threw into the pack he had with him. Then he bent down and heaved the bloody animal over his shoulders and turned back to Emma and Abel.

Without a word he strode past them out of the woods, across the creek, and up to their wagon. He dropped the deer onto the wagon bed then glanced back at them.

"Didn't figger you youngins should get your school clothes dirty," he said gruffly. "The school ma'rm might not let you back in the school." He laughed raucously at his own joke.

"Emma here is the school mar—school teacher," Abel informed him. "Besides, school's over now."

Emma saw surprise cross the weathered features of the man as he looked at her once again. She knew she looked younger than her nineteen years, so she held her head high and stared back. Suddenly remembering her skirt, she quickly pulled it out of her waistband and smoothed it out.

"Who's land am I s'posed to be trespassin' on anyway?"

"You are on land belonging to our father, Russell Newly. I'm Emma Newly and this is my brother Abel," Emma explained. "Would you be good enough to tell us who you are so we can properly thank you for dressing out our deer?"

"Don't need no thanks; I got me my steaks. S'pose I ought a thank you for saving me a bullet." He laughed loudly again. "Pretty good shootin' for a gal."

Emma bristled, and the man laughed again.

"Your name?" she persisted.

"You can call me Jack. Hermit Jack some call me."

Emma nodded. "Thank you, Mr. Jack, for helping us with the deer."

"Confound it, girl! I said Jack, not *mister* Jack. Thet's the trouble with people—they always want to try and change a body. Nobody's happy to let ol' Jack stay the way he is."

Emma started to apologize, but just then Abel whispered in her ear, "Let's invite him home for supper, Emma. Bet he's got lots of good stories to tell."

Emma turned to her brother with a horrified look on her face. "Are you crazy?" she whispered back. "We know nothing about him. Mother wouldn't like it."

"You're the one who says we should be friendlier to new folks."

"I didn't mean a man covered with fur and whiskers!"

"What difference does that make? I'm askin' him. Wha—where'd he go?" Abel ran up to the wagon.

Emma quickly followed, looking this way and that, but the strange man was gone.

Chapter 2

Sand Creek

"Hermit Jack? No, I've never heard of him; I wonder if your father has." Sky Newly smiled at her children. Her face was flushed as she turned from the stove with a pan of warm cookies. She tucked a loose strand of blonde hair back into the bun at her neck. "Well, how does it feel to be done with school for the year?"

"Wonderful! I was ready for a vacation," Emma admitted.

"You? All you had to do was teach. It's us kids who did all the work." Abel teased. "I'm going out to help Rex with the deer." He grabbed a couple of his mother's freshly baked cookies. "See ya."

Sky shook her head and smiled at her youngest child's retreating back. "That boy! No wonder you're glad for a vacation." Sky studied her daughter's face. "Is something wrong, Emma? You look like you have something on your mind."

Emma sat down at the kitchen table and helped herself to one of the cookies as well. She took a deep breath. "Mother, does it ever bother you when Dad leaves on a case? I mean, do you mind?"

Sky frowned slightly then sat down across from Emma. Her daughter's interest in the detective work her father did for the Pinkertons had always been a source of amusement for the family, but Sky was uncomfortably aware that the interest ran deep.

Russ had done many tasks for the Pinkertons over the years, including protecting the wagon train of mail-order brides Sky traveled with to get to Sand Creek years ago. Details of his exploits he was not at liberty to share with his family, but he often regaled them with stories of hunting down bank robbers, watching over gold shipments, or providing security for dignitaries. One job he had refused to do was to battle with the railroads against the unions—something that many of the Pinkertons had done. After their marriage, Russ quit working full-time for the agency, but he continued to take cases when his boss really needed him.

Emma tended to romanticize her father's work. As a child, she and her brothers acted out the stories he told them, and she always played the part of the Pinkerton detective who rounded up the outlaws and saved the day. Sky didn't know what kind of case Russ was on now, and seeing the glint of interest in her daughter's expression, she wondered if Emma would ever outgrow her fascination with her father's job. She answered her carefully.

"It did bother me at first," she admitted. "I couldn't understand why he would willingly leave his family and put himself in danger to help someone else, someone he didn't even know. So finally one day we sat down and talked about it."

Sky smiled at the memory. "I should have known...or I should say, I should have known your father well enough to know the answer. He told me that *always* his family would come first to him, and I really didn't doubt that. But he had made an agreement with his old Pinkerton boss that if he was ever really needed, he would help out. You see, Emma, your father feels that God gave him certain abilities to be used for him. When he works on a case, he prays for God's leading, and often he is able to tell someone about the Lord Jesus and show him the way of salvation. It's kind of a ministry for him. He not only helps people out of physical danger, but he finds a way to show them how to be out of spiritual danger as well."

Emma nodded in understanding. "That sounds like Dad. But don't you worry about him? Aren't you afraid sometimes that he won't make it back alive?"

"Yes, dear," Sky admitted. "Often I worry and I'm afraid for him, but since this is something he feels called to do, I try to leave my worries and fears in the Lord's hands, and I pray for your dad constantly. I pray for his safety, and I pray that he'll be successful in his endeavors. Even though I remain at home, I feel that I'm a part of his work."

She patted Emma's hand. "And you are too when you pray for him." She held Emma's gaze until her daughter gave a slight nod. It was unspoken between them, but Sky knew how much Emma wished she could work with her father as her brother Tyler and her cousin Michael Trent did from time to time. But girls had different responsibilities in life, and Emma had to accept that. "Now, where are those letters Abel brought in?"

Emma went to the doorway and watched the activities of her brothers for a few moments. Rex, who was eighteen, was the caretaker of the ranch while their father was gone. Russ often said that Rex was a born rancher. Emma's thoughts were not on what she was seeing, so she was startled when her mother spoke behind her.

"Lucy put a note in her letter just for you, Emma. But come, listen to her other news first before you read yours."

Emma listened as Sky read out loud from her sister's letter. Lucy was married to Buck Riley, the son of Hank and Randi Riley, her parents' close friends. Lucy said she and Buck were doing fine with the hotel and business was good, but she was tired. Jade and Tyler's baby was due soon, and their two-year-old Eddie was getting impatient for his brother or sister to arrive.

Emma still found it hard to believe that her oldest brother Tyler had found such a beautiful wife as Jade and that he was already the father of one child and soon another. Buck's sister Mallory was married to Emma's cousin Michael Trent, and they were expecting their third. The rest contained tidbits of news about the other members of the growing community of Grandville, a settlement started by some of the young men of Sand Creek several years ago. Like Sand Creek, Grandville was known for the mail-order brides who came and settled there.

"I'm so glad they found a doctor to live there before all these babies started coming." Sky laughed. "Won't Lucy be excited to know that Dorcas and Cavan are expecting too!"

"Won't it disappoint her that her younger sister will have a baby before she does?" Emma questioned.

"Lucy knows that these things happen in the Lord's timing," Sky responded. Then she sighed. "Oh, I don't know. I suppose it might. She doesn't say much about it, but I know she wants to have a family too."

Emma nodded thoughtfully and opened her note from her sister. She scanned the lines quickly and excitement grew in her.

"Mother! Lucy *is* going to have a baby! She says that she wanted me to be the first to know. Wasn't that sweet!" Emma read on further. "And she wants to know if I can come and help at the hotel for the summer because she hasn't been feeling too well. Oh, I'd love to! Would it be all right, Mother? Can you get along without me for the summer?"

Sky laughed at Emma's anxious look. "With only your dad and two boys to feed? I'll be fine. Of course you can go. Maybe this is just the change you've been needing."

"Working at the hotel should be fun! You meet all kinds of interesting people who have been places and who are going places." Emma jumped up and hugged her mother. "I better start packing!"

Sky laughed again as Emma raced off then she sat down and spoke out loud in the empty kitchen, "One grandson and three more grandchildren on the way! Where has the time gone?"

Chapter 3

Way Station

Emma felt herself jostled about in the moving coach as she watched the scenery bounce by through the side window. The thick pine forest on either side of the road remained green all year long in the Minnesota woods, but she could see tufts of new green grass sprouting up here and there on the forest floor, and the once bare branches of the deciduous trees were beginning to fill with the buds of spring.

Her cousin Gabriel was driving, and they would soon be at the way station where his wife, Leigh, and their friends Dugan and Melody Riley lived. When they had planned the coach line, Dugan was going to build a way station between Grandville and Norris, and Gabe was going to operate the one between Grandville and Sand Creek. However, their new wives had become close friends, and neither wanted to be left all alone at a way station to handle customers, so they had built two homes at one way station. That way, one of the men was always there while the other one drove the coach. They hired another family, the Sternes, to operate their second way station.

Emma sighed in relief as she saw the way station come into view. She immediately regretted calling attention to herself.

"Are you all right, Miss Newly?"

"Can I do anything for you, Miss Newly?"

Emma smiled tiredly at the two brothers who had plagued her with their attentions since early that morning when they boarded the coach. Herb and Neil Robinson were on their way to Norris, and they made no pretense of their interest in their pretty blonde traveling companion.

The young men were good-looking in a farm-boyish sort of way. They had the broad shoulders of men who were used to hard labor, and their clothing was simple and rough, yet they seemed uncomfortable as if they were not used to wearing even such finery as that.

"No thank you, I'm fine. I'm just glad we're stopping for the night. It gets tiring just sitting here. How are you faring, Mrs. Findley?" Emma asked the older woman beside her before the brothers could speak again. Mr. and Mrs. Findley were probably in their late fifties. Giles Findley wore a smart black broadcloth suit, now covered with travel dust, and Agatha Findley tucked her plump figure into a gray skirt and jacket. Her once stiff white shirtwaist now was limp and rumpled.

"I'm sore all over! My, but it will be good to stretch and walk around!"

"A hot meal will be welcome too," her husband added.

"I think you will be pleased with the way station," Emma told them. "My cousin and his wife own it along with my good friends. They'll make sure you are comfortable," Emma assured the couple.

"That's your cousin driving?" asked Herb. His suntanned face broke into a relieved smile. "That's sure good to know. The way he was bein' friendly to you and all made me think we had some competition." He and Neil grinned boyishly at Emma, but she just smiled briefly and concentrated on the view out her window. What a bother they were! She had done her best to remain friendly with the two young men, but she didn't want them to think she was interested in them the way they appeared to be with her. She didn't want to give them the wrong impression.

The coach finally rolled to a stop, and Emma waited for the Findleys to exit first. Gabe was waiting to help her out, but Neil Robinson jumped out ahead of her then turned and with a grin held out his arms to her.

Emma was startled, and when she saw Gabe trying not to laugh as he stood behind the overly zealous young man, she put her lips firmly together and descended from the coach with just her hand resting on Neil's arm.

"Thank you, Mr. Robinson, I—"

"Let me help you inside." Herb Robinson had swiftly followed her from the coach and now offered his arm. Emma distinctly heard Gabe smother his laughter with a cough.

"Thank you, but—"

"Aunt Emmie!"

Emma looked up in relief as her cousin's three-year-old daughter ran from the log building toward her, her pigtails flying straight out behind her. Stepping away from her would-be suitors, Emma opened her arms and swept the child up into them.

"Adele! My, but you are almost grown up, aren't you!" Emma walked to the porch with the little girl chattering excitedly and almost unintelligibly. The two young men made to follow, but Gabe stopped them.

"How about a hand with these bags, fellas? These here are Miss Newly's."

Eager hands reached for the luggage, and Gabe hid his smile.

Emma and Adele crossed the log-railed wooden porch to the doorway of the way station's dining room. "Leigh, you look positively radiant!" Emma exclaimed as she hugged Adele's mother. She backed away and smiled at her friend's protruding tummy. "How much longer until the baby is due?"

Leigh Trent tugged at the calico dress covering her enlarged form. Once a city girl from Boston, Leigh had been one of the mail-order brides to come to Grandville along with seven other women, Melody also being one of them. It had taken Gabe Trent only one look to decide which of the women he wanted for his bride, and Leigh had felt the same way about Gabe. It still amazed Emma to think of all the marriages that had taken place as a result of a newspaper ad. Two of her cousins as well as several of the young men she had known all her life were the welcoming grooms.

"I have three more months to go, but I'm feeling great. I wasn't at first, I'll tell you, but Melody took over all the hard stuff around the station for a while. What's funny is that when she was expecting hers, I was able to take over. We're taking turns." Leigh laughed.

Melody Riley backed through a far doorway with both arms full of dishes. She smiled warmly at Emma as she set down her load. "Emma!" She hugged her friend.

Melody was also from the East and had arrived, fashionable and attractive, to this rugged northern area. Dugan Riley had fallen for her in no time. Emma remembered that her sister Lucy had thought she was in love with Dugan. However, the Lord had shown Lucy that Buck Riley, Dugan's brother, was the man who had been patiently waiting for her for years. Now both couples were happily married.

"How was the trip from Sand Creek?"

Emma made a face. "Gabe's a good driver, but I think I'll be feeling it tomorrow."

Melody smiled. "That's what they all say!"

"Where are Jason and Janelle?" Emma looked through the open doorway for Melody and Dugan's two children.

"They're helping Dugan take care of the horses. I think their favorite part of the day is feeding time. They really love the horses."

"I think they love doing anything they can with their daddy," commented Leigh. "Dugan is so good with them."

"And when he's gone on a run, Uncle Gabe takes over and the kids have just as much fun with him," added Melody.

"You two have it all worked out, haven't you?" said Emma. They talked awhile more about the way station; then Emma began to relay messages. "Mother said to tell you both hello, and did you know Dorcas and Cavan are expecting? And you'll never guess who else is."

"We already know. It's Lucy, right?" Melody asked with a mischievous look.

Emma was disappointed. "How did you know? She said I was the first one she'd told."

"By letter, Emma. It took a while for you to get the news. In the meantime, we all found out. Why, Gabe and Dugan are in Grandville every other day or so, and Buck *is* Dugan's brother, you know," Melody explained.

"We're so happy for them. They've been watching all the other families grow for four years now without any children of their own. I think it was hard on them, but Lucy told me that they were praying for the Lord to show them his will in his time. They'll find it was worth waiting for." Leigh patted her enlarged abdomen affectionately.

"Well, there goes all my big news," Emma complained good-naturedly. "Now how about if I help with supper while you take it easy." She led Leigh, protesting, to a chair and set Adele down beside her. Then she headed for the kitchen to wash and put on an apron, despite Melody's assurances that her help was appreciated but not necessary.

"How many passengers were there besides you?" asked Melody.

"Four. Mr. and Mrs. Findley and two brothers, Hank and Neil Robinson." Emma kept her tone even and her head was bent over the washbowl, so she missed Melody's smile.

"Those would be the two who were assisting you out of the coach?" she asked.

"You saw!" Emma groaned. "Now don't you start! Gabe has been laughing at me already."

Melody chuckled. "You've got to expect that a beautiful young woman like yourself is bound to attract the attention of every young male for miles around. Remember, there still aren't that many young women around here, and these men are all looking for wives." She ducked as Emma threw the hand towel at her.

Leigh joined them and began stirring the soup on the stove. "Maybe they'll turn their attentions on our other guest and leave you alone while you're here."

"You have a guest?" Emma asked.

"Sophia Barlow." Leigh carefully enunciated the name.

"Where is she?"

"She's horseback riding again. She's been here two days and she's spent most of them out riding somewhere," Melody said.

"At least she's away from our husbands when she's out admiring the scenery," Leigh remarked. "She has a bad habit of trying to flirt with them."

Emma was surprised at the expression on Leigh's face. She looked…worried. "But Leigh, Gabe would never—"

"Of course he wouldn't! That's what I keep telling her," Melody interrupted. She squeezed Leigh's arm. "Gabe is just being polite to her because she's a guest here. Gabe's friendly to everyone."

"Still, I wish he stayed away from her like Dugan does," Leigh said softly.

Emma was shaken by Leigh's tone. "Gabe doesn't encourage her, does he?" she asked in disbelief.

"No, Emma, he really doesn't. But a woman like Sophia doesn't need encouragement; it's enough for her that Gabe is friendly." Melody put an arm around Leigh as she explained to Emma. "Leigh is extra emotional right now, but it will pass."

"And it doesn't help to look like an overripe watermelon when there's a beautiful and slender woman flirting with your husband," Leigh added as she wiped a tear from her eye. "Goodness, Melody, look at Emma's face! We've shocked her!" She reached for Emma's hand. "Seriously, Emma, I know Gabe would never do anything to hurt me. He loves me, and I love and trust him. It's just that *woman* I don't trust!"

The back door to the kitchen swung open, and Dugan strode into the room carrying a dark-haired child on each shoulder. He grinned at Emma. "These two told me there was someone here who was hugging Adele, so we just had to hurry with chores and come see who it was. Good to see you, Emma."

"Emmie!" Two-year-old Janelle reached for Emma and wrapped her arms about her neck.

Emma snuggled the little girl while she looked over the dark head to the others and said, "I'm surprised she knows me."

"They see your picture every night," explained Melody. "We don't see our friends and family enough, so the kids mostly know you through the pictures we have in our houses."

Jason tugged at Emma's skirt. "Where's Abel and Rex?" he asked.

Emma knelt to look at the young version of Dugan. "They had to stay at home and help our mom with the horses, just like you help your mom and dad."

The little boy's eyes gleamed. "I love horses. We gots lots of horses!"

"I love horses too," agreed Emma.

The little boy decided she must be all right if she loved his horses, so he reached over and patted her arm with his chubby hand and grinned at her. "Good! That Miss Barlow doesn't like our horses. She hits our horses, and she never brushes them and—"

"That's enough, Jason! Miss Barlow isn't used to our horses, so she doesn't love them like we do," explained Melody to her son. "Supper is about ready, Dugan. Has Gabe gotten our guests settled yet?"

"Yes, I have," Gabe announced as he came up behind the group. "They should all have had time to freshen up by now and are ready to eat your delicious cooking." He slipped his arms around Leigh from behind her and kissed her neck. "Missed you," he said softly.

Emma quickly turned to find something to do. She wasn't aware that the two couples were smiling at her embarrassment until Gabe teased, "Maybe Neil and Herb will save you a place between them at the table, Em."

She glanced over her shoulder to give him a dirty look and caught him and Leigh in another kiss. She turned back.

"Why is your face so red, Emmie?" asked Adele.

Dugan couldn't help laughing. "Emma is not used to seeing your mom and dad kissing, Dell."

The little girl took Emma's hand. "They do that *all* the time, Emmie. Will you sit by me instead of with those men?"

Emma hugged Adele. "I would love to sit by you instead of by a man any day, Dell. Come on."

"I wonder if you'll always say that, Em," teased Gabe. "Here come our guests now. I put the Findleys in the south room, and the Robinsons will share the east room; is that okay?" he asked his wife.

Leigh nodded.

"Which room am I in?" asked Emma.

Leigh answered, "You are staying with us at the cabin. We always put family with us so we can visit as much as possible—unless you would rather not?"

"No, I'd like that."

The guests gathered for supper, and Emma helped the ladies serve the meal of fried chicken, mashed potatoes and gravy, peas and carrots, and freshly baked biscuits. Then she sat down by Adele, much to the disappointment of Herb and Neil Robinson. About halfway through the meal, they heard a horse ride up.

"That will be our other guest, Miss Barlow," explained Melody to the group. "She's been out riding."

Footsteps sounded on the porch and the door swung open. Emma looked up curiously along with the others. She immediately saw the reason for Leigh's concerns.

Sophia stood poised in the doorway for a moment, giving her audience time for a good look at her. Dressed in a black riding suit complete with matching hat over her dark hair, she managed to look elegant despite the dust that clung to her clothes and the strands of hair that had slipped from their pins. She had everyone's attention. She, in turn, studied the people in the room. Emma's interest was immediately piqued. Sophia didn't just glance at the newcomers; she studied them each thoroughly. Then she swept into the room and said, "Gentlemen, please sit down and continue with your meal. I'm so sorry I'm late, Mrs. Trent. I'll just run and freshen up and be back in a moment." She flashed a dazzling smile to the onlookers and turned to go, but then she stopped and looked back. "It's getting so dark. Gabriel, would you mind lighting a lantern for me?"

"Not at all, Miss Barlow. Let me get one for you."

Gabe went into the other room, and Emma watched Leigh set her fork down and stare at her plate. Soon he was back with a lantern, which he handed to Sophia with a smile.

"Thank you, Gabriel." She started to go again then stopped once more. "Oh, I forgot to mention to you that the door to my room has been hard to open. Usually I just pull with both hands, but with this lantern I don't see how I'll manage. Would you mind?"

"Of course, Miss Barlow. I'll go with you now and help you open it, and I'll fix it first thing in the morning." Gabe looked at Leigh. "Be right back."

Emma's heart went out to Leigh as Gabe left with Sophia. Leigh picked up her fork again but only pushed her food around. She made no attempt to join in the conversation going on at the table. Now Emma understood Leigh's concerns. Sophia was manipulating Gabe, and he seemed totally unaware of it.

The minutes ticked by, and Gabe still hadn't returned to the dining room. Finally when the meal was almost over, the group heard Sophia's laughter, and she entered the room holding onto Gabe's arm with both of her own while he held the lantern.

"We're back!" Sophia announced gaily. "I'm sorry again, Mrs. Trent, that it took so long, but I asked Gabriel to wait for me so I wouldn't have to walk back alone in the dark. You don't mind, I hope?"

Emma saw Leigh bite her lower lip. "Are you ready for your supper now, Miss Barlow? We've kept a plate warm for you." Leigh spoke graciously. She was about to rise, when Melody stopped her with a hand on her arm.

"No, sit down, Leigh. I'll get it. We kept yours warm too, Gabe. Why don't you sit with Leigh and I'll bring it along with our desserts."

"I'll help you," Emma offered.

As the two women went into the kitchen, Emma passed Sophia, and the fragrance of lilacs drifted to her nose. Apparently Sophia hadn't minded keeping the others waiting while she did a complete toilet. Her hair was even arranged in a fashionable style, and her dress! Emma did not approve of Sophia's taste in clothing. She heard Herb Robinson offering a chair to Sophia.

"Did you see that dress she put on?" Melody whispered to Emma. "Here we all are either in our working clothes or traveling clothes, and she walks in looking like that!"

"She certainly wants to attract attention to herself," Emma admitted. Sophia's dress was cut immodestly low. "Why is she staying here at the way station?" she asked Melody.

"I wish I knew." Melody started filling a tray with the dessert dishes. "Here, would you please take their suppers to them so they can get started?"

Emma nodded and headed back to the large dining room with the two plates. She set one before Gabe and was glad to see him holding Leigh's hand under the table and talking quietly with her. Then she set Sophia's down, and she heard Sophia questioning the two brothers.

"You're not staying in Grandville, then? Why are you going to Norris?"

Emma didn't hear their answers as she returned to the kitchen, but she was amused by the fact that since Sophia's arrival, the Robinsons had appeared to have forgotten *her* presence.

Emma carried the coffee back to the dining room and started refilling cups while Melody served the apple cobbler. She smiled when she saw that Gabe and Leigh still held hands. But when she refilled the cups for the Findleys, she was surprised to hear Sophia questioning them as to their destination. Emma knew the Findleys were going on to Norris to visit their daughter, and she noticed that once Sophia had that information, she quickly lost interest in the elderly couple. So Emma was prepared when she returned again and resumed her place beside Adele. She had just taken a bite of the delicious cobbler when Sophia turned her attention fully upon her.

"I'm afraid I never learned your name," Sophia said with a charming smile. "I'm Sophia Barlow, but I suppose you've already heard all about me."

Emma watched Sophia with interest. Though the beautiful woman acted friendly, her eyes never warmed to match her expression. *It would be prudent to be cautious around this woman,* she thought. All that her father had taught her about reading a person's character came back to her as she returned Sophia's smile.

"I'm Emma Newly, Miss Barlow, and I'm pleased to meet you. What brings you to our area?"

A moment of hesitation and a small flicker in Sophia's eyes made Emma wonder what she had just done. Then she wondered if she had just imagined it when Sophia answered in an even friendlier tone.

"Me? I'm just enjoying the beauty of this countryside, Miss Newly. I'll probably stay in the area awhile longer before moving on. You see, I"—she leaned forward and spoke confidentially—"I'm a writer, and I like to steep myself in the atmosphere of an area before I write about it."

Emma returned her look evenly. "How interesting!"

The others at the table added comments and expressed interest in Sophia's occupation. Dessert was about over when Sophia again addressed Emma.

"Where are you headed, Miss Newly? Please forgive me if I sound nosey." She laughed. "I'm always asking people questions. I get so many ideas that way."

"I'll be staying in Grandville for a time," Emma explained. "I'm afraid you won't find very much exciting to write about from me."

"You never can tell." Sophia's tone was light, but her look was challenging. "Newly." She stared intently at Emma. "Would you be related to Gabriel, then? Gabriel, didn't you tell me that the Trents and Newlys were related?"

Gabe looked from one woman to the other. "Yes, Emma and I are cousins. Her mother and my father are twins."

"Now, see!" Sophia was triumphant. "You never know what interesting things you might find out when you start asking questions." She regarded Emma thoughtfully. "Gabriel's family runs a ranch near Sand Creek, so I'll bet that your family lives nearby and farms or ranches too, right?"

Gabe glanced at Sophia then at Emma.

Emma smiled as she stood to begin clearing the table. "That's a close guess." As Leigh again began to help, she stopped her. "No, Leigh, you let me help Melody with this tonight. Why don't you and Gabe take a walk; there's a beautiful moon out."

"Sounds like a good idea to me. How about it, honey?" Gabe stood and held the chair out for his wife.

"We can't let Emma come here and do all my work," protested Leigh.

"Let me help tonight too, Mrs. Trent. You've been so good to me; it's the least I can do." Sophia began clearing away dishes, but she was tipping cups over and in danger of dropping a serving dish, so Melody protested.

"Please, Miss Barlow, not in that dress! You wouldn't want it ruined."

Emma efficiently stacked the remaining dishes and rescued the serving dish from Sophia's hands. "Why don't you sit in the other room and visit with the Findleys for a while?" she suggested. "I'm sure they have many interesting stories that would be of help to you."

"But, Miss Newly—Emma—may I call you Emma? There's still so much about *you* that interests me. My stories are usually about young women like you, so you'd be the perfect person to learn about." She followed Emma and Melody into the kitchen. "What do you plan to do in Grandville, for instance?"

Something felt odd about Sophia's interest, and Emma made up her mind not to give Sophia Barlow any more information about herself. She disliked the woman's methods of prying, and she was disgusted with the woman herself. Her behavior around Gabe and her immodest attire only served to make Emma more distrustful of her.

"Really, Miss Barlow, I am sure my life would seem very boring to you. But since you'd like to help out in the kitchen, let me put this apron on you. You and Melody can start washing and I'll finish clearing up. We'll get done so much quicker, and I'll have more time to spend with the children."

As Emma prepared for bed that night, she couldn't help chuckling to herself over Sophia's reaction when she was left to actually help in the kitchen. Sophia had quickly made an excuse to Melody and disappeared. Emma later saw that she was out walking with Neil Robinson. They saw no more of Sophia that night.

But there was something that still disturbed Emma. When she had joined Gabe and Leigh and Adele back at their cabin, Gabe had mentioned something Sophia said at the supper table.

"I wonder how Miss Barlow knew that my family had a ranch near Sand Creek," he mused. "I certainly never told her that. Did you, Leigh?"

"Miss Barlow doesn't usually converse with me. No, I never said anything and I'm fairly sure neither Dugan nor Melody has. Does it matter?" Leigh yawned.

"No, not really. It's just odd that she brought it up," Gabe said before dismissing the matter.

But Emma continued to review Sophia's words and her questions. What was that woman up to? Emma finished brushing her golden hair; then she opened her bag to get out her nightdress. Her hands stilled. Someone had gone through her things! Without touching anything further, Emma studied the contents of her bag.

It would hardly be evident to most people, but Emma had learned from her father how to see what others missed. Her lace handkerchief was on top, just where she had put it, but Emma distinctly remembered folding it in a triangular shape before placing it in her bag. It was now folded in a square.

She lifted the handkerchief out and then slowly went through each item. Whoever had searched her belongings was thorough and efficient. Nothing seemed to be missing, and very little was noticeably out of place. But why? Why search her things?

Emma sat on the bed and pondered the situation while she absently ran her fingers over the hand-sewn quilt. Her first suspicions were naturally that Sophia had done this, but her father taught her never to assume. Sometimes the most unlikely suspect turned out to be the guilty person. So Emma sat quietly reviewing the whereabouts of each person after supper while her eyes continued to study her room for clues. Silently she prayed for wisdom to understand the reason behind this intrusion.

After carefully thinking it through, she thought she could eliminate everyone but Neil and Sophia when she became aware of something else in her room. Sitting there quietly, she realized she had been aware of it for some time. She sniffed.

There was a faint scent of lilacs lingering in the air.

Chapter 4

Grandville

The small community of Grandville finally came into view from the window of the coach. Emma welcomed the sight with a thankful heart, and every sore muscle in her body reminded her why she disliked coach travel. The other occupants of the stagecoach echoed her silent sentiments with sighs of relief as they prepared to leave the confinement of the coach and the backbreaking jarring from the hard benches they had endured for several hours.

Emma watched Sophia from the corner of her eye. The beautiful brunette was gathering her handbag and adjusting her hat while she continued her flirtations with the Robinson brothers. Neil and Herb had been delighted when Sophia decided to join the stage to Grandville. Emma had not been too surprised at the woman's sudden decision.

"Will you be staying at the hotel, Emma?" Sophia asked pleasantly. "We could share accommodations if you'd like."

Emma smiled, but only out of politeness. She had no intention of spending more time with Sophia. "Thank you, Miss Barlow, that is kind of you, but I've already made other arrangements. I imagine we'll see each other, though. Do you plan to remain in Grandville long?"

The flicker returned to Sophia's eye, and Emma realized that although Sophia liked to question others, she did not like to be questioned herself.

"It depends on what I find to write about," Sophia answered breezily. "How about you?"

"I'll probably stay awhile." Emma's answer was non-committal.

"Wish we could stay longer than just overnight," complained Neil. "With two lovely ladies like you two here, it makes it very hard to leave."

Sophia accepted the compliment with a light laugh and a flirtatious look at Neil. Emma merely smiled politely.

"It was nice to meet both of you," she said. "I hope the remainder of your journey goes well. And it was nice meeting you also." She turned to the Findleys. "Maybe I'll see you on your return trip."

The Findleys acknowledged Emma's sentiments as the coach halted. Emma accepted Dugan's hand to help her descend from the coach and found herself immediately swooped up into the air by a pair of strong arms.

"Welcome to Grandville, little sis," said a strong, masculine voice.

As she was spun around in the middle of the street, Emma saw Sophia's attention was on her.

"Buck Riley, put me down!" Emma laughed. "Dugan, make your brother behave himself!"

Buck set Emma down after a quick hug. "Lucy is so excited to see you, Emma, but she wasn't feeling well enough to meet you. I'm instructed to bring you to her as soon as possible." Buck stepped back and took a good look at his sister-in-law. Abruptly his arms dropped to his sides, and his face reddened. "Goodness, Emma! You've grown up since the last time I saw you. I was expecting Lucy's little sister, but you've changed."

Emma couldn't help laughing at Buck's expression. Before marrying Lucy, Buck Riley had been the quiet, silent man that no one really noticed. He was bashful and liked to stay in the background, and maybe that was why it took him so long to let Lucy know of his feelings for her. *That* Buck Riley would never have picked up Emma and swung her around in the air!

But with Lucy's love and acceptance of him, Buck was a changed man. He no longer seemed shy and withdrawn but was well respected in Grandville and a favorite brother-in-law of Emma's.

"Did you expect to see pigtails, Buck? I've been teaching school for two years now, so I guess you could say that I've grown up."

"Is that little Emma Newly?"

Buck and Emma turned at the voice. Ralph Tunelle stood behind Buck, and his eyes traveled over Emma in frank admiration. Ralph's clothing was rumpled, and there was at least a day's growth of whiskers on his face. Emma noticed that his eyes were bloodshot as if he hadn't had enough sleep. Buck moved to Emma's side, and she sensed disapproval in his voice as he spoke to the man.

"Hi Ralph. Yes, Emma's come to stay and help Lucy for now. Will you excuse us?"

Emma was surprised at Buck's rudeness to the man. She had known Ralph Tunelle for years. When the men from Grandville had ordered brides, Ralph's prospective bride had left the small town almost as soon as she saw it. Ralph had married Philippa Gray from Sand Creek instead, a girl who had been nothing but trouble to the Newly family and evidently to Ralph as well. Emma held out her hand to Ralph.

"It's good to see you, Ralph. How's Philippa?"

Ralph snorted, and Emma looked at him in surprise. "Apparently you haven't heard the latest gossip, little Emma. My dear wife finally up and left me. She went back to her mother. I thought everyone knew that."

Emma gently withdrew the hand Ralph was still holding. "No, I'm sorry, Ralph, I didn't. How awful! Surely she'll be back soon. Her place is with you."

"How innocent you are, Emma, and how sweet! If only Philippa had been more like you." He continued to stare at Emma until she grew uncomfortable under his gaze. Buck returned to her side with her bags under his arm.

"Are you ready, Emma?" He gently took her arm and led her away from Ralph.

"That's right, Buck. Keep the pretty girls away from old Ralph. I'll be seeing you, Emma." Ralph walked away, and Emma saw him tip his hat to Sophia.

"Emma," Buck's tone was uneasy. "Emma, I don't know how to say this without sounding like a big brother, but I feel responsible for you now that you're here."

Emma looked at Buck and waited for him to continue.

"Look, Emma, Ralph has been pretty down since Philippa took off. They didn't get along too well even when she was here, but it might be better if you stayed away from him. He hasn't been himself at all, and I hear he's been riding over to Norris and visiting the saloon there since we don't allow one here. We've tried to do what we can to help him, but he refuses to pay any attention to us and he won't talk to Pastor Malcolm. I guess all we can do is pray for him."

Emma thought she understood, yet she was horrified at the change she had seen in her old friend. "Don't worry about me, Buck. I'm not about to get involved in any way with a married man."

Buck sighed in relief. "I didn't mean to imply that you would, but I know Ralph and I'm afraid he just doesn't care what he does anymore, right or wrong. Philippa hurt him pretty badly."

Emma nodded in understanding again, and in her heart she asked the Lord to help her friend Ralph Tunelle.

Buck led Emma to a side door on what appeared to be an extension of the hotel and dining room that he and Lucy owned. Emma noticed the newness of the lumber compared to the rest of the building, and she looked inquisitively at Buck, so he explained.

"Lucy and I wanted to have some privacy away from the hotel, yet we needed to still be accessible to it, so I built on this addition last year. It's like we have our own house, but we have a doorway into the hotel so customers can still get our attention when they need us. It will also be easier for Lucy to work in the dining room and kitchen and still take care of the baby." He seemed proud of their arrangements.

Emma breathed in the fresh smell of new lumber. "Mmmm! Still smells new too," she commented.

Buck breathed in deeply. "The whole town still has that smell." He laughed. "Thanks to Tyler and Michael's lumber business, we all were able to build at reasonable prices. Jade's step-father, Palmer Granville, has been a great help with all our banking and loan needs as well." Emma could see the pride Buck had in his community.

Buck led Emma into the house, and after dropping her bags pulled her arm along to a bedroom, where they found Lucy propped up on pillows in the bed. Lucy's eyes were closed, and her long blonde hair fanned the pillow on which her head rested. Hearing their approach, she opened her eyes and instantly held out her arms to Emma.

"I hope you didn't mind me sending for you," she asked Emma. "Jade thinks I'm through the worst part now and that I should start to feel well again soon. I hope so! So you may not even be needed here, but I'm still glad you came."

Emma sat down beside her sister on the bed. She was looking at a slightly older version of herself, she realized. All three of the Newly girls—Lucille, Dorcas, and Emma—had inherited their mother's sky blue eyes and blonde hair. Even the boys—Tyler, Rex, and Abel—had the blue eyes, but their hair was either sandy-colored or darker, like Russ's.

But Emma could see some difference now; there were circles under Lucy's eyes, and she appeared tired.

"You do look pale, Lucy. Don't worry about a thing now that I'm here. I'll take care of everything for you, and as far as me not needing to be here, you've done me a great favor by giving me something new and exciting to do."

Lucy laughed then groaned and held her stomach. "I don't think you'll find working at the hotel all that exciting, Em. We see some odd characters now and then, but nothing too unusual. Buck has built up quite a few head of horses that he cares for in the corrals out back. We've got a side business going with Bernie at the blacksmith shop. We sell or rent the horses out, so we keep busy. And we always provide a fresh team for Gabe and Dugan when they come through."

Emma watched her sister closely. It had been so long since she had been able to see her and talk personally. She realized just how much she had missed her. Letters were great, but seeing Lucy and being able to watch her as she spoke of their business and their lives was so much more satisfying. Lucy practically sparkled when she talked about Buck and all the things he was doing. Yet events of the past few days had left Emma with a question in her mind.

"Are you happy, Lucy? I mean you and Buck. Are you glad you got married?"

Lucy was startled at the question, but she answered her sister honestly when she saw the concern in her eyes. "Yes, marrying Buck was the best thing I ever did. Why? What's on your mind?"

"We met Ralph when I got off the stage," Emma explained.

"Oh." Lucy shook her head. "We've all been praying for Ralph. Philippa made him miserable while she was here and now he's miserable because she's gone. I guess a person can't really say what's right or wrong for someone else, but Ralph probably never should have married her. She never seemed to love him. She still tried flirting with Tyler even after she was married. Did you know that?"

Emma was shocked. "I'll bet that didn't make Jade too happy."

"No. Tyler had a long talk with both Ralph and Philippa, and after that she left Tyler alone."

"How are Jade and Ty?" Emma was anxious to see her brother and his wife, but she also wanted to change the subject.

"You'll see for yourself shortly; they're coming for supper. In fact, I should be up helping Cora get it ready. She's been helping me at the hotel until you came." Lucy started to rise.

"No, stay and rest until it's time to eat," Emma insisted. "I'll go help her. I haven't seen Cora for a long time either, so I'll enjoy a chance to visit with her while we work." Cora was another one of Grandville's mail-order brides. She was married to Ray Tunelle, who was Ralph's younger brother. Together the two brothers ran the general store in Grandville.

Jade, Lucy and Emma's sister-in-law, wasn't one of the famous brides who came to Grandville four years earlier, but she was involved in the process of choosing the women, and she met Tyler and fell in love with him during that time.

The idea of mail-order brides didn't seem as strange to Emma as it did to most people. Emma's own mother,

Sky, had been a mail-order bride back in the days when the town of Sand Creek was being settled.

"Em, you must be exhausted from that long ride," Lucy protested. "Let me get up and help."

"Lucy, you stay put." Buck entered the room. "I know you're looking forward to working with Emma, but you need to rest more. I'll help the ladies tonight."

"You?" Emma was surprised.

"Buck helps a lot with the hotel cooking," said Lucy as she obediently lay back on the pillows. "He's probably a better cook than I am."

"Never! Don't you start flattering me, Mrs. Riley. You can't get out of cooking that easily."

Before Emma knew what was happening, Buck had bent down and lovingly kissed his wife. Once again Emma was an unwilling spectator to a husband and wife embrace. Buck and Lucy seemed unaware of her embarrassment.

Emma enjoyed helping Cora prepare the evening meal for the hotel guests. Cora was just as delighted to see Emma again.

"It's been over two years since you were in Grandville last, hasn't it? You've become a beautiful lady; I suppose you have lots of beaus," Cora teased.

"No, not really," admitted Emma. "I mean there have been some boys—men—who have wanted to call, but none who were...well, you know..."

Cora nodded. "None who were exactly right, is that it? Don't worry, Emma, the Lord can help you in that area of your life. You just need to be willing to follow his Word. Believe me, I know."

Emma worked in silence for a few moments then she spoke hesitantly to Cora. "Nearly all the women here in Grandville were married by the time they were my age. I never thought that much about it before. Here, everywhere I look there are couples and now," she added with grin, "lots of babies! It almost makes me feel like I'm missing out on something."

"I know that feeling too." Cora smiled. "Maybe you don't remember when I first came here with my cousin." Cora shook her head at the memory. "I was overweight and self-conscious. I never really believed someone would actually want to marry me. Everyone else was pairing off, and I began to feel it was hopeless and that I should return home. Then Ray spoke up and we were married. Now I have a beautiful daughter and I've even lost all my extra weight!"

She took Emma's arm and looked closely at her. "I'm a firm believer in trusting that the Lord works in our lives for his glory. Even now, every day brings new challenges, and Ray and I seek the Lord's leading to meet those challenges."

Emma nodded her head slowly as she thought over what Cora said. Then she looked at Cora in surprise and asked, "You were overweight? I *don't* remember that."

Cora laughed, and the two resumed their work. Presently Buck joined them.

"Roast beef, mashed potatoes, gravy, green beans, and—and—apple cake?" His nose was working while he tried to guess the evening's menu.

"You're pretty good! I'm impressed!" Emma praised Buck, and he bowed comically.

"Don't be," Cora warned. "He knew the menu before he came in here; he helped plan it."

"Now, Cora, don't give away all my secrets." Buck laughed. "What can I do to help tonight?"

They had almost finished their preparations, so Buck went to ring the dinner bell for the guests and the town people who were planning to eat at the hotel. Anyone who came in later would have to have their meal warmed over.

"Hey, Emma. Tyler and Jade and Eddie just got here." Buck took the platter of meat from her hands. "Go say hello to them before we serve."

Emma gladly went in search of her oldest brother. "Ty! Jade!"

The couple turned at hearing their names, and Tyler stepped forward to receive Emma's embrace. "It's great to have you here, Em. How are Dad and Mom and the boys?"

"They're fine. They all send their love. Dad's still not back yet, but—"

Suddenly Emma became aware that Sophia was watching them from across the room. She lowered her voice.

"Dad is still out on a case, but Mom and Rex and Abel are managing the ranch pretty well. Ty, have you ever seen that woman over there? No! Don't turn around!"

Tyler grinned at his sister. "How can I answer your question if I don't look at her?" He looked at Emma closely. "Are you playing detective again? I thought you grew out of that years ago. I still remember how mad you made me when you'd follow me and Mike around and hide so you could listen to us talk."

Emma punched her brother on the arm, but her voice remained serious. "I'm not playing! She was at the way station for three days, and while I was there, I think she searched my belongings."

She didn't have time to tell Tyler more, for Jade and Eddie joined them at that moment; but she saw that Tyler was taking her more seriously as he glanced over at Sophia.

"Jade, you're huge! I mean—" Emma blushed in embarrassment at the words that had popped out of her mouth.

Jade laughed merrily. "It's all right, Emma, I know what you mean. This baby is due anytime now according to Doc Arnett, and believe me, I'm ready! Poor Eddie can't even sit on my lap anymore."

Emma knelt down to eye level with her nephew. He watched her curiously, clutching his mother's skirt with one hand.

"Remember me, Eddie? I'm your Aunt Emmie. I'm supposed to tell you hi from Adele, Jason, and Janelle."

The little redheaded boy's eyes lit up. "Jason?"

"Uh, huh. He said you can ride horses with him when you come to visit next time."

"Can we, Pa?" Eddie pulled at Tyler's pant leg.

His father chuckled. "Thanks a lot, Em. Now that's all we'll hear from him."

"You look wonderful, Emma." Jade smiled at her sister-in-law. "How has teaching gone this last year? Glad to be done?"

Emma conversed with Jade, and they caught up on each other's news. All the while she kept an eye out for Sophia, who hovered closer and closer to hear what they were saying. Emma caught Tyler's eye once, and he indicated that he'd never seen Sophia before.

Most of the guests had gathered, so Emma excused herself and returned to the kitchen. She helped Cora and Buck carry the platters and bowls of food into the next room. Most of the people were seated at three main tables with a few scattered at smaller tables around the room.

Before they began, Buck asked the blessing. Emma noticed the surprise on the newest guests' faces. Sophia raised her eyebrows. Cora insisted that Emma sit and eat with her family while she took care of keeping the food platters and the coffee cups full.

It wasn't long after they had begun eating that Sophia spoke to Emma.

"You seem to know so many people here, Emma. Are you related to someone else?"

Emma took time to pat her mouth with her napkin before replying. "Yes, Miss Barlow." She looked sharply at Tyler to warn him. "This is my brother-in-law Buck Riley. He's Dugan's brother. Buck, this is Miss Sophia Barlow, Mr. and Mrs. Findley, and Neil and Herb Robinson. Buck owns this hotel you will be staying in."

Buck acknowledged the introductions and answered some questions his new guests had.

Emma then continued, "And this is my brother Tyler Newly, his wife Jadyne, and their son Edmund."

An unmistakable glint appeared in Sophia's eyes again, and she immediately turned her attention on Tyler.

"Do you live here in Grandville, Mr. Newly, or are you just passing through like the rest of us?"

Tyler answered Sophia's questions in a friendly tone without elaborating. It was clear that Sophia was not satisfied. Her questions became more personal until finally others at the table began to look at her. Neil Robinson thought he should help her out.

"You'll have to get used to Miss Barlow's questions, Mr. Newly. She's a writer."

"Oh, really, Miss Barlow? That sounds interesting. What have you written?" Tyler asked her.

Sophia's face went blank, and she looked at Neil with icy eyes. "Uh, nothing you've probably ever heard of... I'm fairly new at it." She fell silent.

Emma was proud of Tyler for turning the questioning back on Sophia. Whatever the woman was up to, he'd find it out.

The meal ended, and since Emma insisted on doing the cleanup, Buck sent Cora home with Ray and their daughter Minerva, who was affectionately nicknamed Minnie. He said he'd help with the cleanup, and Tyler offered his help too. Jade and Eddie went to visit Lucy, and the hotel guests either returned to their rooms, the lobby, or went outside for some evening air. Herb Robinson took Sophia for a walk.

Emma was clearing away dishes when Ralph sauntered into the dining room and took a chair at a small table. She looked up from what she was doing and found him watching her.

"Did you need to see Buck, Ralph?" she asked, unsure how to behave around him.

Ralph laughed under his breath. "I can see Buck anytime, but *you* are a different story. I like seeing you here, Emma."

The dishes clattered in Emma's hands.

"Does that make you nervous? You've sure turned into a pretty thing."

Emma was rapidly becoming irritated. "What is it you want, Ralph?" she asked in her no-nonsense teacher voice.

He laughed again. "Okay, put away the icy glare. I'll behave myself. I usually come in about this time for my supper. I find that if I wait until Ray and Cora leave, I don't have to put up with a sermon from my brother while I eat. Just let Buck know I'm here; he keeps a plate hot for me."

Emma moved to the kitchen with a load of dishes in her arms. As she backed through the door, she glanced at Ralph again, and in that unguarded moment she saw in his face a mixture of hopelessness and loneliness. She explained to Buck, and sure enough, he had a plate all prepared. His hands were wet from the dishwater, so she waved him away and took the plate herself.

Ralph's gloomy look brightened as Emma approached. Emma could see in his eyes that he was about to say something flirtatious to her again, so she quickly spoke first.

"Ralph, I know you've heard this before, but you have to give your problems over to the Lord. He'll—"

"Not you too, Emma!" Anger flared in Ralph's eyes. "*You!* What do you know about my kind of problems?" He stood to his feet and picked up the plate of food she had set before him. "Tell Buck I'll return the dishes tomorrow." With that, he left the dining room.

Shaken by Ralph's outburst, Emma went back to help the men wash up. She said nothing about the incident other than to inform Buck that his dishes would be returned later. Apparently Ralph often left the dining room to eat, for Buck only nodded.

They finished their work in good time, and the men headed back to Buck and Lucy's home off the hotel. Emma decided to take a short walk first and would join them later, she told them. She had a lot on her mind.

The night air felt cool and crisp, and Emma walked briskly for a while down one side of the small town. She barely saw the lights in the windows, and the murmur of voices behind the closed doors never reached her ears. She was deep in thought.

Sophia was a puzzle. The woman had obviously searched her bag at the way station, and she asked too many questions. Emma noticed that it was she or Gabe or Tyler that held Sophia's interest the most. Sophia seemed to want to know about the Newlys and Trents, but why?

Then there was Ralph. Although Emma knew the kind of person Philippa was, she was still shocked to see their marriage falling apart. That sort of thing shouldn't happen. Emma had always been taught that marriage was for life and that differences could be handled through prayer. *But what if one of them wasn't saved?* The thought struck Emma. What if they couldn't solve their problems through prayer because they didn't know the God they were talking to? That could be it.

Emma petitioned God at that moment for the salvation of either Ralph or Philippa or both. And if they were both saved, she reasoned, they had a foundation to build on. They just had to make some repairs first, and that would be possible with God. She knew even as these thoughts came to her that she was oversimplifying the problems, but she also knew the power of God to change lives.

There was a bench up ahead in front of the General Store, so Emma took the opportunity to sit. Another problem niggled at her brain. Should she teach school next year? She sighed then took a deep breath of the night air. *Lord, what should I do?* she prayed. Was it wrong to be dissatisfied with her life? She felt she needed something new, but what?

"Hello, Emma. Did you come to say good night to me?"

Emma jumped at the man's voice. She had been so deep in her own thoughts that she had not heard him approach. "Who is it?" she asked. She could only make out a form in the darkness.

"I'm glad you came, Emma. I've been thinking about you ever since you got off the stage."

Emma stood and backed away from the man as he reached for her arm.

"No, don't go. Not without a kiss goodnight."

"Ralph?"

He pulled her roughly, and as she was drawn closer to him, she smelled liquor on his breath.

"Ralph, leave me alone! I was just out for a walk!" She tried to pull away.

"Just one little kiss," he mumbled. He lost his balance and pulled sharply on Emma's arm to hold himself up. She was jerked against him, and his face came down to hers. She felt his lips on her cheek as he searched for her mouth.

With all her might, Emma shoved Ralph away from her. In his unstable condition, he couldn't stay upright, and he crashed against the side of the building. Emma wasted no time getting as far away from him as she could.

She arrived at Buck and Lucy's back door panting for air, and she took a few moments to catch her breath while she patted her disheveled hair and waited for her heartbeat to return to normal. She didn't want to worry Lucy, but she was determined to speak to Buck at the first opportunity about what had happened. Ralph definitely needed help.

Finally, Emma felt calm enough to enter the house. She heard voices in the next room and assumed that Jade and Tyler were still there, so she went in to see them. They were there all right, but it wasn't seeing them that made Emma stop dead in her tracks and cover her mouth with her hand.

A man lay on the floor with his bandaged leg out in front of him. It was her father.

Chapter 5

Grandville

"Dad!"

Emma rushed into the room and knelt beside her father. He propped himself up on an elbow and stared at her.

"What are you doing in Grandville, Emma?"

"Dad, are you all right? What happened?"

"He's okay, Em. Lie down again, Pa. I've got to loosen this bandage you've put on. It might hurt some." Tyler carefully examined his father's leg by running his hands gently over the skin. "No bones sticking out, anyway."

"Bones? Will someone please tell me what happened?" Emma insisted.

"Your dad's horse fell on his way here, Em. He was thrown and got his leg twisted under him. It's probably broken; we'll know more when the doc gets here. He hasn't had a chance to tell us any details yet," Buck explained.

He turned to his father-in-law. "Russ, Emma came to help Lucy out at the hotel. She just arrived this evening too."

Russ Newly took his daughter's hand and smiled into her worried face. "I'm okay, Emmie, really, I am. So you're staying in Grandville?" His attention turned to Buck. "There's nothing wrong with Lucy, is there, Buck?" Worry temporarily obscured the pain in his eyes.

Buck hastened to explain. "Nothing serious, except you may be interested to know that you'll be getting another grandchild around about October or November."

Relief leapt into Russ's expression. "That's great news, Buck. Praise the Lord."

"I'll go for the doc now," Buck said.

"No, not yet." Russ stopped him. "As long as the bones are pretty much in place, I can wait to see the doctor. First I need to talk to you fellows. Emmie, maybe you and Jade better go let Lucy and Eddie know that I'll be all right."

Emma obediently ran to Lucy's room and relayed the message to her concerned sister. Jade sat on the bed to soothe Eddie's worries, and Emma hastily returned to the other room and her father's side. Russ had barely begun his story, but he stopped speaking when she sat down.

"Em, uh—maybe you should wait in the other room," he suggested.

But Emma shook her head. "No, Dad. I want to know what's going on too. You know you can trust me as well as you trust Tyler and Buck."

Russ sighed. "Okay, you can stay." Pain flickered over his face as he adjusted his leg and began to speak again. He talked for the next five minutes, explaining his latest case to his listeners. "I don't know the whole story. What I've gathered so far is that there are a couple of men who work in government offices in Washington, D.C., who've gotten themselves into a heap of trouble. Now, remember, this is confidential." He studied each face before him, receiving a nod from both Tyler and Buck. His gaze stayed on Emma.

"Of course, Dad. You can count on me," she assured him. Her mouth felt dry, and despite her concern for her father, she felt excitement building in her.

"These men have somehow stumbled onto a sophisticated counterfeiting ring right there at the capitol, and I don't mean something like the small printers we've dealt with out here. Remember when we turned our greenbacks into the government in exchange for gold coin several years back?"

The men again nodded, and Emma asked, "The Civil War greenbacks?"

"That's right."

"I discussed this with the older children in school," she continued. "The National Bank printed the paper money to help pay the costs of the war, but at first the greenbacks couldn't be exchanged for gold or silver, so people didn't trust them. After that, national bank notes came into effect backed by government bonds."

"Right again." Russ nodded and shifted position without moving the injured leg. "When the greenbacks were called in and the exchange offered in gold, that's when this band of thieves went to work and printed counterfeit greenbacks. They had a man right up there in the office who was in on it, and he let those counterfeits go through.

The group stole hundreds of thousands in gold from the U.S. Treasury, and it would never have been known if the two men I'm talking about hadn't uncovered the plot."

"Good for them!" Tyler exclaimed.

"Good for our country, but maybe not so good for them," Russ acknowledged. "Their testimony is needed to convict the top man and others, but until the trial, they need to be kept safe. Their lives are in danger." He let that statement sink in before continuing. "Like I said, there are two men, a younger fellow and an older man. One of them opted to stay in D.C., and he's being protected by a security agency there. The other knew Mr. Pinkerton and asked for his help personally. I think he felt he would be safer out of the area.

"I've got a hunch there's a lot more going on than what I have been told, but I've kept in contact with the agency, and my next move is to deliver a message to the man in Norris. Apparently my next instructions will be in it."

"You don't know what it says?" asked Emma.

"I was told it was confidential," was her father's reply. "Now with this leg busted up, I'm not going to be able to deliver the message, so I'm asking one of you fellows to go for me." He looked at Buck and Tyler.

"Sure, Pa. I can deliver the message for you," volunteered Tyler.

But Buck was shaking his head. "No, you can't go, Ty. Jade's about ready to have that baby, and you can't leave her now. I'll go."

"You're right. Maybe I better not chance being gone when Jade needs me. It will be my turn next time, then." Tyler slapped Buck on the back.

Emma was about to ask Buck how he could leave Lucy while she was still not well, but just then Jade came in from the bedroom.

"Buck, Lucy said she forgot to give you this right away when you got home. Mr. Dunham from the telegraph office sent it over while we were at supper." She handed Buck a piece of paper. "She said it didn't make any sense to her."

Buck took the message and puzzled over it. The words didn't make sense to him either.

"May I see that, Buck?" Russ asked. He took the message and skimmed over it. "I thought so. I told my boss he might be able to contact me through you or Tyler. This is a coded message." Russ studied the contents of the note more thoroughly then he explained. "Looks like my job has just gotten harder. Now I not only have to deliver the message, but I also have to keep this man hidden, under my protection for the next three months. After that, I have to see to it that he gets to Washington safely." Russ frowned slightly. "You can't be away from Lucy and the hotel that long, Buck, and I don't want him brought here being a danger to any of your families." He forestalled their next suggestions.

"I do believe that my place is here with Lucy these next months," Buck told Russ. "I'm sorry I can't help you, and with Tyler not being able to help, who can do it?"

"I can."

The three men turned at Emma's quiet words and stared at her. Russ took in his daughter's serious expression and spoke with caution.

"Thanks, Emma, but the job will be too dangerous. I couldn't send you, sweetheart." He turned back to the men. "If only there was time to get Hank over here."

But Emma ignored his words. "I could deliver the message, Dad, and then I could bring the man to our place or to the Riley's for safekeeping for the three months. Between you and Rex and Abel, you should be able to protect him even with a broken leg, right?"

But Russ was shaking his head. "I wouldn't have been able to take him back to Sand Creek. There're too many people who know that Hank and I work for the Pinkertons, and he wouldn't be safe there. I do know of a place…but no, Emma, I can't get you involved in this."

Emma's mind was still working. "The message you received indicates that the man is still safe anyway. Have you any idea what he looks like?"

"No."

"How will you know him, then?"

Russ grinned. "Believe it or not, we have passwords that we'll give each other. I'm supposed to meet him at the hotel dining room in Norris in two days."

"Do you think anyone suspects you?"

Russ shrugged. "There's always that possibility. I'm sure that whoever is after this guy is watching for an agent to show up in the area and maybe lead him to where the guy is hiding. Like I said, a lot of folks know that I work for the Pinkertons, and they probably even know that Tyler and Buck sometimes help me. Word gets around, and people like to brag about knowing a Pinkerton man."

"Which is why they wouldn't suspect a woman!" exclaimed Emma.

Russ studied his daughter thoughtfully. "No, they probably wouldn't. You know, Emma, that just might work. There's another agent I know of in the area, a new guy. If I could get him here to take over for you after you delivered the message…" Russ's voice trailed off while he thought, and Emma's heart raced as she realized her dad was considering her suggestion. Tyler and Buck looked doubtfully at each other.

Suddenly Tyler remembered. "What about Sophia Barlow?" he directed the question at Emma.

"That's right! Dad, a woman named Sophia Barlow has been asking a lot of questions about the Newlys and the Trents." Emma explained in detail about the way station and the coach ride.

"Well, that does it, then. You're not going if this woman suspects you."

"Actually, I think she was more interested in me than Emma," said Tyler. "Apparently the name Newly means something to her, and if it's because it's connected to the Pinkertons, I really doubt that Emma interests her."

Russ remained thoughtful while the others waited in silence. Though eager to be of help, Emma waited patiently for her father's decision. Finally, he asked Buck for some writing paper so he could compose a message for his boss. "You'll probably have to get Mr. Dunham up to send this. Ty, I think I'll see Doc Arnett now."

Russ finished writing the message, and when Buck reached to take the note from him, he carefully avoided looking at it. Russ chuckled. "Go ahead and look, Buck. I doubt that it will make any sense to you. There are only a few agents who use this code; your pa is one of them."

Emma looked over Buck's shoulder at the printed message, and Russ watched her lips move as she tried to decipher it. "Injured. Need replacement. Send unknown. Newton."

Russ was astonished. "How did—?"

"You showed me the code once when I was little," she explained. "I had been pestering you with detective questions, and I suppose you thought I would never understand what it was all about, but I never forgot it. Don't worry, I haven't shown anyone."

Russ stared in amazement at his daughter. "Give me that paper," he ordered. Quickly he scribbled out a new message and handed it back to Emma.

She took it and studied the message carefully. Her eyes flew to her father's face in disbelief; then she threw her arms around his neck. "Thanks, Dad! I'll do a good job. You won't be sorry."

"You're only going to deliver the message and take our friend to a place of safety until a replacement arrives, is that understood? I think maybe you're right about no one suspecting a woman."

Emma's eyes gleamed excitedly as her father made her sit and listen to his careful instructions. "Now that I've had a little more time to think about it, I don't want to risk sending Buck or Tyler. The people around here know they've done Pinkerton jobs for me before, and this is too important of a case to assume no one is paying attention to their whereabouts. I'd never get you involved if I had another choice," he explained to her. "And I'll get you out of it as soon as possible, you understand?"

Emma nodded.

"I'll send you a telegram in Norris in code just like this one with your instructions." Russ studied his daughter's face intently. Emma could see the love and concern in his eyes. "Let's pray together before the doctor gets here."

Buck left with the message, and Emma went to gather her belongings while Doc Arnett tended to her father. She took a few moments to join Lucy and Jade.

"I'm sorry to leave you so soon, Lucy. I feel awful about it, but I'm very excited to be working for Dad."

"Don't worry about a thing, Em. I'm feeling better, and Buck said the Morrisons have a daughter who might be able to help us out for a while. He'll check with them tomorrow." She reached for Emma's hand. "I really just wanted to have you around. I've missed you."

"The Morrisons bought land north of town and are going to try raising some cattle," Jade explained. "They have seven children. Maybe in the fall if you're still looking for something different to do, you could teach school here in Grandville. We're going to need a teacher soon the way this town is growing."

Emma grimaced. "It would be fun to stay here for the winter, but I just don't know. I've got to do some praying about what I'll do next."

"I'm worried about you leaving. Dad's already been hurt. What if something happens to you?"

Emma squeezed her sister's hand. "What happened to Dad was an accident. Besides, Dad knows I can handle myself, Lucy. We agreed that I would be a less likely suspect than one of the men, so there shouldn't be any trouble. And I don't expect to be gone too long."

They heard the back door open and close, and Emma said, "Maybe that's Buck back from the telegraph office. I'll go see." She still needed to have a word with Buck.

Finally her opportunity came, and Buck listened quietly as Emma explained Ralph's actions, but she saw anger build in his eyes. "He had been drinking, Buck. I know that doesn't excuse him, but normally Ralph would not have behaved that way."

"I think it's a good thing you'll be gone. I'll have a talk with Ralph. You can be *sure* it won't happen again."

Emma's brow creased. "Ralph *is* saved, isn't he? I mean, I got to thinking about the problems he and Philippa are having, and I wondered if maybe one or the other of them isn't saved."

Buck sighed deeply and put his hands on his hips. "I'm sure Ralph is. When we first came up here to build this town, we had weekly Bible readings and prayer together and all nine of us took turns leading it. I was often encouraged by Ralph's insight into God's Word. Yes, he's saved, and just because he's not serving the Lord now doesn't change that. He's still God's child and always will be. We'll have to pray that he comes to the end of himself soon and turns to God for strength to get through this. Philippa…I don't know. She always seemed to go along with everything we said and did, but I never heard her talk about her own salvation."

Emma looked thoughtfully out the window into the darkness. "We need to pray for her, Buck. Her getting saved may be the key to putting them back together."

"Well, you better get some rest. You'll have a busy day tomorrow."

As Emma climbed into bed in the room Lucy and Buck had prepared for her, she felt a tingle of excitement race through her. Tomorrow she would actually be working for the Pinkertons! Well, for her dad, but it amounted to the same thing, she thought. Thoughts of secret messages, codes, and a mysterious man swam through her mind as she drifted off to sleep.

Chapter 6

Grandville

Emma finished filling a platter with pancakes then carried it into the hotel dining room. They had all agreed the night before that she should continue on as normally as possible until the stage was ready to go. Russ, resting in bed with his broken leg, planned to stay in hiding at Buck and Lucy's, while Tyler planned to distract Sophia when the stage left so that she wouldn't know that Emma was on it.

Steam rose from the fragrant stack on the platter as Emma set it down on the table. Most of the hotel guests were already seated, so Buck led in prayer, and the meal began. Emma turned to go back into the kitchen when her name was called.

"Emma Newly! How's my little cousin?"

"Michael!" Emma opened her arms to receive a hug, but Michael Trent picked her up and twirled her around. Her cheeks flushed as the guests stopped eating to stare at them.

"Michael, stop that! I'm not twelve anymore! Besides, you're embarrassing me."

Michael hooted in laughter. "You're still as short as when you were twelve." He took a step back and studied her from her prim figure to her pinned-up hair. "Ah—but I see you have become a young lady."

"Michael! I'm almost twenty! I'm older than Mallory was when you married her." Emma knew she was being teased, so she put her hands on her hips and glared at her cousin. "Course, you're getting close to thirty, so I suppose I do seem pretty young to you!"

He laughed heartily at her comeback and gave her another hug. "It's good to have you in Grandville, Em. As soon as you're settled, you'll have to come see the house. We've added on already. Did you know Marcy and Marty are going to get a new brother or sister in a few months?"

"Yes, I'd heard that, Mike. Congratulations! How is Mallory feeling?"

"Great! She never gets sick. She—"

"Emma, you never told us you had so many relatives." Sophia stood behind Emma and smiled into Michael's eyes. "I'm Sophia Barlow, a traveling companion of Emma's."

"How do you do, Miss Barlow?" Michael's voice was pleasant and friendly, but Emma sensed his disapproval of Sophia's forward ways.

"So how are you and Emma related?"

"Michael is my cousin, Miss Barlow. He and Gabriel Trent are brothers, and you'll remember that their father and my mother are twins."

Sophia's eyes lit up. "Oh, so that's why you look so famil-iar. You have the same handsome jaw that Gabriel has." She watched for Michael's reaction to her flirtation.

But Michael wasn't taken in by her. "As a matter of fact, my wife thinks it's even better than Gabe's," he joked. "How long do you plan to be in Grandville, Miss Barlow?"

"It's such an interesting place, I may never leave," Sophia responded.

"Excuse me, there's more to get from the kitchen." Emma moved away.

"I'll give you a hand, Em," Michael volunteered as he followed her. "So that's the nosey Miss Barlow," he said quietly once they were through the swinging door. At Emma's look of surprise, he explained. "I was over at Buck's earlier this morning and spoke to your father. I have to tell you, Em, I'm not pleased about you going in Uncle Russ's place. I offered to go for you, but your dad said he's given you the go-ahead. I'm guessing he knows how busy we've been at the lumber mill and doesn't want to take me away from it. Tyler and I will never run out of work, it seems. But you will be careful, won't you?"

Emma nodded, but Michael caught the sparkle in her eyes.

"It's not a game, Em. Look at your dad. Who knows what caused his horse to bolt and fall like that?" Emma shot him a startled look. "You have to be suspicious of everyone while you try to act as normally as possible. You—"

"I know, Mike." She put a hand on his arm to stop him. "I'm not taking this lightly. I don't think it's a game, and I will be careful."

"Here." Michael handed Emma a folded piece of paper. "Before I left Buck's, I jotted down some verses that have been of great help to me when I've felt afraid or alone. Maybe they'll be of help to you sometime too."

Emma blinked back sudden tears. "Thanks, Mike, and thanks for understanding why I want to do this. I may be nervous, maybe even afraid, but I'll never be alone." She took the paper and opened it. Silently she read the references Michael had written down:

Joshua 1:9
Psalms 18:2
II Tim. 1:7
II Cor. 12:9

Some of the verses she was familiar with; others she would look up later.

The stage was ready and waiting with Emma's bags aboard. She stayed out of sight until everyone was inside, then, after a quick look around, she left the hotel and let Dugan help her inside the coach. Sophia was nowhere in sight, and Emma hoped Tyler was keeping her attention away from the departing passengers.

"Miss Newly! I thought you were staying in Grandville." Mrs. Findley exclaimed from her seat next to her husband as Emma slid in beside them.

"I decided to go on to Norris and visit some friends there first," explained Emma. She watched for the reactions of the other travelers. Besides the Findleys and the Robinson brothers, there was one other man. He was someone Emma knew by sight but not personally, a farmer near Grandville, she remembered.

Herb and Neil Robinson were delighted to have her traveling with them again, and they turned all their attention and what she assumed they considered their charm on her. Emma sat back and relaxed. *So far so good.*

After an overnight stay at the Sterne's way station, the next day's travel began with Emma feeling an increase in excitement. True, she would only deliver the message she had carefully pinned on the inside of her dress, and she would watch out for this man for a couple of days until she was replaced, but she couldn't help enjoying an exhilarant feeling of adventure.

The coach stopped for a noonday meal of sandwiches provided by the way station and for a rest for the horses for about an hour. Emma evaded the Robinson brothers' offers of escorting her on a walk and strolled alone by the bubbling creek. It felt good to stretch her legs. She felt as though she had been riding in a coach for months now. How glad she would be to have a few days without having to travel! She grinned at her thoughts. Her desire to have an adventure was certainly coming true, but she never knew dealing with sore muscles would be a part of it.

It was getting time to leave again when Dugan came to fetch her. Emma was instantly alert to the worried expression on his face.

"What's wrong?"

He pulled his hat off and combed through his hair with his fingers. "I'm not sure that anything is, but I thought since you were working for your pa that you should know."

Emma nodded. Dugan didn't know what her job was, but he had been informed to help her if she needed it.

"I was just on top of the coach checking over the cargo, and I noticed that the bags had been moved. I packed them myself, Em, so I know how they should have been. Two were turned around, both of them yours. No," he continued before she could voice her question, "they didn't get bounced around while we were moving. They were actually turned around." He waited for her reaction.

Emma thought hard. Where had everyone been during their break? "Any ideas?" She asked Dugan.

He shook his head. "I was down by the creek getting water for the horses, so I couldn't see the coach. Anybody could have done it. Could be that somebody just wanted something out of their own bags and had to move yours to get to them," he added.

Emma nodded. "Thanks, Dugan. Fortunately, there's nothing in my bags anyway that would make me suspicious to anyone."

"Then maybe whoever is suspicious will search you next," Dugan said pointedly. "Look, Em, I don't like it. If your pa knew about this, he might pull you off your job."

But Emma's look was determined. "I can handle it, Dugan, so don't you go worrying my dad. Whoever is interested in me, *if* someone is, will soon realize I'm just an innocent traveler. You'll see." Emma's tone was confident, and she smiled reassuringly at her friend. "Let's not keep the others waiting." She hoped Dugan didn't notice the tremor in her voice or see her hands shake as she held them tightly against her sides.

Emma tried to appear nonchalant as they approached the other travelers who were reluctantly preparing to enter the confining coach again. Unobtrusively, she scrutinized each one. Mentally, she shook her head. *Who could it be?*

They were about a mile farther down the road when the coach was hailed. Emma stuck her head out one of the side windows and saw a rider racing to catch up with them.

"Oh dear! It's not an outlaw, is it?" Mrs. Findley clung to her husband's arm while he made attempts to soothe her.

"There's only one," Neil Robinson informed them as Dugan began slowing the horses. "Hey! It's a girl!"

Herb leaned over Neil for a look. "It's Miss Barlow! What is she doing out here?" he exclaimed.

Neil pushed his brother off him with a grunt. "She probably missed me," he gloated.

"Ha!" Herb leaned out again. "Slow down, Riley! We got another passenger."

Emma's hands felt cold as she gripped the handbag on her lap. *Sophia!* The search of the luggage no longer appeared to be a mystery. Sophia must have caught up to them while they were resting the horses, gone through her luggage, and waited until now to "catch up" to them again.

Silently, Emma asked the Lord for guidance. Her father was depending on her to handle this job; she must not let Sophia get in her way. The coach finally rolled to a stop, and the Robinson brothers jumped out to greet Sophia.

"Well, where does that young woman think she's going to sit?" wondered Mrs. Findley.

"I could ride with Dugan," offered Emma.

"*I'll* ride on top." The farmer moved to the door, then he looked back at the Findleys and Emma. "I'll leave our new passenger to get elbowed by those two"—he indicated the Robinson brothers—"every time we hit a bump." He flashed a crooked grin and was gone.

The conversation outside the coach was indistinct, so Emma leaned forward a bit to hear better. Her handbag rolled off her lap and onto the floor of the coach. She was so intent on trying to hear what Sophia was saying to Dugan that she didn't reach for it right away, so Mr. Findley picked it up for her. Sophia began to tie her horse to the back of the coach with the Robinsons' assistance. Emma sank back on the seat and was surprised to hear the Findleys laughing at her.

"My dear Miss Newly." Mr. Findley held out the bag to her. "Perhaps you will need this?"

Emma flushed. "Thank you, Mr. Findley. I didn't realize I had dropped it."

"Don't worry, dear," Mrs. Findley whispered to her with a knowing look. "I think the young men will still pay attention to you, even with Miss Barlow along. She's not half as pretty as you are in my opinion."

Goodness! thought Emma. *They think my preoccupation is due to jealousy of Sophia!* She was about to protest then stopped herself. Maybe it would be better to let them think just that.

Sophia stepped into the coach with a cheerful, "Hello! Bet you're surprised to see me!" She settled between Neil and Herb with her skirts taking up most of the room, and she gave them both intimate smiles before turning to Emma, completely ignoring the Findleys.

"Why, Emma! I thought you were staying in Grandville!"

Emma willed her voice to remain calm as she politely answered, "It's nice to see you again, Miss Barlow. I have some friends in Norris I wish to see. After I visit with them for a few days, I'll probably return and visit more with my relatives in Grandville. My summer is pretty much free—I teach school, you see."

"How interesting!" Sophia's feigned admiration irritated Emma even more. *What is she up to?*

"You're a school ma'rm?" Herb was surprised. "Wish my teacher had been as pretty as you; I'd a stayed in school."

Emma smiled at his compliment and was about to reply, but Sophia regained Herb's attention by taking hold of his arm. "I taught school once," she said. "But it wasn't what I wanted to do. Writing is my passion! I love adventure and excitement, don't you?"

The two young men nodded their heads vigorously, and Emma had to stifle a giggle. They reminded her of two puppy dogs trying to win approval from their master by wagging their tails, begging, or sitting up. Mrs. Findley gently patted Emma's arm to console what she thought was jealous anger at Sophia for taking Herb's attention. Emma came dangerously close to bursting out in laughter.

"Why ever did you race after us, Miss Barlow? Why didn't you just join us when we left Grandville?" Mrs. Findley decided to take Sophia's attention away from the men with her questions.

"I hadn't decided if I wanted to leave yet," Sophia answered carelessly. "When I make up my mind to do something, I just do it. So when I decided I wanted to see Norris next, I just started out."

"On your own?" Neil was shocked. "Where did you stay last night?"

"I left early this morning. It doesn't take long to catch up to a slow-moving coach. In fact, I would have kept riding, but my horse was getting tired, so I joined you." Sophia acted as though she did this sort of thing every day.

Emma's lips tightened at the thought of Sophia abusing the horse. *The animal is probably worn out.* Dugan must have thought so too, for Emma noticed that they were moving even slower than usual. *I bet Dugan is furious with Sophia. The horse is probably one from Buck's stables.*

"What will you be doing in Norris, Miss Barlow?" Herb asked.

"Please, everyone"—she held out her hands—"call me Sophia. I hate all this formality. And I'll call you Neil and Herb." She took their arms again. "Norris interests me. I'm sure I'll find something exciting to write about after I get there." Her eye caught Emma's, but Emma calmly looked out the window at the passing countryside.

So Sophia expects to find something interesting in Norris, she mused. *Well, so do I. The question is—how do I keep her from finding out about the man I'm supposed to meet?*

Chapter 7

Norris

The small town of Norris lay nestled in a valley between two rolling hills. The countryside around it was liberally dotted with trees, many of the pine family but others with newly sprouted buds, giving the area the fresh yellow-green color of spring.

Two men walked along the boardwalk, avoiding the soft muddy main street. The afternoon shadows were lengthening as they talked.

"Will he be on the coach?"

"I don't know—maybe. He might just ride in on his own. At any rate, we'll be meeting him tonight at the hotel dining room. Why don't you go back to the room and wait? I want to look over who's on the coach. Don't worry, I'll be careful."

"I'll be glad when we're out of this small town."

The other man only nodded then walked over to the bench outside the hotel. He settled down and tipped his hat forward and appeared to go to sleep.

The sun was sinking behind the hills when the stage finally came into view. The weary travelers peered out at the unimpressive row of buildings with relief. Their trip was almost over. Dugan called to his horses, and the coach gradually slowed down. The swaying hadn't even stopped before the door swung open and helping hands were assisting the passengers out.

The man on the nearby bench was amused by the attention the town gave the stagecoach. The seemingly empty town of Norris was suddenly filled with people. Apparently the coming of the stage was the highlight of the week for them, for they left their homes and their businesses and hurried to the hotel to get a look at the newcomers. All the better for him, he thought. He'd be less likely to be noticed. The man chuckled as he stood and went to lean against a post so he too could get a better view. He watched the elderly couple slowly descend from the coach. They looked stiff and sore from their ride, and he smiled in empathy, thinking of the long ride ahead for himself.

A young man jumped down next, and the man on the boardwalk narrowed his eyes as he studied him. There was a flash of skirts, and a pretty dark-haired woman was helped down. She held the young man's arm closely as they walked away from the coach together. Another young man jumped down, and he scowled after the couple who had just walked away, but he turned and helped the next passenger out.

Suddenly the man on the boardwalk stood up straight, and he stared as Emma stepped down.

"Thank you, Mr. Robinson," Emma said as she smoothed the skirt of her traveling dress. She was aware of the many eyes looking curiously at the passengers, and it made her nervous. Next time she was in Sand Creek when the stage rolled in, she vowed she would remember what this felt like and not stare at the people on it. She glanced around at the faces, and her eyes stopped on the man by the post.

Quickly she looked away and turned back to the coach for her luggage. Her heart was thumping, but she tried to remain calm. The man had been staring at her with something like surprise in his eyes! Suddenly she was frightened.

"You okay, Em?" Dugan held her bags in his hands.

Emma calmed; Dugan was still here. Dugan was still a lifeline if she needed one. She smiled shakily at him. "I'm fine. Here, let me take those; you have the horses to care for."

"Allow me."

They both turned at the man's words, and somehow Emma knew without looking it was the stranger, but she forced herself to meet his eyes. He was standing very close behind her, and he gallantly swept off his hat and made a little bow. To Emma's surprise, she saw amusement now lurking in his eyes.

Dugan waited for Emma's permission before handing over her things; then with a backward glance, he went back to caring for his horses and coach.

"Am I interfering?" The man nodded to Dugan once, and Emma felt her cheeks redden.

"What? Oh—no! Dugan is just a friend—practically a–a relative even. You're not—you're—" She stammered to a stop and willed herself to quit acting like an idiot. She straightened her shoulders and put on her "teacher face," as her brothers teasingly called it. She opened her mouth to speak again when she saw the faintest of smiles cross the man's face. Puzzled at what he found funny, she forgot what she was going to say.

"Miss, I don't mean to embarrass you, and I want you to know that I'm not feeling any pain especially. I'm mostly just interested in your personal safety and everything."

"What's wrong?" Emma looked quickly from right to left and leaned past him to see what possible danger might be threatening her safety. She saw a quick grimace cross the man's face, and she put out a hand to him. "Are you all right, sir?"

"Yes, miss. It's just that—would you mind moving a little? You're stepping on my foot."

Emma gave a gasp and looked down at her small foot resting squarely on the man's boot. She hastily stepped back.

"My goodness, Emma! Do you have more relatives here in Norris too?"

Emma spun around at Sophia's call and, being already disoriented, she promptly lost her balance. The tall man behind her dropped her bags and grabbed her around the waist. She clutched at his arms and got her feet firmly planted under her before daring to look up into the laughing blue eyes again.

"Honestly, Emma! Every time I turn around, some man is hugging you! Who is it this time? Another brother, cousin, uncle?" Sophia stood with her hands on her hips, shaking her head at them while she waited for an introduction.

Emma groaned inwardly. *How does Sophia always manage to be around?*

After making sure Emma was safely on her feet, the man again swept off his hat and bowed to Sophia. "Allow me to introduce myself. I am Simon Chase and..."—He paused slightly—"...Emma"—(he appeared to be testing the name)—"and I are...friends." He smiled at Emma, ignoring her horrified look and turned back to Sophia. "Now, if you'll excuse us, we need to get...Emma...settled."

Sophia's eyes gleamed, and Emma saw the intense interest in them. The sooner she was away from Sophia's inquisitiveness, the better. "Yes, please excuse us, Miss Barlow. I'll probably see you later." And she followed the man named Simon Chase as he carried her bags up the steps to the hotel.

Once inside away from listening ears, Emma stopped him. This time her "teacher face" was ready, and a simmering anger burned in her eyes. "Do you realize what you have led Miss Barlow to believe, implying that we are... are friends and that you had to help me get settled in this hotel?"

"Now, Emma—"

"My name is Miss Newly."

Simon Chase seemed to have trouble controlling his features.

Emma watched him carefully, for if it looked to her like he might even smile a little, she would explode.

"Miss Newly," he corrected himself. "Please forgive me, but it seemed that you didn't wish to converse with the woman at the moment, and it would have been a bit difficult to explain exactly why I was holding you, don't you think, especially since you were the one who was standing on my foot? I'm sure you can explain it all to her at another time. For now, I'll just bid you good night, Miss Newly, and I hope you enjoy your stay in Norris."

Emma said nothing as Simon Chase tipped his hat and strode away. She didn't even turn to watch him, which was a good thing since his shoulders were shaking with laughter. Her face remained impassive as she stared ahead of her, waiting for her temper to cool down. Her brothers knew that look as well and were wise enough to stay away from her until she had it under control.

A hesitant voice interrupted her thoughts.

"I said, may I help you, miss?"

Emma started. The hotel clerk was looking at her strangely. "Yes, please." She cleared her throat. "I would like a room."

"Did you figure out which one is the messenger?"

Simon closed the door behind him and sank into a chair beside the bed. "No. I recognized one of the passengers, and at first I thought she might be the one."

"She?"

"The daughter of an agent I know. I've seen pictures of his family, so I knew who she was when she got off the stage."

"You're a friend of this agent?"

"We know each other. I have great respect for him."

The older man sat on the side of the bed. "So why don't you think his daughter is the one?"

Simon chuckled and stretched out his long legs. "She barely made it into the hotel without having an accident. And that temper! Whew! She'd be the wrong one to send on this mission. No, I saw a man on top with the driver, but he took off to the saloon right away. I'm guessing it might be him."

"Well, we'll know tonight. I'm anxious to move on. These small towns make it hard to be inconspicuous."

Emma hung up a few of her things, but she left most of her belongings packed. She needed to be ready to leave in a hurry, she reasoned. Her father had given her instructions on where to take the man to wait for her replacement. It was an out-of-the-way sort of place, a small farm north of the town. She had wondered what reason they would give people for him living there for such a short while, but her father had suggested she discuss it with the man after he had seen the message she carried. Most likely he would pretend to be a relative who needed help getting started on his own farm. Her father's coded message should arrive by tomorrow too, and that would contain further instructions.

It had worried her father, as well as Buck and Tyler, that Emma would be alone with this man, but they had agreed that she could stay in town and be his eyes and ears while he stayed at the farm. Emma knew her father would send that replacement as soon as possible, especially if it meant protecting his daughter's reputation.

Her thoughts drifted to the man called Simon Chase. Why had he seemed surprised when he first saw her? She was aware that men often noticed her, but her experiences with attention from them had been limited mainly to her own small town and men she knew. She still felt embarrassed at the unusual circumstances when Sophia came upon them. She shrugged. She hoped he wouldn't annoy her further like the Robinson brothers had.

Emma changed into an attractive deep blue dress for dinner. She carefully pinned the message to her undergarments and checked her handbag. Her father had given her a large amount of money to carry. He said she should be prepared for any emergency.

She counted the money carefully; it was all there. She checked her handbag again, this time looking for the verses that Michael had written for her. She could use some encouragement about now. Where had she put that paper? She found two torn pieces of the paper and looked at them in dismay. She must have ripped the paper while she dug in her bag, and now she only had the pieces with the numbers of the chapters and verses, but not the books they came from.

She tried to remember what references Michael had written, but with all the excitement she'd been through, she just couldn't. She reached for her Bible instead and took a few moments to strengthen herself spiritually. Then she prayed for wisdom for the task ahead. One final look in the mirror, and she was ready to go meet the mystery man.

Chapter 8

Norris

The hotel dining room didn't seem too busy, but then for a small town like Norris, it might, in fact, be very busy. Emma stood in the doorway for a few moments wondering who would be the best person to approach. Her father had instructed her that it was to be her job to contact the man and speak first. The man would be waiting in the hotel dining room, and he would be reading a book.

Emma noticed two men reading books and one man jotting down some notes in a book. She decided to ignore him. One of the others was Mr. Findley from the stagecoach; it wouldn't be him, would it? As she passed him, he looked up and smiled. She nodded but went by him. She would speak to the other man first, the one with the large book that covered his face. Perhaps she was too early and the man hadn't even arrived yet.

Her step faltered and butterflies made havoc of her stomach. *What time I am afraid, I will trust in thee.* The words soothed her mind and she reached the table in a calmer state than she had begun. The man still held the book too high for Emma to see his face, so she stood unnoticed for a moment. She started to peer around the book then thought better of it. She cleared her throat slightly.

The book moved, but still the man didn't seem aware of her presence. Emma saw a few people look her way. "Excuse me, sir, may I sit down?" she asked.

The book instantly was whipped away, and Emma's face fell when she found that she was speaking to Simon Chase.

He stood, and there was definite amusement in his face. "Of course, Miss Newly, I would be delighted to have you join me. Please sit down."

But Emma backed away. "No thank you. I'm sorry; I thought you were someone else. I'll—" She jumped as his hand flashed out and caught her by the arm. "What are you doing?"

His pull on her made her trip and fall forward, and again he caught her in his arms. Anger flared through her, and she was about to unleash it when she saw where he was pointing. A wide-eyed young girl carrying a tray filled with steamy bowls of hot soup was standing directly behind her. Emma had almost backed into the serving girl.

Immediately Emma was contrite. "I'm so sorry, miss, may I help you?" But the girl was back in control and moved on to do her serving. Emma sank into the closest chair.

"There now, Miss Newly. How pleasant of you to think of joining me. That soup smells wonderful; I think I'll have some of that. How about you?" Simon spoke politely, but Emma could still see the laughter he was hiding. She had done enough to make herself look foolish in front of him, and she was tired of being laughed at. She started to rise, but Simon put his hand over hers and spoke quietly.

"Isn't there something you wish to tell me, Emma?" His voice was no longer teasing, and his eyes told her he was serious. Still, she was unsure. He watched her struggle to make up her mind.

Hesitantly she spoke the words her father had given her. Simon smiled in reassurance and answered her carefully and exactly so that she would have no doubt that he was the mystery man. Emma sighed. How could she spend several days anywhere near this man? Whenever she was around him, things went wrong and she ended up looking and feeling incompetent.

Simon motioned to the serving girl and ordered the soup for both of them. He sat back and studied Emma silently until she felt her face flush at his scrutiny.

"Do you always blush when you're nervous?" he teased.

Emma felt her temper begin to rise again, and she fought to control it.

"Aha! There's that look again. I've said something to make you angry once more. Please forgive me, Emma, but your blush is quite becoming."

"Mr. Chase, since we'll be working together, I think it best that we remain formal with each other." She missed Simon's amused grin. "I am to take you to a place north of—"

Emma was startled to silence when Simon leaned forward again and took her hand. "My dear Emma, this is not the place to discuss our business." He glanced around. "Too many eyes and ears. You can give me your information later in my room."

Emma's expression was incredulous. "I'm not going to your hotel room!" she hissed.

Simon grinned. "Then perhaps we can take a walk after supper and make some plans. You have the message with you?" At her nod, he said, "You can give it to me now."

A strange expression crossed Emma's face.

"Is there something wrong?"

If it were possible for her face to redden more, it did. Emma cleared her throat slightly. "I...uh...I'll have to give it to you later after all. Um...I..."

"Well, well, Emma! So you two are a little more than friends, I gather." Sophia stood by their table, and interest gleamed in her eyes. She wore the same low-cut dress she had worn at the way station, and Emma's heart sank as she realized that Sophia was looking at Simon's hand over her own. She tried to pull hers away, but Simon held it more tightly.

"Good evening; Miss Barlow, isn't it?"

Simon started to rise, but Sophia waved him back. "Now I see why you sneaked off to Norris, Emma. Do you have any more secrets I should know about?" Sophia showed perfect white teeth when she smiled, and Emma saw her wink at Simon.

Anger flared up within Emma again. Sophia was thinking the worst about her and Simon, and she was going to set her straight! But Simon's next words shocked her to silence.

"Miss Barlow, I see you have a keen eye for observation and no doubt you have guessed already that Emma and I are very fond of each other. I do hope you can keep our secret for us?" Simon's confiding declaration thrilled Sophia. She gushed out congratulations and sent Emma an "I told you so" kind of look. Had Simon not been holding Emma's hand so tightly, she would have run from him, from Sophia, from everything!

"How wonderful! I knew Emma was up to something! Are you a mail-order-bride, Emma, like some of your relatives?" At Emma's quick look of surprise, Sophia giggled. "Oh, I've been asking questions about your family and about Grandville. Did you know most of the couples in Grandville were formed from a newspaper ad?" she asked Simon.

"Ah! But with Emma and me, it's true love that has brought us together. Isn't that right, dear?" Simon squeezed her hand, and Emma winced. She looked at him in anger, but his expression reminded her of the job she was sent to do. She had to protect Simon, and if this was one way to get rid of the nosey Sophia Barlow, then she would go along with it. But he was going to regret it. She placed her other hand over his and smiled sweetly at him while her fingernails dug into the back of his hand.

"Simon, you weren't supposed to tell."

His eyes barely gave evidence of the pain he was feeling, but there was a definite challenge in the way he looked at her.

"Oh, I'm so excited for you! I knew there was a story in you, Emma Newly!" Sophia exclaimed. "Will you be getting married soon?"

Emma's eyes widened, but Simon laughingly said, "We haven't made plans yet, Miss Barlow." He smiled confidently at Emma.

She smiled too and was satisfied when she saw Simon grimace in pain as she pressed her foot down on his toes. Growing up with brothers had taught Emma a few things about standing up for herself.

Sophia looked hard pressed to contain her excitement. "Aren't you excited, Emma?"

Emma just smiled again as Sophia hurried off; then she turned back to Simon with sparks flaring. "What do you think you're doing?"

Simon held up his hand and rubbed the back of it. "Emma, we may be watched even now. You must be careful what you say."

"*I* must be careful? Who's going to stop you?" Emma sputtered.

"Look. Let's eat now and we'll talk later when we have more privacy. The important thing is that I get that message."

Emma bit her lip and refused to look at Simon. "I can't give it to you now," she said through clenched teeth. "It's pinned to—it's pinned under—it's…"

Simon's chuckling stopped her, and she glared at him with icy eyes. She glanced at the other diners, but none seemed to be paying attention. "I had to keep it safe!" she muttered under her breath.

"Guess I'll have to wait until *after* we're married." He quickly held up a hand at her expression. "I'm only kidding. Settle down."

They ate their meal in silence, but Emma was inwardly fuming and it didn't help that Simon appeared to be enjoying the situation immensely. After they finished, he suggested they take a stroll.

As they walked through the hotel lobby, a man approached Simon and spoke quietly to him. Emma watched Simon give him a few instructions, and then the man bowed slightly and went up the steps. She turned to Simon in surprise.

"Is he your servant? What do *you* need a servant for?"

Simon opened then closed his mouth. He seemed to be thinking over Emma's question. "Why shouldn't I have a servant? Of course, now, if I were getting a wife, I suppose I could let Charles go. Can you cook?"

Emma refrained from answering and nearly refused the arm he offered. They walked along the boardwalk without speaking until Simon led Emma to a spot at the edge of the small town, away from the buildings. He looked carefully around and checked to make sure they weren't followed. Emma uncomfortably realized that that should be her job. She was puzzled about Simon and why he, seemingly so capable, needed protection.

As soon as they were settled on a fallen log, he began to ask her questions. It wasn't long before he knew all about her father being hurt and her temporary status as an agent. It was the first time they seemed able to converse normally with each other without any pretense between them. Emma's animosity towards Simon was forgotten.

"And I want you to know how much I admire what you are doing for the government, Mr. Chase. I think it is very brave of you, and I will do my best to see to your safety."

Simon studied Emma's face a moment as if debating how to reply. He acknowledged her compliment with a nod, and they continued their discussion. When he learned that she was to wait with him until a replacement came, he started to shake his head.

"That may not be the best thing anymore. Tell me about Sophia Barlow. You said she might get more suspicious than she already was."

Emma related the events of the past few days, omitting nothing but Ralph Tunelle's interest in her. That was personal.

"Maybe she really is just a nosey writer," he commented. "But it's best not to take chances. I'll know more after I see that message. I do need it now, Emma."

Emma stared blankly at Simon for an instant. "If you'll just turn around for a minute," she muttered.

Simon couldn't help snickering as he turned away, but Emma ignored him. She swiftly began to unfasten the message pinned to her undergarments, but suddenly she stopped. A prickly feeling began in her scalp, and without a doubt she knew they were being watched. Was it Sophia spying on her again?

"Mr. Chase."

He turned quickly at her tone. "What's wrong?" He spoke quietly as she had while his eyes searched the surrounding area without seeming to, and he put an arm around her shoulders to steady her. "Emma, don't pull away. I think we're being watched." He looked down into her widened eyes. "We better give whoever is spying on us something to see."

She was unprepared when his face bent down to hers and he kissed her. She started to struggle, but the pressure of his arm on her shoulder reminded her that he was only acting, and she kept trying to convince herself that it was only an act as the time lengthened. When he finally released her, she didn't know if her heart was pounding because of their danger or because of his kiss.

She was still held close to Simon when she slowly opened her eyes. His hold on her tightened when she started to move away.

"Really, Mr. Chase, I don't think this is all that necessary," she protested breathlessly.

His voice was soft against her hair. "Behind you to your right is a man. I wonder who else besides Miss Barlow has taken such an interest in us."

Emma turned her head slightly to look into the darkness. "I don't see a man," she whispered to Simon's shirtfront.

"He's gone now." Simon still held her. "We must have convinced him that we were a normal couple in love."

Suddenly Emma pushed away from him. "All you've convinced me of is that you're a good actor." She tried to fix her hair by pushing in the pins, and she straightened her collar and adjusted her sleeves, anything to keep from looking at Simon. Thankfully, the darkness hid her flaming cheeks. How embarrassing this was! Since her first meeting with the mystery man she'd done nothing right. She couldn't even deliver the message properly. *The message!*

"Turn around, Mr. Chase." With haste, she unpinned the important paper and with great relief she handed it over to Simon. There! That part was over.

Simon tucked the note into his pocket. "I'll call for you first thing in the morning and we'll breakfast in the hotel and discuss what to do next, all right?"

Emma nodded.

Simon spoke very quietly. "You're a good sport, Emma, to take over for your father like this. I want you to know that you've been a great help. Thank you." Simon leaned over and brushed a light kiss on Emma's cheek. Somehow that simple gesture stirred her more than his previous kiss.

A noise made them both turn with a guilty start.

"I'm sorry! We didn't mean to disturb you. Neil and I were just taking a stroll in the dark before retiring." Sophia's voice was filled with pent-up excitement and there was not a bit of regret evident in it. "It seems I'm always finding you kissing men in the dark, Emma Newly." There was a malicious note in Sophia's words, and she laughed gaily as they went on their way.

Emma scowled at Sophia's words. Sophia must have seen Ralph try to kiss her! How cruel of her to bring it up in front of Simon; after all, she thought Emma and Simon were in love, or did she? Was she testing them?

Simon shifted his position beside her on the log, and Emma realized he was waiting for her to speak. She started to explain then stopped herself. Why should she? Why did he need to know anything about Ralph? The silence lengthened.

Finally Simon said, "I guess we should get back to the hotel." He stood, and Emma followed. They didn't speak on the short walk, and it wasn't until Simon had delivered her to her door that he spoke again.

"Good night, Miss Newly, and thank you again."

"Good night, Mr. Chase."

Emma watched him walk down the hallway. "Miss Newly" he'd called her after saying "Emma" practically since he met her. Glumly, she closed the door. How different he now acted from when he had given her that small kiss on her cheek. But had he known Sophia was approaching them even then? Had that been an act as well? Emma's thoughts ran rampant until she quelled them with a request to God.

Lord, please help me to know and understand what is true and what is false. Help me— A quiet knock on her door made her jump. She moved swiftly to it and asked, "Who is it?"

"It's Dugan, Em."

Quickly she opened the door, and after a moment of hesitation, Dugan stepped in, but he held the door open with one hand. Emma appreciated his concern for propriety, and she knew he must have a pretty good reason to risk it.

"What is it?"

Dugan looked at her carefully. "Are you okay, Emma? Is there anything you need help with?"

Emma was puzzled. "You mean about my job? No, things are fine and I'm okay."

But Dugan persisted. "Are you sure, Emma? Because I saw you with that man…" At Emma's horrified look, he stopped what he was going to say.

Emma quickly closed the door and faced Dugan squarely. "You have to believe me, Dugan, that I'm fine." As briefly as possible she explained the circumstances under which Dugan had seen her and Simon.

"Okay, Emma, I hope you know what you're doing!" He shuffled his feet and fingered his hat. "I'm supposed to pull out of here early in the morning, but if you need anything from me, I'll stay."

"No. Really, I'll be fine. Remember, the Lord is with me too."

"Well, you just remember to be careful." He opened the door. "You're family, you know." Then he gave her hand a quick squeeze and left. Emma looked after him with a smile on her face. It was good to have a friend like Dugan.

A noise at the other end of the hallway made her turn, but no one was there. *Sophia again?* Next she'd be announcing to Simon that Emma had men in her hotel room! Emma sighed. She wasn't going to worry about Sophia anymore tonight. She was getting some sleep.

Chapter 9

Norris

"Do you have the message?"

"Yes. Here, take a look."

Charles took the paper Simon offered him and read it eagerly. A scowl creased his forehead.

"This isn't good."

"I know, and we have to keep hidden until September or October. Any suggestions?"

Charles grinned. "You're the man with all the ideas. Who was the messenger boy?"

Simon frowned. "It _was_ the woman I told you about, and here's some news for you. Her father was hurt trying to get that message here, so we'd better be on our toes. By the way, you're my butler."

"Your what?"

"My servant, you know—my man. At least that's what Miss Newly thinks, so we might as well let her. Poor kid!

She thinks she's capable to protect *me*. I think she should just go home; you and I have been doing okay on our own. Listen." Simon stood and stretched. "I've got some messages to send. You stay here and watch for anyone who might want to search our room. Seems somebody might want to know more about our business than we wish to share. Good night."

It was early, very early. Emma struggled to open her eyes. One blurry glimpse told her it was still dark out. She burrowed deeper under the blankets and prepared to sleep several more hours.

Tap...tap...tap...tap

Her eyes opened again. She listened while she struggled to focus.

Tap...tap...tap

There was someone at her door! Emma came wide-awake as her feet hit the cold floor. She hadn't brought a robe with her, and she searched hurriedly for something to put over her nightdress. Her coat!

Tap...tap

"Who is it?" she whispered from her side.

"Emma, it's Simon. We have to talk."

Simon! For a brief instant, Emma debated what to do. There would be nothing left of her reputation if someone saw him there; then she realized she had a job to do. She opened the door.

Simon stepped in and shut the door softly behind him while Emma watched with wide eyes. He looked tired, as if he hadn't been to bed all night. His clothes certainly hadn't been changed. Something must be wrong.

Emma placed a hand on his arm. "What is it, Simon—I mean, Mr. Chase?"

He turned from closing the door and for a moment he stared at her. Emma put a hand to her hair for it appeared to be what he was staring at. She must look a fright, she reasoned, with her long hair flying all about her.

Simon cleared his throat and shocked Emma with his next words. "Will you marry me, Miss Newly?"

Now it was Emma's turn to stare.

"The message you brought me informed me that I must stay in hiding for several months yet. I tried telegraphing, but I received the same answer."

"But you're not supposed to use the wires," Emma protested. "Neither am I." *Marry him?* She looked away while the thought raced through her head.

"Apparently our bosses have changed their minds. I have two telegrams for you too."

Emma took the papers. Distracted a moment from his astounding question, she asked, "There are two for me?"

"Yes, they were sent to me and other than your name, they appear to be unreadable."

Emma looked at the messages written in her father's code. She studied them for several moments, trying to decipher them while Simon's question still hung in the air between them.

Meanwhile Simon took the opportunity to catch his breath. The sight of Emma with her blonde hair cascading nearly to her waist had caught him off guard. Even now as she concentrated on the paper in her hands, her coat had opened and he saw a glimpse of delicate white lace next to her pink skin. He looked away. The impropriety of his being in her room at this early hour stood out in his mind. He must not be detected here for her sake, but the matter was urgent and he needed to speak to her before the morning was fully underway.

Their situation had gotten worse. The other man in Washington under protection had been found out and murdered. Now there was only one left to testify, and Simon's instructions made it clear that extreme measures may be necessary to protect him.

"This one is from my father's boss." Emma's words gained his attention. "It says no replacement is available and that I'm supposed to stay with you and your man until the fall. He thinks because I'm a woman, it will make an even better cover for you."

Simon watched Emma digest the information. He wondered what her thoughts were. He had had a little more time to get used to the idea. In fact, he had spent half the night trying to decide what to do, but it was his boss who made the final decision for him. *Stay hidden at any cost. Find some kind of cover and stick to it.*

He waited while Emma studied the second message, and he could almost understand her hesitancy in revealing it to him. Finally she spoke, and her voice reminded him of a little girl's.

"It's from my father," she said with a dazed expression. "He says he understands the predicament we're in and asks that I go along with the…the…marriage to you."

Simon was well aware that Emma refrained from telling him the rest of the message. He knew the code and had read it carefully for himself, so he knew Russ Newly was telling his daughter to trust Simon and even be willing to put her life in his hands. Simon wondered if Emma would now realize that Simon wasn't the man who needed the protection but that it was Charles, the man she thought was Simon's butler. If she didn't catch on, he wasn't about to reveal the truth to her yet. She was not a trained agent and could easily give them away.

Simon tried to stifle a yawn, and Emma turned to him as if just remembering his presence.

"So, Emma—Miss Newly—are you willing to be my wife for the next few months?"

Emma shook her head. "I don't understand."

"It would be a cover. See, if we pretend to get married and live in one place for a while where people get used to us, we won't be suspected anymore…hopefully. And Miss Barlow already is expecting something like this, so we might as well not disappoint her." He smiled at her.

But Emma turned away. "I don't think that's funny, Mr. Chase. There must be some other way. Maybe you could just come home with me and stay with my folks as a guest or a relative or something."

But Simon knew even as Emma spoke the words that the Newly home would not be safe. He could see that she was clutching at straws. Not even Hank Riley—another agent he knew—would be able to house them safely. One of the reasons Simon had become a Pinkerton agent himself was because of the reputation of men like Hank Riley and Russ Newly. They were perhaps two of the best in the organization. Their names were well known in the area, and he knew their homes would be under surveillance by those men who were looking for Charles.

Maybe I should take Charles farther west or maybe south. But, no, they had to stop somewhere and set up as established residents to throw off any suspicion, and this place was as good as any to do that. And with Emma posing as his wife, it just might work.

Simon put his hand on her shoulder and turned her to him. "No, Emma. Remember, your father may already be known." She nodded her head in agreement. "I think the best thing we can do is stay away from your family completely so that no one connects you to your father's job." He took a deep breath. "I've been thinking that we should let people believe that you ran off and married me against your family's wishes." At Emma's protest, he continued. "That way your suspicious actions can be accounted for and even Miss Barlow should be convinced."

Emma pondered his words. "Yes, that would explain a lot, and my father…" she indicated the telegram, "seems to be telling me that it's okay, but…really, isn't there any other way? Getting married seems rather drastic. I mean, I'm willing to do whatever it takes to help you, but…*marriage?*"

Simon sighed in relief that she had halfway consented, but her full cooperation was going to be necessary. "I don't want to alarm you, but I see you need to understand the seriousness of our situation, Emma. I was just informed that my colleague in D.C. was murdered."

Emma gasped.

"I don't want you to feel you must go along with this charade if you are afraid of being in danger yourself, so if you want to get out, you just say right now and I'll go on my own, but frankly, I think having us pose as a married couple and settling down will take suspicion away from us." He paused. "Can't you send your family a coded message like that one to explain it?" he suggested. "Then after that, I think there should be no more communication with them for now. You understand, don't you? It would all be just for a cover."

He wondered what battles were being fought in Emma's mind as he waited for her decision. Surely she was concerned about her reputation and her future. He had thought of that as well. He knew it was a lot to ask of her and wanted to withdraw the suggestion, but he also knew the importance of his mission and could not. Finally, Emma reluctantly nodded.

"But, Mr. Chase, how do we pretend to get married?"

Chapter 10

Norris

Emma wasn't satisfied with her hair, so she uncoiled it and tried re-pinning it again. Her hands were shaking and she was disgusted with herself for being nervous. After all, she wasn't *really* getting married this morning; she was only pretending to get married.

Only it would be a real wedding. She sat down on the bed in her hotel room and stared at herself in the bureau mirror. Simon had explained that if they were to convince Sophia and anyone else who was interested in them, they would have to do more than just pretend. It would have to be a real ceremony. It could be annulled later, he said, if they wanted it to be. Emma had looked sharply at him, but he had continued his explanations in that same tired voice until they had made all their plans. He had been up all night and was so tired he probably hadn't realized what he said, she decided. Of course they would want it annulled!

Sleep had been impossible after Simon left. Even though she had finally given her consent to the pretend marriage, she was still looking for a way out. There had to be another way! Her mind raced, trying to come up with other solutions to Simon's safety. Every idea came up short, and she knew they were out of time. With Sophia's interest and the murder of Simon's friend, they had to act now.

And there was her father's message.

Emma shook her head almost in disbelief. The situation was indeed serious for her father to allow her to not only continue on his behalf but also to now take on such a provocative role. Indeed, it was because of her father's instructions that she was able to agree to the masquerade at all.

A bird chirped, and Emma glanced over at the window. A bright sun was already shining gaily and warm spring breezes were making this a perfect day for a wedding. Emma sighed. Just the way she had imagined her wedding day to be.

Oh, what a farce this was! This pretending and acting didn't seem right. It was lying! How could she live a lie for the next three or four months? Her eye caught her Bible resting on the bureau. What was that verse Michael had given her?

Determined, she picked up her Bible and looked for the verse. "Ah, here it is. Joshua 1:9, 'Have not I commanded thee? Be strong and of a good courage; be not afraid, neither be thou dismayed: for the Lord thy God is with thee whithersoever thou goest'." Emma thought about Joshua in the Bible. He had been a spy, one of twelve spies sent into Canaan land. And she remembered the two spies whom Rahab protected in Jericho. She hesitated to put herself in the same category as men who were on a mission for God, yet she felt some peace in knowing that there is a time to spy.

Lord, I don't want to be a liar, yet I know I have a job to do. Please give me the strength to do it and the ability to be good at it. Protect Simon, for I cannot. Help us both protect our secret from harmful people.

Emma waited a few moments in silence; then she continued in prayer for her family and her other needs. Peace filled her, and when she was finished, she smiled at her reflection and made some last-minute adjustments to her hair. Now she was ready.

She found Simon waiting for her in the hotel lobby as he said he would. What she didn't expect to find was Sophia in deep conversation with him. Sophia laughed softly at something Simon said, and she put her hand on his arm in a familiar gesture. Emma's eyes narrowed.

Whether Sophia knew that they were pretending or not would depend on the way Emma and Simon behaved toward each other now. Emma wondered what a bride-to-be would do if she found another woman flirting with her future husband on their wedding day. Then she saw Simon begin to speak and Sophia place her fingers over his lips to stop him, and Emma felt something inside her snap. Swiftly she crossed the room to their side.

"Good morning, darling! You know I hardly slept a wink last night; I was so excited about today!"

Simon rose to his feet with a puzzled yet amused expression on his face that quickly changed to surprise as Emma reached up on her tiptoes to lightly brush his cheek with her lips. He saw the quick wink she gave him before she took his arm and turned back to Sophia.

"Oh hello, Miss Barlow."

Sophia slowly stood and looked from one to the other with a knowing smile on her face. "So, it's today. You're getting married today, aren't you? You will let me come, won't you? Unless—I mean, will you have room? I know Emma has a large family."

Emma moved away from Simon and took Sophia's arm. "Miss Barlow—Sophia, can you keep a secret?"

Sophia's eyes glinted with interest.

"You see, my family doesn't know why I'm here. They haven't approved of my seeing Simon and have tried to keep us apart, but"—Emma looked lovingly at Simon— "we love each other so much, we just know we want to be married, despite their wishes."

"Why ever wouldn't they approve of Simon?" Sophia was incredulous. "I see absolutely nothing wrong with him."

Emma bristled at Sophia's visual inspection of her intended. Before she could form an answer, Simon slipped his arm around her waist and replied.

"I'm sorry to confess that at one time I was a gambler, Miss Barlow. The Newlys naturally didn't approve of my vocation, but I've given that up for good, and Emma and I are going to live and work together to make a happy home." To Emma he added, "I was able to put money down on the cabin you wanted, dearest. We can move in today."

"Oh, Simon! That's wonderful! Our own home."

"If you'll excuse us, Miss Barlow, we have many things to do. You may attend the ceremony if you wish. It will be in…"—Simon consulted his pocket watch—"in exactly one hour."

Giddy with excitement, Sophia finally left them. Emma stepped away from Simon. She was a little unsure of what his reaction would be to her performance; she was a little unsure of it herself. His certainly had convinced her, which reminded her. "You were a gambler?"

Simon laughed. "No, *dearest*, I wasn't. Unless you count the time I won candy from my brother in a bet. But it was the best I could come up with at the time. The bad thing about acting like we are is that we have to keep it up and try to remember what we've said. We'll have to work out a plausible story together so we don't catch each other by surprise in the future. You were very convincing, by the way."

Embarrassment crossed Emma's features. In a quiet voice, she said, "I had a battle this morning trying to convince myself that I wasn't really lying, just pretending. I hate lying!"

"But it *is* only an act, Emma. You have to realize how important this job of yours is. When you agreed to take your father's place, you agreed to do whatever was necessary to fulfill his job. Backing out now could put the whole project in jeopardy."

"I'm not backing out! My father always used a different name, and he had to act many parts over the years. He told us about some of them." Emma took a deep breath. "I can handle this; it's just that it's one thing to discuss it and quite another to do it."

"Maybe the best thing for you to do is to try to think of it as real. I mean, try to think of us as a couple really in love or maybe that we're in a play and this is our part. It's going to have to be an ongoing thing for the next few months, and we don't know who will be watching us. Like now, for instance, we can be seen from the dining room. I don't know if anyone there is watching us or not, but if we only act like we're a couple in love when we think we're being watched, we'll be found out sooner or later. The people who are after us are not stupid, and we won't always see them before they see us."

Fear touched Emma. "How can we possibly know who they are?"

"We can't. That's why we have to live our act, Emma. I can't tell you how important it is that we not be discovered." Simon studied the silent face in front of him. "I always find security knowing that the Lord is with us, Emma," he said softly.

Her face brightened as she looked up at him in surprise. "You know the Lord, Simon? Oh, that's wonderful news!" She gripped his hands in her excitement. "I feel so much better knowing that!"

Simon squeezed her fingers. "And you're already *acting* naturally."

A step behind them made them turn.

"Good morning, Miss Newly, sir." Mr. and Mrs. Findley stopped on their way through the lobby. "Miss Newly, you look positively radiant this morning." Mr. Findley looked pointedly at their clasped hands.

"Good morning, Mr. and Mrs. Findley." Emma slipped her arm through Simon's. "I'd like you to meet Mr. Simon Chase. Simon, the Findleys were on the stage with me; they have come to Norris to visit their daughter."

The men shook hands, and Mrs. Findley smiled knowingly at Emma. "I can see now why you didn't give that Miss Barlow any competition for the Robinsons."

Emma laughed lightly. "There was no need to; you see, Simon and I are getting married this morning."

Mrs. Findley clapped her hands in delight. "I knew it! I told Giles that you two must be in love when I saw you from the other room. You look so perfect together! But, this morning? Aren't you going back to Grandville to be married or to Sand Creek? Isn't that where you are from?"

Once again Emma explained their elopement, and the elderly couple nodded in understanding.

"But don't let hard feelings come between you and your family," Mrs. Findley admonished. "You might regret it for the rest of your lives." Her hand flew to her cheek, and a look of rapture was on her face as she said, "I just love weddings!"

Emma graciously thanked her for her concern then as an afterthought she said, "Why don't you both come to our wedding? We'd love to have you there."

"Yes, please do." Simon insisted. "I think since none of our families will be there, it would be nice to share our day with some of Emma's friends. Miss Barlow is coming too."

"Could we, Giles?"

"I suppose we could," Mr. Findley agreed. "I would be happy to give the bride away, that is, if you have no one else."

"I would be delighted!" Emma smiled. "And, Mrs. Findley, would you stand up for me?"

"Oh dear! You want an old woman like me? Are you sure?"

"I would love to have you!" Emma was suddenly very fond of the older woman.

"Then I will, and thank you. But call me Agatha, please." Suddenly she was all aflutter. "Giles, we must go back and change. We can't be in a wedding in these clothes. When shall we meet you?"

Simon and Emma decided to part ways for the next half hour. Emma wanted to deliver her message to the telegraph office, but Simon offered to take it for her.

"You go pick out what we'll need for food and supplies for the farm until we can make a trip back to Norris. I'll send Charles to help you."

"Charles?"

"Yes, remember my man? One of the reasons I believe this masquerade is possible is that Charles will be with us and can serve as a chaperone to later defend your honor, Emma. He'll not only stay with us but also help out around the place."

Emma couldn't help the frown that crossed her face.

"What's wrong?"

"Why do you have a servant, Simon? What do you need one for?"

Simon lowered his voice as he explained. "He's been with my family for years, Emma. Please, try to make him feel useful."

"But—"

"Thanks, Emma." Simon leaned over and gave her a quick kiss on the cheek. "I'll see you at the wedding."

Emma stared after him, lost in thought for a few moments. Was this the way it was going to be? She was allowing a man she barely knew to kiss her and call her endearments. She had always believed that those privileges would and should be reserved for the man she truly loved and would marry. She had never been kissed before, except for that one unpleasant experience with Ralph, and somehow she thought she should feel terribly guilty about allowing Simon to kiss her, but strangely she didn't.

"Miss Newly?"

Emma realized she was still staring out the door while Simon's servant had approached and was waiting to speak to her. She turned and held out her hand to him.

"Please call me Emma. And you're Charles, right? Or would you like me to call you something else?" She took in his dark suit and tie and the way he held himself ramrod straight.

"Charles will be fine, miss. Mr. Chase asked me to accompany you on a shopping trip."

Shopping trip? Emma was puzzled by the man's choice of words. Shopping in Norris meant going to the general store. "You're not from around here, are you, Charles?"

"No, miss. I'm from the East, miss. Is it so obvious?" He allowed himself a brief smile.

Emma returned the smile. "I'd love to hear what it's like there. Please tell me sometime."

Charles nodded.

"After you, miss."

Emma had expected Charles to offer her his arm, so she was surprised when he waved her ahead of him. She led the way to the store with Charles two steps behind her. How odd she felt! She stopped on the boardwalk and looked back. Charles stopped also.

"Why don't you walk beside me, Charles, and we can talk a little," she suggested.

"Begging your pardon, miss, but it wouldn't be proper."

"Proper!" Emma put her hands on her hips. "Is that the way Simon wants you to behave?"

"Excuse me, miss?"

"Stop calling me *miss*, for Pete's sake! Listen, Charles, if we're all going to be together for the next few months, then I think we should start out right. I'd like to be called Emma, and you might as well know that I don't need a servant and neither, in my opinion, does Simon. You are Simon's friend; I can tell by the way he talks about you."

Charles blinked in surprise.

"And I want you to be my friend too." She told the older man. "You shouldn't act so servile with your friends."

"But miss—Emma, I mean." Charles stepped closer and lowered his voice. "I *am* Mr. Chase's servant, and I wish to continue to be so. I'm sorry if I have offended you."

Emma sighed. "No, I'm sorry, Charles. I was raised quite differently than Simon, I guess. I have never cared for the idea of people having servants. We'll have to discuss this later."

She turned and continued on to the store and was not surprised when Charles resumed his two-pace distance behind her. She'd be sure to speak to Simon.

Emma's upbringing served her well for the next half hour as she compiled a list of supplies they would need for the next month or so. Charles, evidently out of his element, was in awe of Emma's capabilities. She ordered staples in food and kitchenware, bedding, lamp oil, feed for the horses that Simon was buying, and she even purchased some chickens and garden seeds. Charles seemed perplexed, so she explained.

"We might as well have fresh eggs and garden produce. Wish we could get a cow too. I'll ask Simon. Do you know how to milk a cow, Charles?"

"No, miss!" Charles shook his head in befuddlement.

"I can teach you. Now, how about some sewing things and maybe some reading material? Would you care to help me choose some books, Charles?"

The store's supply of books was limited, but they took what was available. Charles surprised Emma by saying, "I have some of my personal favorites with me, Miss Emma. Perhaps you would care to borrow them sometime?"

"Thank you, Charles. And I have my Bible too. There's always good reading there."

A doubtful look crossed the servant's face.

"You don't care for the Bible, Charles?"

"No offense, Miss Emma, but Mr. Chase and I have discussed the Bible many times, and I frankly find it very difficult to believe."

Emma digested this information. Charles apparently didn't believe the Bible, but evidently Simon did and was trying to convince his servant. Maybe that was why he kept

Charles with him, to witness to him. Suddenly Emma was looking forward to sharing that privilege with Simon.

A checkerboard caught Emma's eye as she reviewed their inventory, and she added it to their growing pile. Their supplies were finally in order, and Emma instructed the storekeeper that a wagon was being purchased and would be brought to the store for loading soon. It was now time to get to the church.

Emma again led the way down the boardwalk. She started to cross the town's main street with Charles at his two-step distance behind her when she noticed a rider approach from the southern end of town. He looked from side to side as he walked his horse down the street, and when he saw Emma, he reined in beside her and swung down. At first Emma didn't pay much attention to the man; her mind was on her upcoming wedding. Then the man spoke her name, and she turned to him in surprise.

"Ralph!"

Ralph whipped his hat off his head and crunched it in his hands. "Emma, I wouldn't blame you if you never spoke to me again, but I need to talk to you. Please! Only for a few minutes, if nothing else," he pleaded.

Emma didn't know what to say. She looked at Ralph's dusty clothes and haggard features and knew he had ridden day and night to get to Norris. She had a moment's discomfort as she remembered him trying to kiss her in his drunken state then she saw the misery in his face and she knew he was still Ralph Tunelle, an old friend.

"What is it, Ralph?" she asked quietly. She had forgotten Charles standing behind her.

"Em, I had to come apologize to you. I really, truly am sorry for the way I behaved, and you have my word I will never do anything like that again. Buck laid into me real good! I've never seen him so mad! And then I found out you left the next morning and I felt just awful, Em! I'm really sorry. I didn't mean to make you leave. Will you forgive me?"

Emma saw the sincerity in Ralph's eyes. "I forgive you." But at his quick sigh of relief, she added, "But everything is not all right all of a sudden. Ralph, you have to stay away from whatever you were drinking that made you act that way; you have to stop being bitter and feeling sorry for yourself because Philippa left you, and most importantly, you have to put your trust back in God to lead you through this. God is the only answer here, Ralph, and you better see that. I don't know if Philippa will ever come back, but I know it won't do any good even if she does if you don't have Christ as the foundation for your marriage." She took a deep breath.

Ralph nodded. "You're right. Buck and I had a long talk after he got done chewing me out. Everybody else in Grandville was getting married left and right and I didn't have anyone to marry since Cora's sister ran off, so I just kind of grabbed at the chance to marry Philippa when she started flirting with me. I don't know if I even knew what love was all about, but I found I loved her despite the way she treated me. When I married Philippa, I did everything I could to make her happy. She hated going to church, so I quit going. She hated me reading my Bible, so I stopped."

Ralph paused and stroked his horse's neck. "I may never win Philippa back, but I'll do my best to win her back to the Lord. I heard she and her mother went to Chicago, so I'm going there to find her. Maybe she'll listen, maybe not. But I have to try. And I couldn't go without making things right with you first, Em. I was a fool."

Emma put out her hand to Ralph, and there were tears in her eyes. "I'm so happy you're trusting the Lord again. I'll be praying for you and Philippa. You're doing the right thing and God will bless."

Ralph took her hand. "Funny thing is, even though I didn't want anything to do with God, he never left my side. He stayed patient and loving through all my anger and bitterness. He'll be with me now." Ralph paused and looked past Emma. "Can I help you?" he asked someone.

"Oh, this is Charles," Emma started to explain. She turned and was unprepared to see Simon standing behind her with a stern look on his face as he pointedly stared at Ralph's hand holding her own.

"Simon! Where did you come from?" she asked stupidly.

"When Miss Barlow pointed out that the man you were holding hands with was the same one you were kissing in the dark, I thought I owed it to myself to come and meet him and to find out what he wanted with you on our wedding day."

"Wedding day?" Shocked, Ralph looked at Emma.

"Did Emma forget to tell you she was getting married today?" Simon's voice was icy.

"Emma, what's this all about? Who is this man?" Ralph demanded as he returned Simon's glare.

But Emma was silent. If either man had taken the time to look carefully at her, they would have seen the anger simmering under her calm façade. Instead, they were concentrating all their attentions on each other.

Simon took Emma's arm. "If you will excuse us—"

"Hold on!" Ralph took Emma's other arm. "I don't know who you think you are, mister, but you're not taking her anywhere until I get some answers."

If she hadn't been so angry, Emma thought she might have appreciated the humor of the moment. As it was, she saw the Findleys and Sophia Barlow headed their way, and Sophia's face was alive with curiosity. Emma knew she must get the situation under control and resume her act no matter how angry she was. She'd deal with that later.

"Simon, darling," she said sweetly, turning to him with a cold glare, "I want you to meet an old friend of mine, Ralph Tunelle. Ralph is on his way to meet with his wife."

"His *wife*?"

Emma ignored Simon's outburst. "Ralph, this is Simon Chase, and yes, we are getting married this morning. We met some time ago and decided we really must be together." She looked at Ralph's bewildered face and some of her animosity vanished. She spoke honestly. "I really want to be with Simon, Ralph. My family knows this and understands. I'm okay, really."

"Then it's not because of me?"

"No, you had nothing to do with my decision. I came to Norris to be with Simon."

"Emma." Ralph was very serious. "Be very sure. Don't make the mistake I made." He hesitated a moment as if trying to decide what to do; then he turned back to Simon and abruptly said, "Do you know the Lord, mister?"

Emma saw the surprise on Simon's face, and she awaited his answer too. She was unaware that Charles had headed off Sophia and the Findleys and was escorting them back to the church.

"I was saved three years ago when a friend of mine explained the gospel to me. I accepted Jesus as my Savior from sin, believing that he died and rose again for me." Simon stated the facts to Ralph, but his eye caught Emma's too, and he returned the genuine smile she gave him. "So you're a believer too?" he asked Ralph.

At Ralph's nod, Simon boldly continued, "Then can you explain to me why you, a Christian and a married man, were kissing my girl only three nights ago?"

Emma didn't understand nor try to analyze the warm feeling those words *my girl* gave her.

Ralph looked uneasy but proceeded to tell Simon his story and his reason for riding to Norris to apologize to Emma. Simon held out his hand. "Forgive my earlier rudeness. Emma and I will pray that you find your wife and can restore your marriage."

Ralph took the offered hand, and Emma was relieved and pleased to see that the two men now respected each other. Her previous anger was forgotten. Suddenly, she remembered the time.

"Simon, we're going to be late for our own wedding! Ralph, come with us."

Ralph looked down at his dusty, wrinkled clothes and ran a hand over the whiskers sprouting on his chin. "I'm in no shape to go to a wedding."

"Please come," Simon coaxed him. "No one cares how you're dressed."

Ralph grinned. "Okay."

The preacher of Norris's only church seemed very relieved to see the bride and groom finally arrive. He was very businesslike and had people seated in no time. Ralph's appearance gave him a second's pause, but nevertheless he seated him and proceeded to arrange Agatha Findley and Charles up front with Simon. Giles Findley and Emma stood in the back waiting for their cue to walk forward.

Emma felt butterflies in her stomach, and she gripped the small white Bible she held in her hands. There was neither piano nor organ, but the preacher's wife sang a beautiful hymn in a clear, sweet voice that brought tears to Emma's eyes.

Giles took her hand and put it through his arm. He smiled a fatherly smile and proceeded with her down the aisle. Emma felt the butterflies in her stomach flutter again as she realized Simon was watching her closely with a strange look in his eyes. She smiled nervously at him. His returning smile put the butterflies to flight once again.

The ceremony was brief but unforgettable. Emma felt every word spoken was searing her with its reverence. She determined that for the duration of their time together, she would play the part of a wife to Simon as sincerely as those words suggested except, of course, for—

Emma's eyes widened as she realized that not once had she considered that marriage included more than just living together. Surely Simon didn't expect—No, of course not! He said they could have the marriage annulled *if they wanted to!* She shot him a worried look, and as though he understood her concerns, he squeezed her hand reassuringly.

What was she doing? What did she know about this man? Up until a few minutes ago, she didn't even know for sure that he believed in God. For that matter, what did he know about her? Emma felt the pressure of Simon's fingers on hers and realized that the preacher had stopped speaking and was looking at her expectantly.

"I do," she blurted out, hoping it was the right time. The preacher continued on, and Emma sighed with relief. Simon was going into this as blindly as she was. If he could accept her and trust her to do her part without knowing a thing about her, then she would do the same.

"I now pronounce you man and wife. You may kiss the bride."

Emma was still looking down at the Bible she held when she realized that Simon had turned to her and was waiting. She timidly looked up and saw the amusement he was trying to hide. *He thinks it's funny,* she thought.

She turned and reached up on tiptoe and surprised him with a brief kiss. *There, that will teach him to laugh at me.*

But Simon's arms went around her, and before Emma knew what was happening, he gave her the kind of kiss any bridegroom was expected to give when he kissed his wife for the first time.

There were more kisses and hugs as the well-wishers congratulated the couple. After that, Simon and Emma went back to the hotel to gather their personal belongings and load them on the wagon with their supplies. Charles was waiting for them in the wagon when they came out.

"He's not going with you, is he?" Sophia stood on the boardwalk and looked incredulously at Charles.

Before Simon could form a reply, Emma said, "Of course he is. He's Simon's right hand man, and we're going to need all the help we have to get our home into shape, what with getting my garden in and fixing up the house and all."

"But don't you want some time alone?" Sophia insisted.

Emma was becoming irritated with Sophia's persistence, but Simon calmly answered, "I wanted to take a trip right away, but Emma convinced me that we needed to stay and work on our place first. We'll just have to postpone it for a time."

"I see. Well, maybe I'll just pop out for a visit after you get settled."

"You do that. Bye for now."

They left without any further fanfare other than a wave from Ralph as he leaned against the railing by the hotel watching them go. Emma wondered what he was really thinking about her hasty marriage.

On their way to the cabin that Emma's father had told her about, Simon informed her that Charles knew about his situation and the circumstances of their marriage. Emma was relieved that she wouldn't have to pretend in front of the servant. About an hour later they arrived at the cabin, and Emma was relieved to see that it was larger than the one-room affair she had feared it might be. There were two bedrooms off the living area. Everything was dirty and musty from disuse.

"Looks like we got our work cut out for us, hey, Charles?" Simon went out to the wagon and hunted for one of his bags. "I'll just get changed into some work clothes and we'll get started cleaning this up for you, Mrs. Chase."

"Cleaning it *for* me? I intend to do my share, Mr. Chase, so if you will bring in the smaller of my two bags please, I will also change."

Simon stopped by the wagon. "Really, Emma, Charles and I can handle it. I didn't mean to saddle you with a load of work the first thing."

"My bag, please," Emma insisted.

Simon shrugged and found her bag for her. Emma went into the smaller of the two rooms, leaving the two men the larger. She was pleased to see that the cabin was partially furnished with beds, tables and chairs, and even two bureaus. Her father had told her these things would be there, but it was possible to have found the cabin ransacked and everything gone.

She pulled out one of the dresses she had brought to wear while working in the hotel kitchen, and she tied a kerchief about her head. Then she went out to the wagon and found the broom, pails, and rags she had brought from town, as well as a cake of soap.

She had two pails filled with water from the well before the men appeared. Simon looked ruggedly handsome, she noticed, but—and she had to suppress a giggle—Charles looked out of place and ill at ease in his store-bought work clothes. Emma was sure he would have been happier working in his suit and string tie.

"I guess we should start by carrying these things inside," suggested Simon.

"You will not! Nothing else goes inside that filthy cabin until it is cleaned top to bottom." Emma informed him. "Your first job, Simon, is to take care of the horses and chickens and carry anything to the barn that belongs there. Charles and I will start on the house."

"Yes, ma'am." Simon grinned and hurried off.

"May I take those for you, madam?" Charles asked, pointing to the pails in Emma's hands.

"No, you may not. You may take that broom though and brush down the ceilings and walls before you sweep the floors, starting with the small bedroom. I'll follow you and scrub everything down."

"Yes, madam." Charles grabbed the broom and practically ran into the cabin.

A couple of hours later, Emma threw out yet another pail of dirty water and rubbed her aching back muscles. A ring of stones not far from the cabin indicated that campfires were often lit there. Emma had quickly started a fire and filled pot after pot of water to heat on it. The ceilings, walls, and floors were done, and she was finished with the windows in the bedrooms. All she had left were the windows in the kitchen and living area. Simon was cleaning out the fireplace and inspecting the chimneys for both it and the kitchen's woodstove. Charles, looking a little more normal now that his stiff clothing was rumpled and dirty, was on his knees scrubbing the front porch.

Emma smiled and went back to work. It wasn't long before she felt satisfied that the cabin was clean enough to bring in their belongings, and she gave the two men permission to start unloading the wagon. She felt like she was playing house as she began arranging the food they had purchased on the shelves and setting the newly bought dishes in the cupboards.

Charles had hauled the mattresses outside and had spent half an hour beating them until he was red in the face. Emma inspected them and claimed them ready to go back, and she told the men she would make up the beds after she had fed them some supper.

"Supper?" Simon sniffed the air. "I'm starving, but I didn't realize until you mentioned supper that I'm smelling food cooking."

"What is that tantalizing aroma?" Charles followed Simon into the kitchen.

Emma dished up the stew she had left simmering. Living in a family of eight, she had long ago learned the mechanics of running a household and the delicacies of keeping everyone happy with a well-cooked meal.

"That smells delicious, Emma! Where did you get it? Did you buy the stew from the hotel before we left?" Simon's face was innocent of any teasing, though Emma looked sharply for it. Her brothers had been great kidders, and she was always on her guard for their tricks.

"No, I didn't buy it from the hotel. I cooked it myself."

"When?" Charles asked the question in amazement.

"In between jobs, I came in here and added things to the kettle. Why?"

"You are an amazing woman, Emma Chase. I can't believe you accomplished all this and a meal too!" Simon praised her.

"*We* accomplished it. You two were working pretty hard yourselves." Emma sat down and waited patiently.

Charles still stood by the table, and when Emma looked questioningly at him, he said, "I will dine when you and Mr. Chase have finished."

Emma was incredulous, and Simon quickly wiped the grin off his face when she looked at him. "Simon, make him stop acting like that, for goodness' sake!"

Simon was hard put not to laugh out loud. "Better do what she says, Charles."

"But, sir!"

"No, Emma is my wife and if that's what she wants, that's what she gets."

Charles took his place at the table, though disapproval was written all over his face.

Simon smiled. "Shall we ask the blessing for the first time in our new, *clean* home?"

Emma smiled back and blushed slightly. *Our home,* he had said. She bowed her head.

"Lord, may our lives together please you as we seek to serve you. Bless this delicious smelling meal and bless Emma for providing it. We ask for your continued protection and guidance in your precious Son's name, amen."

A warm feeling stole over Emma as she ate and conversed with the men. Simon was really very nice, and she looked forward to some interesting talks with him.

Simon and Charles insisted on cleaning up the kitchen and told her to take it easy for the rest of the evening. She laughingly agreed to leave them the kitchen work, but only because she said she had beds to make. The bedding had been brought in from the wagon and was waiting to be put on the beds, so she got to work.

After the last blanket had been tucked into place, Emma stood back in satisfaction and surveyed her work. Her muscles were aching and tired, but she felt good about all they had done. Tomorrow she would begin work on curtains and rugs, but for now, she was ready for a good night's sleep. She went to the closet for her things so she could set out her nightgown.

Emma stood at the closet door and stupidly stared at its contents. She fingered the clothing there and recognized Charles's suit. She pushed aside other garments, searching for Simon's things. Were the men going to share the small room and leave the larger one for her?

She went to the larger bedroom and opened the closet door. Her hand went out then stopped in mid-air. Her things were there all right, and hanging alongside them were all of Simon's things.

Chapter 11

North of Norris

How long she stood looking at those clothes, she didn't know, but eventually Emma came to herself and tried desperately to get a hold on the anger she felt creeping up inside her. How dare he think she would pretend this far!

But even as the anger made a sweep through her, another more powerful emotion begged for her attention. This was not the Simon she was beginning to know and respect. Answers were needed, and she headed for the kitchen in a confused state.

Simon and Charles were in deep conversation as they finished their work, and Emma stood silent, wondering what to say. It was Simon who noticed her first.

"Oh, you've found us out, Emma! You were done sooner than we expected." At her puzzled look, he explained. "I found this bathtub in the barn, and Charles and I are heating water so you can have a nice, hot bath." Evidently the two men were extremely proud of themselves. "Just let me move it into your room and we'll start filling it."

"Which room would that be?"

She was unsure if it was her tone, her expression, or her continued silence that made the men stop what they were doing. Simon moved to her side.

"What's wrong, Emma?"

"I found my clothes," was all she replied, and there was hurt in her voice.

"Oh." Simon uttered the single sound.

"I'll go...uh, I'll go...check on the animals." Charles found an excuse and left with haste.

Emma's lips were stiff, and her expression hard when Simon turned back to her. For just the briefest of moments amusement lit his eyes, and he quickly quelled it, but not before Emma saw, and the anger in her boiled over.

"I don't know what you see that you find funny, Mr. Chase. I want an explanation. If you think—"

"Whoa, Emma!" Simon held up a hand to stop her tirade. "I don't think anything of the sort. Listen. I had Charles put the clothes away like that so that any snoopy guests like Sophia Barlow would be convinced we are really husband and wife. You may have that bedroom to yourself. Charles can take the smaller room, and I'll sleep out here by the fire. Okay?"

Emma didn't reply at once. The anger was slowly seeping out of her, and she was beginning to feel every bit a fool. Simon must wonder what kind of help she was going to be to him if he had to always explain himself to her. "I'm sorry. I—"

"It's been a long and eventful day. What you need is a hot bath and a good night's sleep." Simon dismissed the matter lightly and proceeded to carry the tub to Emma's room and then to fill it. Emma moved about the kitchen aimlessly, trying to find something to occupy herself with until he was done. She berated herself for her quick temper, and she wondered how she could ever act normally around Simon again after the last embarrassing moments. A knock at the cabin door made her jump.

Simon stepped into the main room and looked at her then at the door. "Charles wouldn't knock," was all he said, but from his look Emma read much more. The act was on.

Emma nervously watched from beside the stove as Simon called through the door. "Who's there?"

"My name's Brady!" The answer was shouted back. The voice—a man's—was crackly and high pitched. "My horse went lame 'bout half a mile back."

Simon glanced once at Emma then opened the door. A short, thin man in dirty, well-worn clothes took a step inside.

"What can we do for you, Mr. Brady?" Simon asked politely.

"Aaaah! A fire!" The man named Brady hurried to stand before the blaze. "Gettin' a mite nippy out there tonight. Hard to believe it's really spring." His glance flashed in all directions, taking note of everything in the small cabin, but he appeared not to notice Emma until she spoke to him.

"Are you hungry, Mr. Brady? I have some stew I can warm for you."

Emma was unprepared for the response from the man. He looked her up and down with a puzzled expression on his face. Then he pointed a finger at her and said, "I know you! You're one of Russ Newly's little girls, ain't ya?"

Surprised, Emma darted a look at Simon, who gave her a quick nod. "Yes, that's right. How did you know who I am?" she asked.

"Your pa carries pictures of his whole family. He's even got one of your ma inside his watch case. Fine man, your pa."

"How do you know Russ Newly?" Simon asked.

"Russ and me have gone trappin' together here in these woods. We even used this cabin once in a while, so I was mighty surprised when those people told me it had been sold! Now that I see Russ's daughter here, I can understand."

"What people told you about us?" Again Simon asked the question.

Brady frowned at Simon. "Who's this fella? Are you in some kind of trouble here, missy?" He looked around the cabin again as if he were looking for answers.

Emma reached out her hand and Simon stepped over to her and clasped it in his own. "This is my husband Simon Chase, Mr. Brady. I'm not in any trouble; why do you ask?"

Brady rubbed at the stubble on his chin. "What's the deal?" he mumbled to himself. He appeared to be making up his mind about something as he looked from Simon to Emma and back again. "You two are *really* married?" he asked.

Emma resisted the temptation to glance at Simon. "Yes, of course. In fact, we were married just today."

"Ya don't say!" Brady slapped his hat against his leg, raising a small cloud of dust in the clean cabin. "Well, if I know anythin', I know I can trust Russ Newly's daughter to be tellin' the truth. Confound those people! Why would they doubt you?"

"What people?" Simon tried questioning again.

"I don't know, mister. Some feller got a hold of me in town and said he'd pay me money to check you out. He kept sayin' to me, 'we,' you know, like 'we want some information' and stuff like that. So I figgered there was more than just him. Anyways, I agreed 'cuz it looked like easy money to me. I reckon I can tell him you're okay."

"Do you know what he looked like?"

Brady studied Simon thoughtfully but made no answer.

Again Simon questioned him. "Where are you supposed to meet him?"

"I've said all I'm gonna say." Then, surprisingly, Brady smiled and his grin revealed a missing tooth. "I'll be goin' now, what with this bein' your weddin' night and all."

"But, your horse…" Emma's voice faltered. *Wedding night!*

"I was lyin', missy, I mean missus. My horse is fine. I'll just be goin'."

The door opened, and Charles cautiously entered. He eyed Brady curiously, and Brady, in turn, studied him.

"Who's this?" Brady spoke the words, but Charles asked them with his eyes.

"Mr. Brady, this is Charles. He's our…man. Charles, meet Mr. Brady, who was just traveling by." Emma made the introductions.

"Your *man*? Beggin' your pardon, folks, but you really don't need no hired help to run a small place like this."

Emma smiled politely. "Charles will be excellent help to us, I'm sure."

"Oh!" Brady shared a knowing look with the newly-weds. In a not-too-quiet whisper, he confided, "He needed the job, huh?"

Simon coughed, and Charles appeared indignant. Emma wondered how to get rid of their unwanted guest before he asked any more questions, but Brady solved the problem by starting for the door.

"Would you folks mind if I bed down in your barn for the night? I promise to be outta here first thing in the mornin'."

"You're more than welcome, Mr. Brady," Simon readily agreed.

Charles edged away from Brady as he approached, and Emma thought she detected a wrinkling of Charles's nose as the grizzly old man passed him. She suppressed the urge to smile.

"If that will be all, sir, madam, I shall retire for the night." Charles made his announcement; then, upon receiving Simon's nod of consent, he moved toward the smaller bedroom. But it was not to be.

"Now hold on there!" Brady's look and words were now expressing his own indignation. "I don't know what kind of hired hand you are, mister, and maybe these good folks are gonna be kind enough to share their home with ya, but for goodness' sakes, man! This is their weddin' night!"

Charles was startled by this outburst, but no more so than Simon and Emma. He looked to Simon for help, but Simon was carefully studying his fingernails, and Emma refused to meet his eyes. He turned to the outraged Brady with a blank look.

Brady was exasperated. "Where was you born and raised, mister? Ain't ya got no manners? Go grab a blanket and bunk down in the barn for one night at least."

"But—" Emma started to protest, but Simon squeezed her hand, and her voice faltered.

"Now, don't you worry about a thing, missus. I'll see to it that he's tucked in for the night," Brady assured her.

Simon gave Charles a quick nod, and the red-faced man went to his room for the required blanket. Emma felt her own face flush even more when Brady winked at Simon before he herded Charles out the door in front of him.

"Night, folks! Sleep well!"

The door banged shut behind them, and Emma snatched her hand away from Simon's. "You could have said something!" she accused. "Oh! What have we done to Charles!"

Simon could only laugh as he sank into a nearby chair. "Did you see his face?" His shoulders shook as the laughter rolled through him. He pointed at Emma. "And your face!"

"I don't find it so funny." Emma crossed her arms in front of her while she tried to keep the disapproving look on her face, but Simon's mirth was contagious, and before she knew it, she was laughing as hard as he was.

"Ohhh!" Simon held his side as if he had a pain. "Charles better find a spot upwind of him!" And he started off again.

Finally Emma breathed a deep cleansing breath of air. How much better she felt! How good it was to laugh away their problems rather than to fret over them! She smiled at Simon and found him watching her.

For a breathless moment they looked at each other, and Emma felt something stir inside her at the look in Simon's eyes. Then he stood, and the moment was past.

"I better do a quick check on the men before we turn in." He informed her casually. "Remember, Brady was asked to check up on us, so we're still being suspected by somebody. Wish I knew who! In fact, I'll probably keep a watch on Brady all night to be sure *he's* telling the truth."

"Shouldn't I be the one to do that?" questioned Emma.

But Simon only smiled at her.

He left, and Emma went to the bedroom and finished filling the tub with the now lukewarm water. A quick wash-up would feel good even if it wasn't a hot one, so she laid out her nightclothes before she undressed and sank into the water.

Ahhhh! That felt good. But she didn't dare linger. She grabbed the store-bought soap and went to work, even washing her long hair thoroughly. Then she used one of the buckets to dip water and rinsed her hair by bending her head forward and pouring the water over it. She didn't hear the knock on her door, so she jumped when she heard her name spoken.

"It's okay, Emma. It's just me!"

She turned to the door behind her and tried to see through the mass of wet hair hanging over her face. She was outraged! *How dare he!*

The door was open only a slight crack, and Simon's amused voice reached her ears from behind it. "Sorry to frighten you, Emma. I called several times and you didn't answer. Are you all right?"

Emma shoved the dripping hair out of her face as she stared at the door. "Yes," she choked out the word while she reached for the towel.

"I've got more hot water for you. It was still on the stove when I went out. Would you like it?"

The cooler air coming through the partly open door was making Emma shiver. Hot water! The thought was very appealing. "How?" she asked.

She heard Simon chuckle. "Well, that does present some difficulty, doesn't it? I could bring it in with my eyes closed, but I might trip and spill it all over the floor. I could just carry it in and tell you I promise not to look, but I might forget, I could—" The door squeaked.

"Simon!" Emma let out a shriek and she heard him start laughing.

"Sorry, Emma. I bumped the door. Look. I'm only teasing. I'll just set this pot of hot water inside the door and you can figure out how to get it from there, okay? I promise not to look."

Emma's eyes were large as she watched the door. "Okay," she said in a small voice. She held the towel tightly while she waited for Simon to finish his task. Presently she saw the door move open a little more and Simon's hands, holding the handle of a steaming pot of hot water with two of their new towels wrapped around it, appeared. The pot was carefully set down and the hands retreated. Emma breathed a sigh of relief as the door closed, and she was about to call out her thanks when the door creaked open again. She held her breath.

Simon's amused voice came through the crack. "By the way, Emma, you might want to hang something over that window in case our guest gets to snooping around tonight. It's amazing how much of the room you can see when you're outside behind the cabin." The door shut.

Emma's eyes flew to the black square on the wall indicating the bare window. The night was dark and she had given no thought to anyone snooping around their little cabin. Suddenly she was in motion. She stood and wrapped the towel around herself, and then, shivering, she looked through the packages of material she had bought in town. She found a piece large enough, and taking several pins and a heavy book, she pounded the pins through the material and into the wall around the window. *There!*

By now Emma was shaking with cold, but she wasn't about to get back in the tub. She grabbed a bucket and filled it with the hot water then kneeling beside the tub she poured the clean water over her hair until it felt thoroughly rinsed. Then she dried off and dressed as quickly as her shaking fingers would allow her in the chilly room. Again she put her coat on as a robe and grabbing her comb she headed out of the room and straight for the fire.

Simon was spreading a blanket before the fire when Emma burst into the room. He immediately saw her blue lips and shivering form.

"Emma! You're shaking like a leaf! Here." He picked up the blanket and wrapped it around her shoulders; then he gently pulled the wet hair out away from her neck. "Give me that towel," he commanded.

Emma let him take the towel from her shaky fingers, and he began to rub her head and hair until her teeth were rattling.

"Ouch! Simon, that hurts."

"Sorry." His voice was curt. "This blanket is wet now too. Wait. I'll get a dry one." He went to the bedroom and returned with another blanket. Emma was still shivering as he pulled the damp one away from her shoulders. He wrapped the dry one around her then turned her to face him. Without warning, he wrapped his arms around her and began rubbing her back briskly to warm her up. Emma couldn't resist snuggling up to his warmth.

"You should have bathed by the fire or the kitchen stove," he told her. "Next time we'll set something up."

The front door squeaked, and they both turned toward it. Simon's arms were still around Emma, and she realized that somehow her arms had found their way around him. They made a very cozy picture for the two men who were staring wide-eyed at them. Brady grinned widely, and Charles's eyebrows disappeared into his hair. Instinctively Emma tried to pull away, but Simon kept a firm hold on her.

"Something wrong in the barn, gentlemen?" he asked coldly.

"We're awful sorry to disturb you folks," Brady explained. "But this pansy foot of a hired man you got needs another blanket." As apologetic and disgusted as he sounded, Brady's eyes were alert to the scene before him. He appeared to miss nothing of the embarrassment on Emma's face; in fact, he seemed pleased about it.

Charles avoided his employer's eyes as he quickly grabbed another blanket from his room and stomped out of the cabin again. Brady followed more slowly with a satisfied look on his face.

Simon's hold on Emma relaxed, and she heard him chuckle. "That should finally settle the matter of our marriage to Mr. Brady. You all right now?"

She nodded without looking up at him.

"Good. I'll empty the bath while you stay here and let your hair dry."

He moved away, and Emma stared into the flames. Absently she began combing through the long strands of her hair. From behind her she heard Simon carrying the buckets to the door and emptying them.

The dancing fire mesmerized her as she sleepily watched the flames, and her hands dropped to her lap while her mind swirled with the emotions she was feeling. She relived the moments of the day: Simon saying 'I do,' Simon kissing her, Simon laughing, Simon looking at her, Simon holding her.

Moments later Simon found Emma asleep before the fire. Her comb had fallen to the floor and her long, blonde hair lay swirled around her like a blanket. He touched it and found it almost dry. For a long moment Simon looked at his bride. Then gently, so as not to wake her, he picked her up in his arms and carried her to the bedroom. She instantly cuddled up to him.

Emma's curtain had come undone in one corner, Simon noticed as he entered the room. The lantern burned on the small bureau, and Emma turned her face into his neck away from its brightness. He felt her breath on his skin and he stopped abruptly. His heart raced.

He looked down at her, but her face was completely hidden against him. Tenderly he kissed the bare skin on the back of her neck before he set her down on the bed. He pulled the blankets over her, coat and all, and she immediately wrapped her arms around the pillow and began to breathe deeply.

Simon blew out the lamp then with a sigh he left the room and closed the door behind him.

The black triangle, revealed by the drooping of Emma's makeshift curtain, presented a view of the night outside. Now a few stars appeared, and occasionally a glimpse of the moon. Then eventually the form of a man became evident as he stood back in the trees, watching with keen interest as the light went out in the little cabin.

Chapter 12

North of Norris

Emma briskly finished wiping off the table and putting away the dishes from their breakfast. Brady had finally left after joining them for their morning meal, and Charles could barely contain his relief. Emma smiled as she recalled the surprise on both their faces when Simon had taken his Bible and read a short devotional before they left the table, but she had been very pleased. Simon was full of surprises.

The men headed out to the barn together. Both were tired from their night. Charles, because he had obviously never slept in a barn before and hadn't slept well; and Simon, because he had kept an eye on the two men, wary about Brady's interest and concerned about Charles's safety.

The cabin was quiet, and Emma stared out the window, but she wasn't seeing the view before her. Yes, Simon was full of surprises…bits of memory floated through her mind as she relived the night before. She remembered her bath and warming up by the fire in Simon's arms. She frowned. She had awakened in her bed with her nightgown and coat on, but she had no idea how she got there or why she had slept in her coat. Somewhere in the recesses of her memory she recalled the feeling of warm lips on her neck and tender, gentle hands wrapping her in warmth. She shook herself as she reached for the broom and quickly cleaned the little cabin's floor.

The garden was next. She wanted to get a garden under way as soon as possible so they could enjoy fresh vegetables. She envisioned crisp radishes and crunchy carrots and peas and beans and garden lettuce to liven up their meals. She had no idea just how long they would actually be staying, but it didn't hurt to be prepared.

Once outside, however, Emma took a deep breath of the fresh spring air and decided a walk in the woods would do her good before she got started. Simon and Charles were busy with the animals in the barn, so they wouldn't care. The birds were chirping, and the new buds on the trees were stretching out to her. She couldn't resist the call of the forest.

Emma walked for several minutes, enjoying the fragrant morning air. Born to study the wilderness, she kept track of her progress so she could retrace her steps. All around her were the signs of spring, and she often stopped to admire the view and revel in the beauty she saw. She was delighted when she spotted the early bloom of a flower, and she knelt down to admire its delicate petals.

"Good morning."

The man's voice was unexpected, for she had thought herself alone. Her hand holding the new flower jerked in surprise, and the blossom was torn from its stem and dropped to the ground. Dismayed, Emma turned from it to the intruder. Her mouth fell open.

"Ralph!"

"Hi, Emma." Ralph looked sheepishly at her.

"What are you doing here? I thought you were on your way east."

"I was…I am. Emma, don't be mad, I'm only looking out for you."

Emma was puzzled. "What do you mean?"

"Well, this marriage, for one thing." Ralph began pacing in front of her. "I couldn't sleep. I kept thinking that somehow I was responsible for you rushing off to get married. I know you said different"—he forestalled her protest—"but I wasn't sure. I had to find out for myself. So…" He gave her a guilty look. "I checked up on you."

Emma blinked. "What do you mean you 'checked up on me'?"

Ralph was evidently embarrassed, but he doggedly continued his confession. "I hid behind the cabin last night—"

"You what?"

"I know, Emma, it sounds ridiculous, but I had to know for sure. I mean—look—I drove you away from Grandville with my stupid actions, and I couldn't live with myself if I found I drove you into an unhappy marriage. I'm glad I was wrong," he added.

Emma's temper was rapidly building, but at his last words, she swallowed hard. "What do you mean?"

Ralph dug his boot toe into the dead leaves, pine needles, and moss on the forest floor. "You know. I saw Simon carry you into the bedroom, and you had your arms all wrapped around him. After he kissed you and blew out the lamp, I left. Honest, Em. I had seen enough to convince me. I'm really sorry again for butting into your life, but, you understand, I had to know. I just had to be sure."

The words sounded far away to Emma as she stared at him, trying to recall what he had seen. Did Simon know someone was watching them? Was that why he had been so convincing? Or—her heart stirred at the thought—had he genuinely been that tender with her, that…loving?

"I'm leaving now, Emma, but I just want to say I'm really happy for you and Simon. I only hope once I find Philippa that we can be as happy. Please, don't be mad at me for spying on you."

Emma heard the worry in his voice, and she shook her head. "I'm not mad. I think it's pretty special to have a friend who cares so much about me." She held out her arms. "We'll be praying for you and Philippa."

Ralph grinned and gave her a brotherly hug. "Thanks, Em," he said in her ear.

"Whoeee! No wonder I can't find any critters in these woods—they're full of people!"

Ralph swung around, and Emma jerked away from him with a guilty start. She stared in amazement at the old man in the coonskin cap.

"Hermit Jack?" she asked in disbelief.

The gray-bearded man peered closer at her. "Wal! Iffen it ain't the youngin' who shot my buck!" He moved closer to her and looked her over carefully. Then he pointed to her skirt. "I see you figgered out how to wear thet thing."

"Who is he, Emma?" Ralph asked her quietly.

"Emma! Thet's right! Lemme see—Newly, right? Emma Newly. I never forgit a face, but sometimes I have trouble rememberin' the names."

"That's right, Mr., I mean, Hermit Jack." Emma smiled at the old man, but she moved closer to Ralph's side. "What are you doing here?"

"Whaddya mean? I live 'round here, back up in them hills. I was out lookin' for some tracks and found the woods full of people. Why, someone even went and moved into thet old cabin. Gettin's so a body can't move around without runnin' into folks."

"I live there now." Emma's smile wavered when a frown appeared on Jack's face.

"You? You livin' there alone?"

"No," she hesitated then plunged on. "I'm married now. My husband and I and a hired hand live there now."

Hermit Jack's bushy eyebrows drew together in a deep vee. He turned his attention to Ralph.

"I 'spects you're the husband since I seen ya all cozy'n up together." His stained teeth indicated he was smiling.

Ralph started to answer, but Emma interrupted.

"No. No, he's not my husband. I'd like you to meet Ralph Tunelle, a good friend of mine. Ralph, this is Hermit Jack." The situation was becoming uncomfortable, especially as the old woodsman scowled at the two of them. Emma felt guilty about being caught in Ralph's arms, yet she hadn't done anything wrong. Why did the hermit have to show up now?

"*Friend*, huh?" Jack looked critically at Ralph while the silence lengthened. Then, "So where's the husband?"

"He's at the cabin, or I should say, the barn with Charles; that's our hired hand. Well, really he was my husband's servant, but now he's just helping out. My husband's name is Simon…" She frowned, trying to remember as she rattled on. "Chase—Simon Chase." Emma babbled on while she avoided the old man's eyes. He made her feel guilty, and she could tell he disapproved of her. "Would you like to come meet him?" she offered lamely.

"No."

"Oh, well, you're welcome to drop in anytime and join us for a meal." Why had she said that?

"No."

Emma pressed her lips together tightly. The old geezer didn't have to be so rude. Who did he think he was anyway, prowling around, sneaking up on people? She turned to Ralph. "I have to get back."

"Me too. I mean, I have to get started." Ralph smiled at Emma. "Take care, Em, and best wishes." With that, he moved quickly through the trees and out of sight.

"Well, I—" Emma stopped. Hermit Jack had also disappeared. She spun around but couldn't spot him anywhere.

"Why, of all the nerve!" Childishly she stomped her foot. The hermit man had succeeded in putting her in a bad mood, and she went back to the cabin and attacked the garden plot with a vengeance. By the time she was done, she was dirty, cross, and hungry. *Hungry!*

Emma pushed back her hair with a dirt-stained hand and looked at the position of the sun. "Goodness! It's nearly suppertime and I never even fixed a lunch for the men!" She looked over at the barn but couldn't see Charles or Simon, and now that she thought about it, she hadn't heard any noises from the barn in a while either. Where were they? They must be starved.

"Fine wife I've turned out to be; I can't even remember to feed my husband," she mumbled. She hurried to the well for water and brought a bucket to the small porch where she had set out a wash pan, soap, and towel. As she rushed to scrub the dirt out from under her fingernails, her stomach growled and her nose became aware of delicious aromas coming from inside.

Curious, she grabbed up the towel with her still dirty hands and opened the door. She was met by the sizzling sound and fragrant smell of frying chicken. Pots were steaming and boiling on her small stove, and the table was neatly set for two with a small, delicate flower boasting as centerpiece. She stared in confusion at the sight until Charles spoke from behind her where he had come from his room.

"It's not quite ready, madam. You still have time to, uh, freshen up," he suggested delicately.

"Charles, you can cook?" She was astounded.

"Quite well, actually. My…my mother's friends taught me. It may not be exactly what you're used to, but I did my best with what commodities were available to me."

Emma stared dumbfounded at the servant. "When did you come in here? When did you—I never heard a thing. Why didn't someone tell me what time it was?"

"You seemed preoccupied, my dear." Emma turned as Simon spoke behind her. "Charles and I both tried to get your attention, but you were so involved in stabbing holes in the ground and muttering something about men being impossible that we decided it best to just leave you alone. Charles took it upon himself to start the evening meal a little early since we all missed our lunch." He turned to the servant. "Smells great, Charles. I'm sorry I didn't offer my help to you, but the barn repairs took longer than I anticipated."

There was a strangely flat sound to Simon's words, and Emma supposed he thought her a poor partner to be saddled with. Indeed, why shouldn't he? She certainly had failed to be an asset to him in their first two days together. She looked down at the dirt she had rubbed into her towel.

"I'm really sorry. I don't know how I let the time escape from me like that. I guess when I get involved in something, I forget about everything and everyone around me. And, I *was* letting my temper get the best of me. I have a hard time keeping it under control sometimes."

"Really."

Emma looked sharply at Simon, but he was walking to the door. "I'll just put away a few things outside, then I'll be in, Charles," he said over his shoulder.

The door closed behind him, and Emma stared at it. "Did I say something wrong?" There was a slight tremor in her voice.

Charles sighed and smiled kindly at her. "He's got a lot on his mind, madam. I wouldn't worry about it."

"Is he upset that I didn't get you both some lunch? I mean, of course he is! Who wouldn't be? Oh Charles, what a disappointment I must be to him! He knows I'm not much good at my job, and now I look like I can't even run a house!" She shook her head slowly. "I'll just have to do better. I have to."

"You're doing fine, madam. May I make a suggestion?"

At her nod, he continued, "Why don't you clean up and change and just enjoy the evening? Forget the things that are bothering you and start over. Fresh."

"Well, I suppose…I should help you finish."

"I can manage. Go. You've only got about fifteen minutes."

Emma saw Charles scan her windblown hair and smudged face. She couldn't help laughing.

"You think I can repair the damages that quickly?" she joked.

"I think you can do anything you put your mind to, madam," Charles assured her.

With another laugh, Emma hurried to get ready. By the time the fifteen minutes were up, she was scrubbed clean and in a fresh dress with her hair neatly brushed and hanging in a ponytail down her back. Her face glowed with a touch of sun and her disposition was greatly improved. Somehow she knew she could face up to the challenges again.

Simon and Charles were waiting when she joined them in the small kitchen. She looked hesitantly from one to the other. Charles nodded his approval, but Simon only reached for her chair and held it for her without saying a word. Emma glanced at him then away. Was he really that upset that she had forgotten the time?

Charles began placing the steaming dishes of food on the table, and Simon attempted to help him.

"Please, sir, allow me."

Emma saw Simon scowl, but he sat down. It was then that he noticed the place settings were for only two people.

"Where do you intend to eat, Charles?" he demanded.

"If you please, sir, I will dine in my room this evening. I have a lot of reading I'd like to do; then I'll retire early. That Mr. Brady snored loud enough to wake the dead. I don't believe I slept at all."

"Go ahead, Charles." Simon even chuckled. "You deserve a break."

"And I'll clean up in here," Emma added. "Thank you, Charles."

When they were left alone, Emma waited for Simon to speak first. He looked at all the food placed before them and simply said, "Let's give thanks, shall we?" After his short prayer, they began their meal and a heavy silence settled over them.

This is ridiculous, thought Emma. *He's acting worse than some of my front-row students!* She opened her mouth to ask him about his day, but he spoke first.

"Did you have a nice walk?"

Emma closed her mouth. Something in the way he spoke those words told her he knew about Ralph. Suddenly she understood.

"You could have let me know you were there. You could have spoken to Ralph yourself instead of spying on me."

"I never spied on you."

"Then how did you know I talked to Ralph?" Emma's eyes narrowed.

"You just told me."

Emma set her fork down and glared at Simon. "Then why are you upset with me? Is it because I forgot to cook some lunch?"

Simon exhaled deeply and looked directly at Emma. She saw disappointment in his eyes. "No. I don't expect you to wait on me or cook for me if you don't want to. You only need to provide a believable cover for Charles and me until we can go to Washington. But, Emma, no one will believe us if you are found in the woods in another man's arms."

Emma stared at him. "You said—"

"I know you have other interests in your life, but I'm afraid they will have to be set aside for now, because this job is simply too important to be destroyed by them. I'm sorry, Emma, but I have to insist that you act your part more convincingly. When this is all over, you can go on with your plans. Excuse me."

Before Emma could voice her outraged reply, Simon pushed his plate aside and left the small cabin. She stared down at her unfinished food. Did he really think she was the kind of girl who got involved with someone else's husband? How did he know she had hugged Ralph? He said he wasn't there. Then who?

Emma's lips tightened. Hermit Jack!

Chapter 13

Norris

The livery was closed for the night, the blacksmith having hung up his tools and retired long ago. The back room had no window, making it an ideal location for the clandestine meeting being held there. The single lantern's light threaded its way under the door and between the cracks in the wooden walls but not enough to draw attention from outside.

One of the two men within pulled out his tobacco pouch and sliced off a chunk with a short-bladed knife. He tucked the tobacco in his cheek and passed the bag to the other man, who proceeded to do the same.

"When's she gonna git here?" he questioned around the wad now under his lip.

"She said she'd come after dark."

"Wal, it's dark. Where is she?"

"Jes hold yer horses."

The second man scratched at the nubs on his chin. "Iffen she'd have nabbed the girl in Grandville, we'd be outta here already."

"Sophie knows what she's doin'."

"Don't you mean *So-fee-yah*?"

The other man snorted. "She is gettin' kinda high-falutin', ain't she!"

"Wal, I'm getting' sick of her bossin' us around—"

A noise outside silenced them. The man holding the knife moved to the side of the door and held his weapon ready as the door slowly creaked open. A dark-haired young woman peeked into the room and, seeing the one man, she quickly entered and closed the door. Turning, she came face-to-face with the second man, and she stifled the scream she almost let out at the sight of him.

"Fergus! Why'd you try to scare me like that?" she hissed at him.

Fergus grinned, finding amusement in her fright. "Ya told us to be careful. Jes doin' what ya said," he explained innocently.

Sophia Barlow smacked her brother on the head with the back of her hand. "Don't get smart with me, Fergus. Your brains couldn't handle the strain."

The other man guffawed but quickly squelched his amusement when Sophia glared at him. "Mind yourself too, Horace."

"Aw, Sophie, we was jes havin' fun with ya."

"We don't have time for that. Listen, we can forget about the Newlys and Trents for now. I've come across something bigger."

"Whaddya mean forget them? We've bin workin' on this too long to let it go now," Horace protested.

"Yah," Fergus agreed. "Iffen ya woulda snatched thet girl in Grandville, we'd be rich from all the ransom money already. Ya sure didn't git any of them fellars to fall fer ya."

Sophia bristled at her brother's words. "What more could I do? They're all married and wouldn't dream of cheating on their wives. I tried my charm on them, believe me! When little Emma Newly turned up, I thought it would be an easy thing to take her and ask for ransom from all that inheritance money they've got, but she turned out to be slipperier than a fish at getting away from me. But forget that for now. I've got big news."

Horace rolled his eyes. "We've heard thet before. Why can't we jes rob the bank and skedaddle outta here?"

"You stay away from the bank; you hear me, Horace?" Sophia stared down her brother. "There are already posters out on us calling us 'The Barnes Gang,' and people are wising up, watching for the three of us. That's why I don't want us to be seen together. Now listen, I've come across some people who will pay us well just for doing a little job for them."

"What kinda job?"

"Just listen!" Sophia stared her brothers to silence. "You two just have to grab Emma Newly's new husband and hold on to him until these people come for him. I'll check out their place and get you all the details soon. It's a sweet deal and we'll get paid well." She waited while the two men looked at each other. "Maybe if this works out, we could still get the Newly girl and try for the ransom money later." She offered a further bribe.

"Whaddya think, Horace?" Fergus waited for his brother's nod. "Okay, Sophie. But then we wanna git outta here."

"You'll leave when I say; you hear me?" Sophia glared at the men. "I set up the deals and make the plans. You do as I say or you won't get your cut. Now get back to your camp before someone in town sees you." She turned swiftly and left the room.

Fergus spat a stream of tobacco juice at the closed door. He looked at Horace and shook his head. "We never shoulda let her go to school."

Chapter 14

North of Norris

The next week passed slowly. Simon and Emma only spoke when they had to, and Charles ended up mediating most of the time.

Emma was hurt by what Simon thought of her. More hurt than she believed possible. It was becoming more and more important to her that Simon should respect her, and she resolved to settle their misunderstanding and get rid of the tension building between them as soon as possible. Her opportunity came when Simon announced he was going hunting the next morning.

"May I come with you?" she asked.

Charles looked up from the game of checkers he and Simon were playing, but Simon continued to study the board. Emma was working on a rug to put in front of the fireplace, and her hands moved rhythmically though she held her breath waiting for his answer. Simon took his time making his move in the game before he replied.

"We'll leave a little before sunup," was all he said.

The next morning Simon set a fast pace through the woods, but Emma was prepared. She wore her riding skirt for better mobility and moccasins for silence in traveling over the forest floor. She was impressed with Simon's skill in moving through the forest.

Occasionally he turned to check on her, and though he made no comment, she could tell he was surprised that she stayed with him. It wasn't long before they came upon a pond and Simon found a hiding place for them to wait. The deer would come here to drink.

They hadn't spoken all morning, and Emma felt the silence weigh them down. Now was not the time to talk, however, so she spent some time beseeching the Lord to relieve their misunderstandings and put them back on the right footing again. She felt rather than saw Simon's movement, and she was prepared when the gun roared and a doe dropped to the ground.

"Good shot, Simon!" she exclaimed. "You must have been doing that since you were a kid."

"Actually, no." Simon looked at her fully for the first time that morning. "I grew up back east and didn't spend much time in the forest until the last half a dozen years. I've learned a lot from a friend of mine."

"But if you haven't been back east in so long, how did you uncover the counterfeiting plot in Washington?" Emma wondered out loud.

She was sorry she'd asked a moment later when Simon's face closed up like a mask. "Sorry, Emma, that's not for me to tell," he said dryly. He rose from their hiding place and went to take care of the deer.

Emma could have kicked herself. Why had she asked the wrong question the first time he started talking with her? Somehow she had to try again. She followed and watched while he cleaned out the animal. Summoning up her courage, she spoke to his bent head.

"Simon, Ralph means nothing more to me than a friend. He was here the first night we came because he wanted to make sure he hadn't driven me to an unhappy marriage. When I took my walk, he followed me and apologized. That's all there was to it. I wished him well and hugged him goodbye like I would any of my friends. That's when Hermit Jack saw us, and I suppose he was the one who told you what he saw."

She waited, but Simon made no reply, though she noticed that his hands had stilled.

"I'm sorry, Simon, that I didn't play my part very well, but I promise I'll do better in the future. I want to do a good job. I really do. And just so you know, I would never be involved with a married man. Never. I know God's Word is against it, and so am I." Emma was breathless by the time she had finished speaking.

Simon resumed his work, but he spoke over his shoulder. "I'm a married man, Emma. I'm married to you."

Stunned for a moment by his choice of words, Emma then spoke, "I know." The words were barely a whisper.

Simon stopped his work again and glanced at her. Her head was down, and she refused to meet his eyes. He walked to the pond and washed off his hands then came and stood before her.

"I've been a bear, haven't I? I'm sorry. I guess I never really believed you were getting involved with Ralph. I think I'm getting to know you well enough to know that. But having him show up right after Brady was here—and Brady said a man sent him out to check up on us—and Ralph just happens to be going east…it all seemed too coincidental."

Emma was incredulous. "You mean you suspected Ralph of being a spy? Ralph Tunelle?"

"From what you told me, you would never have expected him to act like he did with you either. Who's to say he hasn't sunk even lower?"

Emma's look pierced Simon. "Then you suspected me of giving him information about you."

Simon's eyes dropped; then he honestly looked Emma in the eye. "I did. Even a moment ago when you asked about my work, I was suspicious." He took a deep breath. "But there comes a time when you have to trust each other, and I think I'm beginning to know you well enough to trust you, Emma. There's just one thing."

Emma waited. She was aware of Simon's hesitancy to continue, and despite her anger at his suspicions of her, she was nervous about what he would say next.

Simon shifted his feet, but again he looked squarely at her when he spoke. "It's your temper."

Emma's mouth dropped open.

"It's so very important that we succeed here, Emma, and I'm afraid that if your temper gets the best of you just once, it could spoil all our plans."

The anger seeped away from her. "I know." She swallowed hard. "I've always had a problem with it. I get really quiet and try to hold everything in; then some little thing causes it to explode. And you're right. *I* need to be in control, not my temper."

"Well, it could come in handy if we are ever attacked by an invading army," Simon teased. "As long as it's not directed at me, we'll be okay. Remember, I'm not one of the bad guys."

Emma smiled.

"Will you forgive me for suspecting you and for being rude to you this past week?"

"Only if you'll forgive my temper."

"Done!" Simon grinned back at her then suddenly frowned. "We may both have some explaining to do to Charles. I know *I* owe him an apology. Here I've been trying to be a good testimony and witness to Charles, and lately I've been acting like a spoiled child who didn't get his way." He shook his head. "How can I win Charles for Christ when he sees no difference in the way I act from the way an unbeliever acts?"

Emma also became sober. "I have to apologize to him too, Simon. He needs to know that Christians will still sin because we still have our old sin nature but that God's forgiveness has already taken care of our sin. I'm ashamed that I've allowed my temper to cause me to lose sight of how important my testimony before Charles is."

"Thankfully, God can still use us despite our faults."

Emma smiled again and found herself looking into Simon's eyes. The time lengthened, and Simon took a step closer to her.

"Emma." He reached up and brushed a wisp of hair from her face. Her eyes closed.

"I knew I could find you!"

They turned with a start, and Emma's heart sank at the sight of Sophia striding toward them. Simon's hand dropped to his side, and Emma saw him scowl.

"Miss Barlow! What brings you way out here?" Simon sounded welcoming, but Emma heard the annoyance in his voice.

"Your hired man told me I could find you here. Goodness! Is he ever a stuffed shirt! He was reading a huge book and acted like I was some kind of criminal for bothering him. I left the Findleys with him at your cabin, and I came looking for you. We've come for a visit."

Emma saw a hint of worry in Simon's face. "We better get back to the cabin then and entertain our guests. Emma dear, will you show Miss Barlow the way back, please? I'll finish here and be with you shortly."

"Of course. Are you sure you don't need any help?"

"I'll be done in no time. You go on ahead."

Emma was reluctant to leave. Simon had been about to say something to her; something special, she was sure. The moment had held promise. *Oh! Why did Sophia have to show up now!*

"You go hunting together! How quaint. But I suppose being newlyweds you do just about everything together, or did you just need to get away from your hired help? You know, he was very rude to me. I think you should speak to him."

Sophia rambled on as Emma led her back through the forest. Once again, Emma wondered how long Sophia had been watching and listening to them before she spoke up. They really did have to act their parts all the time like Simon said, not just when they knew they were being watched.

The Findleys were enjoying coffee at the table when the two women returned. Emma looked around for Charles, but he wasn't there, and the door to his room was open.

"Your man made us coffee then said he had work in the barn to do, chores or something." Agatha explained with a smile. "My, Emma! You are looking wonderful! How do you like married life?"

"I couldn't be happier! It's awfully nice of you all to come for a visit. Simon will be with us shortly; he's dressing out a deer he shot this morning. Now, tell me, how is your daughter and her family?"

Emma refilled their cups and poured for Sophia and herself as she listened to the Findleys talk about their daughter. All the while she kept a look out for Simon. She was more aware than ever that she was there to help protect him and to make sure he wasn't discovered.

Emma had always suspected Sophia, and she kept an eye on her as Sophia moved about in the small cabin examining their belongings. Emma wouldn't put it past her to check the closets, and she was thankful for Simon's wisdom in putting their clothing together. Finally, she saw Simon, carrying the deer over his shoulders, walk into the clearing around the cabin.

A sensation of having stood and watched him do that very thing before came over her. She smiled to herself. Perhaps it was because she wouldn't mind doing it for the rest of her life. Her eyes widened at her thoughts, and she had to swallow. Could she actually be falling in love with her husband?

"My, he's strong," remarked Sophia. "I think I'll go chat with Simon for a bit. You don't mind, do you, Emma?"

Sophia was out the door before Emma had a chance to answer. Emma took a step after her, but Agatha Findley asked another question and as hostess, Emma turned again to her guest. The thought of Sophia flirting with Simon upset her, and it must have showed on her face, for Agatha said, "Don't worry about Sophia. Remember, Simon chose *you*. Where did the two of you meet anyway?"

Caught off guard, Emma searched for an answer. Because she and Simon had spoken very little to each other the past week, they hadn't thoroughly gone over their story, and she didn't know how to begin. She was rescued by Charles.

"Madam, Mr. Chase would like your assistance for a few moments, please."

"Yes, of course. Excuse me, please." She left the inquisitive Findleys with relief and headed to the barn with Charles. Sophia's giggling could be heard before they even reached the building, and though Emma's teeth grit together because of it, she reminded herself to keep her temper in check. She had a job to do.

Sophia was leaning against a post very near Simon, talking to him in low tones. Whatever he replied, she found amusing, and she covered her mouth with her hand and giggled again. Then she gave Simon a playful push on the arm and said, "You're teasing me, Simon."

Simon simply smiled, but when he saw Emma, he stood and reached for her hand.

"Sorry to take you away from our other guests, my dear, but I was wondering what you would like from this deer for our lunch. I'm sure the Findleys would enjoy the fresh meat, and Miss Barlow already said she'd stay for our noon meal."

Emma nodded pleasantly to Sophia and discussed what cuts of venison she wanted, all the while aware of the pressure of Simon's fingers on her own. She turned to go back to the cabin, but Simon pulled her close for an instant and kissed her cheek. She found it was no longer acting on her part when she gave him a loving look. Simon's answering smile and nod conveyed that she was very convincing.

Their lunch together went smoothly, for the Findleys were enjoyable guests. Sophia was endured, and Emma wondered if the young woman was even aware that she was becoming a bother with all her questions. Her flirtations with Simon annoyed Emma, and she marveled that Simon could handle Sophia's attentions without seeming bothered by them. He was a better actor than she was!

It was with relief that they finally bade their guests farewell. Simon slid an arm about Emma's waist as they waved to the departing carriage.

"Do you think we passed the test?" he asked her.

Emma smiled dispassionately in response. "That Sophia! I think she knows every inch of our cabin inside and out. Do you know I found her in my bedroom when

I got back from the well? She said she was admiring my handiwork, meaning the curtains and rug I made. Can you believe that? I'm so glad she's gone; I'm always afraid I'll lose my temper around her."

"You handled her very well, Emma. I think she's convinced that we're who we say we are. The Findleys certainly believe it," he added with a grin.

Emma cast a sideways glance at Simon, and her face reddened. Agatha had made mention several times that Emma simply glowed like a woman in love. She even mentioned that no doubt babies would be coming along soon! Emma had evaded responding to the older woman's remarks by turning to work on the meal she had cooking on their stove, but Simon had replied that they hoped the Lord would bless them with a family soon. Emma hoped her flushed cheeks would be blamed on the heat from the stove. It took her several minutes before she could join the conversation again, and even then she avoided Simon's eyes.

"You did a great job," Simon repeated. "I don't think we'll have any trouble from Sophia for a while." He reached inside the door for his hat. "I need to finish in the barn. See you later."

The rest of the day passed quickly with Simon and Charles out in the barn and Emma working in the little cabin. At some point during her work, Emma found a time to speak with Charles about her behavior, apologizing to him for her temper and her failure to look to the Lord, as she and Simon had been trying to demonstrate to him through their daily devotional and prayer time in his presence. Charles had responded with graciousness, although he seemed uneasy about listening to her apology.

Simon found his opportunity as he and Charles worked together in the barn.

"Charles, I need to apologize to you for the way I've been acting this last week," he began.

"No need, sir. Madam has already spoken to me, and though I appreciate your concern for my feelings, I see no reason why either of you should feel you need to apologize to me for what you do."

Simon stopped his work and looked at Charles curiously. "Sir? Madam? Aren't you carrying this butler thing a little too far?" He chuckled at Charles's embarrassment.

"I am rather enjoying playing my part. I'm good too, aren't I! It's a good thing I've had a butler myself most of my life so I know exactly what to do." He joined in Simon's laughter.

"Seriously, Charles, I do need to apologize. I've been telling you about Christ and how knowing him as your Savior can make a difference in your life. Then I slip up and show you the many faults in my life and leave you wondering if I know what I'm talking about." Simon prayed for the right words as Charles studied his face.

"It's that important to you?"

"Yes, it is."

"Why?"

"Because if the way I'm living my life discourages you from accepting Christ, you would be turning your back on eternity in heaven and face an eternity without God. I don't want to cause that to happen. It's *that* important!" Simon let his words sink in.

Charles nodded slowly. "Well, I accept your apology and Emma's too. I never expected either of you to be perfect, Simon, just because you believe in the Bible. I know enough of the Bible to know that people can't achieve perfection, and I certainly know that I'm not perfect either. But I'm a good person, and that has to count for something. After all, look what I'm doing right now. I'm risking my life to testify at that trial. Nobody's making me do it. Surely that accounts for something in God's eyes."

"What you're doing is good and right and noble, Charles, but you yourself admitted that you're not perfect either. God doesn't have a balance scale that he uses to weigh the good over the bad to let you into heaven. The Bible tells us that all our righteousness is like filthy rags to God. He only sees the goodness of his Son's sacrifice on the cross for our sins as acceptable payment because Jesus Christ was without sin in the first place.

"If you could get to heaven on your good works, Charles, how good would you have to be? How would you know when you had done enough? And are you willing to take that chance?"

Charles appeared to think that over. "I guess I wouldn't know," he responded.

Simon nodded. "Exactly. But you can know you're assured of heaven by accepting the gift of salvation that

Christ offers you. Ephesians 2:8-9 says, 'For by grace are ye saved through faith; and that not of yourselves: it is a gift of God: Not of works, lest any man should boast.' Does that seem clear to you, Charles?"

"It seems clear enough," he admitted.

"Do you believe it?" Simon persisted.

Charles paused before answering. "I'd like to think it is that simple, but I can't say that I'm sure that it is."

Simon nodded in understanding. "Then will you do me a favor, Charles, and read some verses that I'll write out for you? Read them and think about them and let me know what you come up with. I'll be praying for you."

After supper Simon lit a lantern and returned to the barn while Charles settled down with a book in his room and Emma picked up her sewing. She was determined to finish the curtains for the kitchen window before she went to bed.

As she worked, Emma thought over the events of the day. It was so good to be speaking again with Simon. Those days of silence between them had been the most miserable she had ever spent. She vowed she would not let her temper interfere again. Her thoughts returned to the morning by the pond when Simon looked as if he were about to say something to her. Was he going to tell her that he was falling in love with her like she was with him? Emma sighed. Sophia had ruined the moment, and she wondered when or if Simon would finish their conversation. She looked up as Charles came out of his room.

"Hasn't Mr. Chase returned yet, madam?"

Emma's hands stilled at the apprehensive look on the servant's face, and she glanced at the window. It was pitch black outside.

"What time is it, Charles?" she asked as she went to the door and looked out at the barn. There was a faint glow of light coming from the partially open doorway. "There's his lantern. He must still be working," she said in relief.

"Madam, it's after midnight. I better see if Mr. Chase needs my assistance."

"After midnight! I had no idea! I'm coming with you; he may be hurt! He probably tried to call to us and we didn't hear! He—"

"Steady, madam. He's probably just engrossed in what he's doing like we were and didn't notice the passing of time. Let's not worry until we know."

Emma had her coat on and the lantern ready and was out the door, making Charles run to catch up to her. They entered the barn together.

"Simon! Simon, where are you? Simon, are you there?"

Emma saw that the lantern Simon had brought out with him was hanging on a peg, but Simon was nowhere in sight.

"Mr. Chase! Sir, are you in here?" Charles called. He cast Emma a worried look. "May I take one of the lanterns, madam? I'll check around outside while you look in here."

The pounding of her heart hurt Emma's chest, and she found breathing difficult. Fear for Simon's safety tried to engulf her, but she warded it off and took up her lantern to begin a thorough search of the barn. Carefully she checked through each stall and every nook and cranny in the small building. Simon was not there, but she found something that sent a chill down her spine. She crouched down to look more carefully.

"He's not outside, nor in any of the out buildings, madam." Charles spoke breathlessly, and Emma heard the worry in his voice.

"Look here, Charles." Emma pointed. "Hold your light over there."

"What is it, madam? What do you see?"

Emma's finger traced some markings near the barn door. "See these, Charles? Here's where Simon dragged the deer before he hung it up. But look at these." In the dirt were two furrows parallel to each other. "These were made by someone's boot heels. Someone who was being dragged." She followed the markings out the doorway and around the side of the building. "And here's where they stop, right by these horse tracks." Emma straightened up and stared at Charles. "Someone has taken Simon."

Chapter 15

North of Norris

Emma had never experienced a more terrible night in her life. She and Charles had to wait until dawn to begin their search for Simon. The tracks were too difficult to find in the inky blackness of the night, and Emma had to fight the desire to start out by lantern light. She had to calm down. She had to think rationally.

Her father's training helped her prepare for the mission ahead of her. She set Charles to work packing the supplies she knew they would need while she readied her weapons and herself. She didn't sleep. Once everything was ready, she sat and waited and prayed. It was no longer a job to her to see to Simon's safety. The man she loved, her husband, was in danger, and she would do anything to help him. Anything. For now she put aside the fact that though Simon was her husband, he knew nothing of her love for him, and she had no idea of his feelings for her.

They ended up starting by lantern light anyway. The sun would soon appear, and Emma was determined to be well on the trail when it did. She circled the area where the horse tracks were until she found the direction they were headed. Charles stood back, completely out of his element, and waited for her leading.

"This way, Charles. They've made no attempt to hide their tracks; apparently they think you and I pose no threat in following them."

"They would be partially right, madam."

"There are three horses. Simon was put on one, so we'll assume there are two men—or women." Sophia Barlow flashed through Emma's mind. Sophia had looked the barn over rather well too.

As the light of the new day washed away the black and gray of the night, Emma and Charles were able to increase their speed in following the trail left by Simon's abductors. Emma paused frequently and jumped off her horse to study the ground. When she found the hoof prints that were the same as those by the barn, she would mount again and be off after them. Charles somehow managed to keep up to her.

Several hours passed. The going was slowed by the continual stopping to check the trail. Emma constantly checked their surroundings, for though she had never been in this area, she would be sure to find her way back again. It was while she was off her horse checking the tracks that she sniffed something in the cool air.

Charles was slumped wearily in his saddle, but he straightened and looked about him as he too caught a whiff of something.

"Wood smoke," Emma said softly. She walked ahead slowly leading her horse, and Charles dismounted awkwardly, muffling a groan as he hobbled after her.

Through the trees they could see a clearing, an open meadow surrounded by woods. Rolling hills blocked their view, but in the distance there was smoke, and Emma made out the top of a chimney.

"The tracks go out into the open," she told Charles quietly. "We'll stay in the trees and circle around to the building. I think we've found them."

"What do you want me to do, madam?"

"Stop calling me *madam*! That's what I want!" Emma rubbed her forehead wearily then placed a hand on Charles's arm. "I'm sorry. I don't know exactly what to tell you to do. Stay down and out of sight as much as possible. We may have to shoot at them, but I'd rather take them by surprise without any bloodshed. Above all, we have to keep from hurting Simon or letting them hurt him. We've come this far with the Lord's leading; we'll have to trust him to get us through these next minutes."

"Yes, mad—Emma." Charles corrected himself with a nervous grin at her. "I'm not much good at this sort of thing, but I'm ready for whatever it takes to get Mr. Chase back."

Emma nodded. "Let's go, then."

The smoke led them to an old shack that was leaning to one side. A bit of cloth waved in the glassless window and open chinks in the logs allowed the chipmunks and squirrels easy access to the inside. A door hung crookedly on its hinges.

Emma led Charles as close as they dared go and still be covered by the surrounding brush. They waited and listened. Emma's senses were fully alert now. She glanced at Charles's tight features and gave him a small, encouraging smile. Her head swung back to the shack as an angry shout rang out.

"Git up, Horace! I've been up all night too! You watch him for a while. I jes can't stay awake no more."

A groan followed the words. Emma motioned to Charles and held up two fingers. Two *men*, she thought. Hopefully there were only the two of them.

There was a loud thud followed by a string of curses.

"I told ya to git up! Go stick yer head in a bucket of water or somethin'! I gotta get some sleep. Git!"

Emma and Charles watched as a man stumbled out of the cabin wearing nothing but his long underwear. The door swung back against the wall with a screech and a crash, but before it slammed shut again, Emma saw a glimpse of a man settling down on a bed and a man sitting in a chair with a handkerchief tied around his mouth. *Simon!*

Emma gripped Charles's arm as the man approached their hiding place. Her pistol was ready in her hands, but the man stumbled past them, bleary-eyed and cussing, and headed for the well. Emma motioned Charles to stay put, and she silently rose and followed. The man named Horace was bending over the well opening when Emma clicked the pistol in his ear.

He straightened up with a start and with a speed Emma hadn't expected, he snatched her gun away. There was a flash of movement behind the man, and suddenly he was lying on the ground and her pistol had flown out of his hand. She made a dive for it and swung it around. Quickly she lowered it as Charles stood white-faced over the fallen man with a stick held in his hands like a club.

Emma scrambled to her feet and to Charles's side in a moment. "Thank goodness you thought of that, Charles!" She spoke in a whisper. "I nearly ruined everything."

Charles continued to stare in shock at the man. "Is he dead?" he choked out the words.

Emma bent over the man. "No, but he's out cold. You pack a pretty mean wallop, Charles." She stopped and put a finger to her lips. From the shack came the unmistakable sound of snoring—loud, raucous, dead-to-the-world snoring. Emma grinned. "Come on."

They approached the front door with caution. Emma cringed as a board squeaked beneath her feet, but the snoring continued rhythmically, undisturbed. She inched the door open slowly until she could make out the occupants of the room. Simon's eyes grew large, but she looked away from him to the man on the bed and then made a quick sweep of the room. With her pistol gripped firmly in both hands, she edged nearer to the bed and held the gun steady on the sleeping man while Charles worked on untying Simon. From the corner of her eye, Emma saw Simon work the feeling back in his fingers then he reached for the gun in her hands and nudged the man with it. She stepped back out of the way.

"Get up, Fergus. Come on! Get up! You've got some questions to answer."

As the man named Fergus rolled over with a groan, Simon spoke to Emma and Charles. "There's another one outside. Take that rifle and—"

"Charles already took care of him," Emma answered hastily.

Simon's eyebrows rose. "Charles?" He motioned to Fergus. "Think you can tie this one up, Charles? You can use what's left of the rope they used on me."

Charles fumbled with the ropes until the man was secured. Then he nodded to Simon. "That should do it."

"Good! Let's get him to a horse and pick up the other man—Horace. I think the sheriff in Norris would like to hear what these two have been up to. I know I have a few questions, like who sent them after me. Care to answer that one, Fergus?"

Angry curses were the only reply, so Simon said to Charles, "Get him out of here, will you? If that keeps up, we'll gag him. I'll be right out."

Charles took the rifle Simon handed him and with a determined look, he motioned for Fergus to precede him out the door.

Simon finally turned to Emma, who was still standing quietly out of the way in the corner. He took in her white face and shadow-rimmed eyes. "I'd be lying if I said I wasn't glad to see you. I was running out of escape ideas by the time you and Charles showed up." He took a deep breath and continued to hold her gaze. "But, Emma, if you knew how frightened you made me when I saw you come through that door." He stopped as if to collect himself. "You have to promise me you'll never do such a stupid thing again!"

Emma had started to take a step toward Simon. The relief in seeing that he was all right and her newfound love for him were in her eyes. At his words, her step faltered and her eyes dropped. Uncertainty crossed her face.

"Emma, have you any idea what could have happened?" Simon's words were harsh. Fatigue and worry lined his face, and concern for her was in his eyes, but Emma failed to see it, for her eyes were still on the floor like one of her school-children after a good scolding. She was only aware of the anger in Simon's voice.

Simon raked his fingers through his hair. "Please, Emma, never risk yourself or Charles for me again. I would have gotten away somehow. I can take care of myself."

"I thought that was my job." Emma's words were barely audible, but Simon heard them.

"No! As far as I'm concerned all you are is a cover for me. That's all, okay?"

Simon missed the hurt in the blue eyes that quickly glanced at him and then away again. His fear for her was so great that he still spoke sternly, not realizing how the words sounded to the white-faced woman a few feet from him.

"I see." She was just a cover. Simon didn't love her; how she had begun to fool herself into believing that he might! He didn't even look glad to see her. Her heart ached with the pain of rejection. She couldn't let Simon see how she felt about him. How could they ever continue living their charade if he knew she would like to be married to him for real? Emma held back the tears she felt stinging behind her eyes. "I'm glad you're all right," she said quietly.

Simon studied her bent head for a few moments as though not sure what he had done but suddenly knowing that there was something wrong. In a gentler tone, he began, "What I mean is—"

A rifle shot outside snapped both their heads up. Simon ran for the door with the pistol in his hand. To Emma he yelled, "Stay there!"

Emma stood motionless for less than a second; then she flew into action searching the shack for another weapon. Finding Horace's clothes on the floor, she brushed them aside and found his gun belt with two pistols. Grabbing one, she quickly checked the chambers and started after Simon.

The pounding of hooves was the first thing she heard as she stealthily crept out the door. She glanced all around looking for Simon and Charles, but only Charles was in sight. He was standing with the rifle held awkwardly in his hands, and he was staring beyond the shack with a frustrated look on his face. Emma ran to him so that she could see what he was watching. It was Simon racing away on horseback.

"Charles! Quick! What happened? Where's Simon going?"

"Those two got away from me. I don't know what happened!"

"Stay here!" Emma commanded. She rushed to her horse and was away after Simon before Charles could stop her.

Emma had been riding ever since she could sit on a horse, and the horse under her was fleet footed. She saw Simon ahead of her and started gaining on him. Soon she realized that Simon was slowing his horse, and she bridged the gap between them. Her horse snorted as she reined in beside Simon's horse. Her eyes flashed, and she made no effort to hold back her anger as she glared at Simon.

"Do you want to get yourself killed?" she demanded to know.

Simon stared at her, speechless.

"Look, I know you think you can take care of yourself, but I was hired to do a job and I intend to do it." She looked to where Simon's kidnappers had disappeared. "There's no sense chasing them now. I think we should get you back to a safe place."

Simon started shaking his head.

"Mr. Chase, you're not my boss; you're my responsibility." Emma turned her horse and headed back for Charles.

Chapter 16

North of Norris

Emma sighed with relief as she slid off her horse at last. Her body slumped like a limp rag doll, but she forced herself to straighten up and schooled her features so that they not reveal her weariness. Simon and Charles were in no better shape, and from the corner of her eye Emma saw Simon rub at his neck muscles then stretch out his arms. Charles limped painfully to the steps of their cabin and sank down with a groan.

"I'm so tired my eyelids feel like lead weights; I can't keep them open. But my muscles are so sore, I don't know how I'll ever sleep," complained the servant.

"I'm afraid you won't get a chance to find out." Simon took the reins of the three horses and started walking them to the barn. The two by the cabin looked at him then at each other before they followed him. Charles moved awkwardly, his legs still bowed from riding the horse.

Emma wasn't as sore from the ride as she was frazzled and worn from her sleepless night and turbulent emotions. The ride home had been mainly in silence with only a word or two spoken now and then to give directions. Emma led most of the time when Simon admitted that he had been unconscious for much of his journey to the shack. No wonder he didn't seem as tired as they did!

Emma was unwilling to let him see her fatigue. After what had happened, she was more determined than ever to succeed at her job and prove to him that she was a capable protector, not just a cover. Her feelings for him she would hide, but she knew deep down that she couldn't dismiss them. They would be an ever-present ache within her, something she would just have to try to ignore.

Simon was already stripping the saddles off the weary horses when Emma and Charles approached him. The evening shadows were filling the stall where he worked, but he did not light the lantern. He worked methodically and thoroughly on the animal before moving to the next one, but he didn't speak. He waited, knowing from the expression on Emma's face that she would soon question him. He didn't have to wait long.

"What did you mean about Charles not getting a chance to sleep?"

Simon watched her help Charles to a bench before she turned to face him. She squared her shoulders then picked up a brush and began to work on the horse nearest her.

Simon wanted to stop her, to tell her that he knew how tired she was, to make her go and rest, but he held his tongue.

Her determination to do her job amused him, but he also had to admire her. She was truly skillful in the woods and had led them back without mishap, all the while keeping a look out on their back in case Fergus and Horace should return. He wanted to tell her that he was already watching, but he didn't. He let her handle it on her own. She wasn't going to like what he was going to tell her now.

"None of us will sleep tonight, I'm afraid." Simon continued to work as he spoke. "We have to leave tonight, as soon as possible."

Emma said nothing, but she paused in her brushing to look at Simon.

"They aren't playing games anymore, Emma. I heard Fergus say that after they brought me wherever they were supposed to bring me, they were going back to make sure you two didn't cause any trouble. They'll be back, or if not them, then someone else. We have to find a new place, a new way to hide." Simon moved to the horse that had remained in the barn and began readying it to pull the wagon. "We'll have to use one of these tired horses too, but we'll stop and trade off with the other one along the way," he explained.

"Where are we going?" Emma asked.

Simon glanced at her over his shoulder before looking away.

"To Grandville," he replied.

"Won't take them long to discover that we're there," she protested.

"We're not staying. We're only dropping you off. Then Charles and I will move on."

Charles's sleepy eyes flew open at the last remark, and he looked from one to the other with intent interest.

"Dropping me off? What are you talking about?" Emma moved to stand in front of Simon. Her hands were planted firmly on her hips.

Simon stopped harnessing the horse and straightened up before her. "Emma, try to understand. You'll be safe there with your family. I—"

But Emma spun on her heel and left the barn. Simon watched her go into the cabin, and he sighed. "I can't let anything happen to her, Charles. You understand, don't you? I never should have let her get involved."

Charles made no reply, but there was a glimmer in his eye as he looked at Simon. He rose painfully and started for the door. "I'll pack what we'll need."

Simon laid his head against the post he leaned on. *Lord, don't let anything happen to her because of me. Help me protect her.*

In the cabin's small kitchen, Emma was working by moonlight, rapidly packing the supplies they would need for their journey. Her mouth was set in a stubborn line, and she grumbled to herself under her breath while she worked. When she was finished, she moved into her bedroom. Charles had already been in and removed Simon's things, so she grabbed her bag and started filling it with her belongings. She worked fast, thrusting and poking the clothes into her bag with vehemence until she grabbed up the Bible beside her bed to pack it as well. Her hands stilled, and she sank to the bed slowly as she looked at the Book she held.

Oh, Lord! What's wrong with me? Her eyes closed and her head drooped to her chest. *Lord, I know I'm acting selfishly. I'm angry because Simon doesn't think I can help him. No, that isn't right, is it? He's worried about me, I guess, maybe as much as I am about him. Father, I'm supposed to protect him, but how can I do that if he won't let me?*

Emma sighed deeply. She opened her eyes and gently fingered the cover of the Bible on her lap. *Lord, you show me what to do. Your Word is my guide, and I trust what it says to me.*

Chapter 17

Near Grandville

Charles snored continuously in the back of the wagon as it rolled along in the moonlight. Emma's head kept drifting back or forward, and she jerked herself awake again and again, a problem that was fast annoying her. Simon seemed unaware of her battle with sleep as he kept the horses moving along in the right direction, but he smiled to himself each time she glanced at him to see if he noticed.

There was relief in his face as well. He had been so sure that their ride would be filled with tension because he had insisted on Emma staying in Grandville, but when he had helped her into her seat, she had smiled and thanked him and informed him she was ready to go. There was no doubt that he was relieved. Now he wouldn't have to argue with her about it. She would stay behind. He and Charles would go away. She would stay; he would go. *She would stay.* He glanced at her just as her head dropped back again.

He scowled. He didn't want to leave her behind! He never wanted to be without her again!

Emma saw the scowl and shook herself to wake up. What a child she must seem to him! She couldn't even stay awake. No wonder he didn't trust her to be of much help.

The sun was peeking over the horizon in front of them when Simon started to rein in the horses. He turned them off the road and they bumped along in a meadow until they disappeared down a hill and he stopped them by the edge of the trees. The road was no longer in view.

"We'll rest here during the day. I believe there's a small lake through these trees, and we can hide the wagon and horses. It's not likely we're being followed yet, but the fewer people who see us, the better. Why don't you and Charles get settled, and I'll see what I can do about making our tracks less noticeable from the road." Simon hopped down from the wagon and gave each of the horses, including the one tied behind, pats of encouragement before walking back up the hill to the road. Emma watched him until he disappeared before she moved.

Charles had come awake now that the wagon was still, and he looked around curiously.

"We're camping here during the daylight," Emma explained. "I bet you're as hungry as I am. We better fix something to eat as soon as we can." She yawned and shook her head. "Then we better get some rest."

She sent Charles to find the food supplies they would need, and she began caring for the horses. She took the one from the back first and led him through the trees until she came to the lake. The horse drank thirstily, and Emma breathed deeply of the early-morning freshness and reveled in the calm of the water and the chirping of the birds. A noise behind her startled her, but it was only Simon with the other two horses.

"I backed the wagon farther into the woods before I unharnessed these fellows. Go ahead and drink, boys. You've earned yourselves a good rest, maybe a brushing too if I can stay awake for it."

Emma looked quickly at Simon. Why was it that she hadn't noticed before how tired he was? He seemed never to tire.

Simon saw her concern. "I'm okay. We all need a good nap, though, except maybe Charles. He's been sleeping pretty well."

Emma smiled. "Poor Charles! I don't think he's cut out for this wild life we lead."

Simon grinned too. "He's doing all right, isn't he!" They picketed the horses and headed back to Charles. "Emma, thank you again for everything you've done. Things haven't gone just the way we've planned, have they?"

Emma shrugged. "No. But maybe our plans weren't God's plans. We'll just have to trust him to get us—I mean, to get you and Charles—through this. I know he will, Simon."

Charles had a small fire going and held the coffee pot in his hands. "That's the way to the water?" he asked.

Simon directed him then went to the wagon for a couple of blankets.

"Here, Emma. Why don't you sleep under the wagon; it'll have a bit more shade as the sun gets higher. I'll throw mine over here." He spread out another blanket under a tree. "As soon as Charles gets back, I'll give him a hand. Meanwhile…" He lay down on the blanket and sighed deeply. "Yep, this spot will do just fine."

Emma laughed then looked at her blanket under the wagon. She looked again at Simon and saw that he was already asleep. It looked too inviting.

When Charles returned moments later, he found Emma sound asleep under the wagon. Simon's hat was over his eyes, and he too was dead to the world. Charles looked at the pot in his hand and at the fire crackling merrily. He shrugged, put the pot on the edge of the flames, and went for his blanket.

It was late afternoon before Emma began to stir. Her sore body protested against the hard ground, but that wasn't what woke her. She was hungry and the aroma of cooking food was making her stomach gnaw and clamor for attention. She turned her head to see who was at the fire fixing their meal, Simon or Charles? But as she turned, she saw that Simon was still asleep under the tree and not far from him was Charles. She suddenly became very still.

There was a scrape of a utensil against a pan and then the renewed sizzling of meat as if it had just been turned.

A moment ago Emma's mouth had watered at the smell of the cooking food; now it was dry, and her heart flipped before starting to race.

Someone was at their fire! But who? She dared not turn around yet. She thought quickly to where the nearest weapon would be while she scolded herself for going to sleep with no thought to protecting Simon. Her hand was inching toward a small, inadequate stick, when she felt that she was being watched. Her eyes flew to Simon.

He stopped her action with his look. Then she saw him turn his attention back on the person by the fire behind her. He slid his gun from the holster beside him and leveled it over her head.

"You gonna let that guy shoot me, Emmie?"

Emma spun around and sat up, banging her head against the underside of the wagon. She cried out in pain as she tried to get a better look at the man who was still crouched before the fire with his back toward her.

"Tsk! Tsk! Em! Thought you were more graceful than that."

"Tyler?" Emma scurried out of her bed on her hands and knees. "Tyler, how did you find us? Why are you here? I'm so glad to see you!"

Emma flung herself into Tyler's arms while Simon and Charles approached more cautiously. The lowered gun was still in Simon's hand, and an outrageously jealous expression was on his face. Tyler was quick to notice it and just as quick to pretend that he hadn't. *So that's the way it is!*

"Em, maybe you better explain who I am to the guy with the gun," he said dryly.

Emma turned quickly back to Simon, but his expression was under control and he was already putting the gun away. "Simon, Charles, this is my brother Ty—Tyler Newly."

Like a cloud had been lifted, Simon's face cleared and he held out his hand to Tyler. Looking him fully in the face, he recognized Russ Newly's eldest son. "Looks like you've been here awhile," he noted, pointing to the sizzling venison steaks. "I can't believe we didn't hear you."

"Well, I can be pretty quiet when I want to be, though you folks probably wouldn't have been awakened by a herd of buffalo stampeding your camp. Care to tell me why and why you're not at the cabin anymore?"

Simon hesitated to answer, and even Emma's "It's okay, Simon, he's my brother," didn't reassure him. Tyler appreciated the man's caution.

"I don't blame you, Simon. In fact, I'm relieved to see that you're being careful. You have every reason to be. Here, maybe this will help." Tyler pulled a folded paper out of his hat and handed it to Simon. Quietly he said, "I understand you can read this coded message."

"At least he keeps it in a safe place," Simon muttered as he opened the paper. Emma gave him a dirty look, but Simon only grinned. She and Charles peeked at the note over his shoulder, but Emma, not hearing her brother's words, was too distracted to even notice that Simon's message was coded.

"Another change of plans, Charles. Looks like you and I will be headed back east sooner than we thought. We—"

"Not you and Charles," Tyler interrupted. Simon waited, searching the other man's face for a reason. "You and Emma."

"Me?" Emma's heart made a quick turn.

"What about Charles?" Simon continued to study Tyler's expression.

"Well, the boss figures that since they're on to you"—he pointed at Simon—"that the three of you shouldn't travel together anymore. They'll be looking for two men and a woman. He figures the two of you…I understand you're *married*." He gave Emma a look she couldn't interpret. "The two of you could travel together without drawing too much attention to yourselves." Emma's blush didn't escape Tyler's notice.

"What about Charles?" Simon repeated.

"Charles is going to stay with us in Grandville," Tyler said simply. "It might be kind of boring for you, Charles; not too much happens there, but until this thing is over and Emma and Simon are out from under suspicion, you might as well stay somewhere out of the way. We've got a lot of room, but it does get noisy now and then, especially with the baby."

"Jade had the baby?" Emma asked eagerly.

"Yep! A girl." Tyler's pride was evident.

"What's her name? How's Jade?"

"We named her Pamela, and Jade's fine, a little tired is all. Lucy is staying with her while I'm gone."

"I'm so happy for you, Ty! I bet Eddie is thrilled."

"Well, he'd rather get a new horse, he says, but, yeah, he loves her." Tyler stopped and looked at the two men, who were still standing there watching them. He was aware of the unspoken exchange between them by the nod and shrug he witnessed. "So, what do you think, Simon? Can you trust us to take care of Charles for you?"

Emma laughed. "Actually, Charles takes care of Simon, Tyler. He's his butler. Can you believe it? Would you mind, Charles? If it would help keep Simon safe, I mean. Would you do it for him? Boy, I'm hungry!"

Emma missed the looks that passed between the three men as she knelt over the fire to turn the meat once again. Charles nodded to the two men, indicating his approval of the plan, then moved to help her dish up while the other two walked a little way away.

"She doesn't know?" Tyler asked Simon quietly. "She thinks *you* are the one?"

Simon nodded. "I've given that impression to more than just her. I'm the one who got kidnapped, but that's okay. Charles is the one who matters here."

"I think that's partly the reason the boss wants to send you traveling, as a decoy. We'll take good care of Charles, Simon. Buck, Mike, and I are all on the case now. We should be able to handle it. You and Em are the ones I'm worried about. Don't you think you should tell her that you're an agent too?"

Simon studied the ground a moment, and Tyler saw his indecision.

"When you want, Simon. You know what's best on that end, but there's something I think you should know." He waited until Simon looked up at him. "Emma's my sister, and I love her. You do anything to mar her reputation, and you'll have me to deal with; you understand me?" Tyler's voice was low, but there was no mistaking the threat in it.

Simon nodded.

"I'd just as soon take Emma out of the picture now along with Charles, but both my dad and the boss think she should stay on." Tyler shook his head. "I don't understand my dad. He wanted Emma out of this right away when he first sent her to Norris. Now he seems to think it's okay that she's with you. You know anything about it?"

Simon hesitated; then he answered Tyler slowly. "I think your father knows my intentions are honorable."

They went back to the fire, and Tyler's thoughts ran riot while he watched the others eat. When he had heard about Emma staying with this man as his wife, he had been furious. But when his father explained to him who Simon Chase was and his special regard for him, Tyler had reluctantly altered his opinion. Simon's actions went further to convince Tyler of his character. At the same time, he realized that the man was in love with his sister.

They devoured their meal while Simon and Emma, with Charles's help, explained to Tyler about their adventures the night before. Tyler told them that he had been sent to bring them the new instructions. When he found the cabin deserted, he had started hunting, guessing that they were headed to Grandville. "The Lord put me on the right road or I never would have found you," he said.

"You'll be hunted," he went on, looking directly at Simon and Emma. "Whoever it is that wants to stop you will have men out looking for you." He grinned suddenly. "Jade and Lucy came up with an idea to throw them off the track, but they said Em would never go for it."

Emma looked suspiciously at her brother. "What are you up to now, Ty?"

"Well, think about it, Em. Maybe they'll figure out that the three of you split up, so they'll be looking for two men or a man and a woman traveling together or even a man alone. They already have a description of both of you, so we figured Simon could grow a beard and change to eastern style clothes, but we didn't know how to change you until the girls came up with an idea."

Tyler fought to keep the smile off his face. "Jade and Lucy think you should pretend to be in the family way."

Emma's mouth dropped open, and Simon stared blankly at the man in front of him. Charles started poking at the fire with a stick while he suddenly had to clear his throat.

Red in the face, Emma stood. "I'm not going to pretend I'm having a baby! Honestly, Ty! What a thing to say!" She walked away with her arms crossed in front of her.

"Wait! It might work, Em!" Tyler insisted. He grinned openly now. "They said you'd be embarrassed, but they sent some of their clothes—you know, the big ones—in case you got up enough nerve to try it. You can just pad in the area that needs it." He motioned with his hands to show a large abdomen.

"Tyler!" Emma was horrified, and she glared at Charles for having a coughing fit just then.

Simon remained quiet, but his hand went to his chin and he rubbed it thoughtfully. "Well, I've already got a start on a beard. How about it, Emma? Would you do it for me?"

Emma stared in shock at Simon until she realized he meant it. She gave her head a negative shake, but he approached her and took her hand in his. He waited until she met his eyes.

"I'm sorry to embarrass you, Emma, but it is important that you and I and Charles disappear. If we can't be found, we can't be stopped. I'm sure your resourceful brother has a disguise worked out for Charles too; am I right?" he asked Tyler.

"He's going to be Jade's Uncle Vern from Chicago, come to visit. Okay with you, Charles?"

Charles nodded, and the men waited for Emma's decision.

"Emma, if I had my way, I'd leave you in a safe place, but it seems you have to come with me and you have to look different. Unless you have a better idea? What do you say?" Simon coaxed, and Tyler watched with interest.

"Leave it to Jade," Emma muttered. "She's the one who ran around disguised like a boy."

Simon's eyebrows rose.

"Well, she suggested that too," admitted Tyler. "But I didn't bring clothes for that."

"I'd rather be the boy," Emma mumbled.

"I'd rather you wouldn't." Simon grinned. "I think I can be a convincing loving husband and proud future father."

Tyler slapped his knee. "That settles it, then. Here are your things, Emmie. Better get ready. Charles, I mean—Uncle Vern and I have to get back to Grandville. Simon, I brought an extra horse. I think you—"

Their voices faded as Emma disappeared into the cover of the trees. What an awful thing to ask her to do! She felt she could never look Simon in the eyes again.

She undid the bundle with reluctance. There were four dresses that she recognized as Jade's. All of them had loose waists. Emma knelt down on the ground before them and wondered how she was ever going to get up the courage to go through with this. Her longing for an adventure was coming true in the oddest of ways. Then she spotted a note tucked between two of the garments. It was from Jade.

Emma, I know you're wishing I hadn't thought up this stupid idea, and I don't blame you. When I was dressed like a boy and tried to fool Tyler, I felt pretty stupid too, but I did it because I wanted to help someone. Em, your dad was here and explained that this man's life is in danger and that yours could be too. Please put away your pride and do whatever you have to to keep safe. We'll be praying for you. Love, Jade.

Emma warily eyed the bundle Jade had made for the padding. She figured out how to fasten it on and then she slipped one of the dresses over it. She looked down at her protruding abdomen then looked up at the fading light of day.

I know I said I'd follow your leading, but are you sure about this?

Chapter 18

Near Freesburg

Simon and Emma rode in silence. Simon kept silent mostly because every attempt he made at conversation soon died from the lack of response of his companion. Emma's silence was due to her chagrin at the plump figure she now possessed. Goodness! She not only was pretending to be this man's wife; she was now pretending to have his child! It was taking all her energy to keep from succumbing to her embarrassment. There was no possible chance that she could engage in idle chitchat as well.

It was their second night since leaving Tyler and Charles. Emma and Simon had traveled mostly at night and rested during the day. The fewer people that saw them the better, but Tyler recommended that Emma begin her new act immediately; anything to throw their pursuers off the track.

"We'll be in Freesburg tomorrow, and we can catch the train from there. I hope my beard will be full enough by then," Simon remarked.

No answer.

"Do you think the suit Tyler brought me and the Derby hat will help?"

Emma glanced sideways at Simon. She knew he was trying to help her overcome her embarrassment, but she couldn't. Not yet.

"I've heard that women in your condition could be difficult to get along with," he remarked.

Emma felt a giggle bubble up inside her. She glanced at Simon again, and his grin was her undoing.

"Simon! Don't make me laugh; this is not funny!"

But once the laughter began there was no stopping it. Simon reined in the horses and lay back on the wagon seat. Emma's giggles turned to hiccups, and Simon reached over and patted the padding.

"Careful. That might not be good for the baby," he cautioned.

Emma slapped his hand and groaned. "Oh, Simon, stop! It's hard enough to breathe with this thing on. Quit making me laugh too."

"Emma," he asked, while she wiped tears from her eyes, "are you still mad?"

Emma took a moment to answer. "I was never really mad; I was just so embarrassed. And honestly! Tyler was no help!"

They nearly burst out laughing again as they remembered how when Emma rejoined them back at their camp,

Tyler had begun to show her how to walk and how to stand. He made little moans and groans as he imitated Jade's behavior while expecting their baby. Emma had walked away in a huff without telling her brother good-bye.

"We'll get through this together, Em." Simon tried out the shortened version of her name. "One way or another."

"You're right. I guess I'll do just about anything to help you. Keeping you safe is the important thing."

Simon looked uncomfortable for a moment. "Look, Emma—"

"There's a good place to camp." Interrupting him, Emma pointed ahead. Now that she had gotten over her shyness, she seemed relieved to talk. "I think we better start calling each other by other names too. 'Simon' and 'Emma' are going to give us away, disguise or not; don't you think so? What should I call you?"

Simon studied the sky. "My grandfather's name is Joshua. How about calling me Josh?"

Emma tried it. "Josh." She looked at him quizzically. "Josh what?"

"Um…Josh…Smith?" he suggested. He laughed at her frown.

"Smith?" She wrinkled her nose in disgust. "How about Josh…Josh…Bailey?"

"Bailey, okay. Josh Bailey. And you, Mrs. Bailey, what would you like to be called?"

Emma stared off into space, and Simon watched with interest as her forehead wrinkled in concentration. Finally she said, "I can't think of anything. What's your grand-mother's name?"

There was a mischievous glint in Simon's eye. "Gertrude."

Emma bit her lower lip and refrained from eye contact with Simon. "That's a nice name, but I think 'Sally' will do."

"You don't like Gertrude? Gertrude Bailey sounds okay to me."

"Sally Bailey is fine, Simon, I mean, Josh. You can call me Sally from now on."

Simon moved the wagon forward to the spot where they would camp. "If you say so, Em, but Grandmother Gertrude will be awfully disappointed."

Only then did Emma realize Simon was still teasing her. "Well, Si—Josh, we can always use it if the baby's a girl."

They planned their arrival in Freesburg to coincide with the train's departure. Simon sold the wagon and horses at the livery, an occurrence that happened frequently with travelers since Freesburg was one of the few towns with a train station. One-way travelers had little choice.

Although Emma had gotten over her embarrassment with Simon, she felt foolish as other people smiled at her and men tipped their hats. She was sure someone would notice that she was a phony sooner or later, and she grew icy cold at the thought. Since Freesburg neighbored her town of Sand Creek, she kept her hood pulled up over her blonde hair and far enough forward to hide her features. She only hoped that there would be no one she knew on the train.

Emma had never ridden on a train before. As she took her seat by the window, she realized that since she had wished for something more exciting to do with her life, that it had come true. Here she was traveling east. She thought over the amazing events of the last month and all the unexpected turns her life had taken.

Without a doubt the most amazing was that she was in love. Emma stole a glance at Simon. Yes, she loved him, even though he didn't return that love. She watched as he casually studied the passengers in the car with them. His neatly trimmed beard altered his appearance somewhat, but it was his attire that completely changed him from the Simon she had met in Norris to a gentleman from the East. He seemed perfectly at home in his Derby hat and eastern suit, and Emma wondered how that could be when he seemed so right in his western clothing. She wondered who the real Simon Chase was.

Simon moved from the seat across from her to Emma's side as another couple entered their compartment looking for a place to sit. He took her hand and spoke softly to her.

"How are you doing, little mother?"

Emma appreciated the comfort that his hand gave her. She answered with a sheepish smile. "A little scared, I think. Can you believe that I've never ridden on one of these?"

Simon was amazed.

"I never had anywhere to go before," she explained.

"We can change that," Simon assured her, and he proceeded to describe to her places he had been and places he would like to take her. Emma listened in fascination and felt excitement build in her at his words, but at the same time she had to remind herself that Simon was only acting out his part.

The couple across from them finally got settled in and proceeded to introduce themselves. Emma liked the middle-aged couple, especially Thelma, the wife. She was a talkative, friendly woman who came well prepared for travel with a lunch basket, books, and knitting things to keep occupied. Her husband, Carl, was quiet and immediately settled down for a nap.

Simon introduced themselves as Josh and Sally Bailey, and Thelma began discussing her children with Emma. She and Carl were on their way to visit their oldest son, who was married. The miles clicked by as Emma's attention was divided between the vivacious woman and the fascinating scenery flying by her window. Simon took his cue from Carl and napped for several hours.

As night approached, the porter came around to make up the berths. Simon squeezed Emma's hand when the porter spoke to her with a sympathetic smile. "Hope the little mother won't have too bad of a night. These beds can be rough on a body. Now, if you need anything, missus, you just call."

The pressure of Simon's fingers helped Emma to politely thank the kind man before she hid her blazing cheeks.

"Oh, it's not so bad, Sally," Thelma patted her arm. "Why, I traveled with a wagon train with my first one! Now those were rough times!" Thelma proceeded to relate the misfortunes of travel to Emma, who was silently thankful for the diversion.

Simon's hand, while offering comfort, was also upsetting her emotional balance. She had been keeping a tight rein on her feelings, but there was no denying the yearning she felt to openly show her love to him.

When Simon didn't release her hand, Emma stole a glance at him. She blinked and looked away; then again her eyes searched his hesitantly. Thelma spoke, and Emma forced her attention back on the older woman while she struggled to understand the look she had seen in Simon's eyes.

"I'm ready to turn in for the night, though why I bother I don't know. I won't get any sleep anyway on this swaying, noisy contraption. Come on, Carl; wake up so you can go to sleep again. Good night, Sally, Josh. See you in the morning."

Emma and Simon sat in silence after the couple left. Emma kept her head turned to the dark window of the train, but she wasn't watching the shadowy images outside beyond the glass. Her thoughts were in turmoil. Did Simon mean what his eyes were telling her? Was she seeing only what she wanted to see? Or was this just another part of the act?

Her hand was still nestled in Simon's, and she felt him rub his thumb over her knuckles. Her fingers tightened on his instinctively, and her staring eyes suddenly focused on her reflection in the window. No, not hers; it was Simon's eyes that stared back into hers.

The mirrored reflections remained motionless but for the bouncing of the train until Emma saw and felt Simon lean toward her. With his eyes still on her reflected ones, he whispered, "Emma, I—"

Suddenly his eyes shifted to a reflection behind them, and he stopped. Emma forced herself to breathe again. Her heart raced. What was he about to say? She followed the direction of Simon's gaze and now saw that a man had settled in the seat across the aisle from them and was watching them with furtive glances.

Simon pulled on Emma's hand. "Ready to turn in, Sally?"

Surprised, she struggled awkwardly to her feet. The weight of her padding made her back ache, and she rubbed the pain with her free hand, for Simon still held her other. The man watched her with interest and when he caught her eye, he tipped his hat politely then turned to the window beside him. Simon helped her walk down the swaying aisle to their curtained berth.

"He's checking out the people on the train, I'm guessing," Simon said quietly after he had closed the curtain around them. "I think we're off his suspicious list. That act of yours with rubbing your back and waddling really fooled him!"

"I wasn't acting!" Emma whispered back. "This thing is heavy and my back really does hurt! And I don't waddle!"

Simon chuckled just as the train lurched and sent him sprawling forward into Emma and her backward into the bunk behind her. Her head smacked against the upper bed.

"Ow!"

Simon was entangled with his arms about her and was trying to get his balance.

"Simon, you're squashing the baby!" she whispered with a giggle.

His arms tightened about her, and he put his mouth near her ear. "I love you, Emma Newly," he whispered.

She pushed him back to look into his face. There was no need for him to act now. No one was around to convince. It was just the two of them. Emma looked into his eyes and again saw the love shining from them that she had glimpsed earlier. Her hands tightened on his shoulders.

"Really?" she asked stupidly.

Simon smiled and nodded and pressed his lips to her temple. "Since the moment you stepped off that stage, I knew. I've wanted to tell you, but with all the pretending there was never the proper time. But I'm telling you now. I love you, Emma."

Emma's eyes closed, and she drank in the words thirstily. Her heart overflowed with her love for him, but suddenly she was shy. She buried her face in his shoulder.

Simon paused in smoothing her hair. He looked down at the blonde head against his chest. "Emma, I'm sorry. I didn't mean to upset you. I won't speak of it again."

Emma heard the change in his voice and realized she had given him the wrong impression. She pulled back and held onto his arms to keep him from moving away from her. Swallowing, she slowly met his eyes. "I love you too."

The words were barely audible, but Simon heard them. He bent his head to her, and their lips met in their first true kiss. Simon's kisses had stirred Emma before, but as she responded to his love openly, the kiss became a sweet promise of a future with this man for the rest of her life. Apparently Simon was thinking the same thing.

"Emma, will you marry me?"

Emma couldn't help the teasing smile that came to her lips. "I already did, Mr. Chase. Don't you remember?"

Simon grinned back and he whispered, "I mean for real, you idiot."

"I thought you said it was a real ceremony," Emma pointed out.

"Well, it was, but—"

"So we're really married."

"We are, but—"

"You said we could get it annulled *if we wanted to*. What did you mean?" Emma stopped her teasing and questioned Simon with serious eyes.

"I was hoping you would come to love me as much as I had come to love you."

"You knew then? You knew you wanted to marry me, so the wedding was real?" Emma paused for only a moment. "I don't want it annulled, Simon."

He watched her closely and knew she was telling the truth. "But don't you want a ceremony with your family and your friends, and don't you want to say 'I do' and mean it?"

Emma thought a moment then shook her head. "I already said 'I do,' and I mean it now. I think maybe I meant it then too, Simon. I just wasn't as sure as you were."

Simon's arms tightened around her again. "So we're really married," he said.

Emma nodded happily.

Simon bent to kiss her again then abruptly stopped. He looked around him. "This is no place to begin married life." He stroked her hair. "We'll be staying at my parents' home in Boston, so I'll have to telegraph ahead and prepare them for the news." He laughed softly. "If I know my mother, she'll have the whole east wing redecorated for our visit. They're going to love you, Emma."

"Parents? Boston? You live in Boston? I mean, you grew up there? Well, of course, I knew you lived somewhere in the East, but—is it safe for you to go there? Won't that be the first place they'll look?"

There was hesitancy in Simon's voice as he whispered back, "Emma, there are still many things about me that you don't know." He paused. "My name, for instance."

"Your name?"

He nodded. "My real name is Simon Chappell. I was advised to use a different name, and I couldn't tell you sooner. I'm sorry."

Perplexed, Emma studied her husband. "So when we got married…Am I Mrs. Chase or Mrs. Chappell?"

Simon smiled. "You're really Mrs. Chappell, although to the people watching us our name was Chase. Don't worry, the marriage papers are correct. I saw to that."

Simon saw that he had astounded Emma with this news and felt that he had told her enough for now. "You have to trust me to know what I'm doing. We'll be perfectly safe at my parents' home. I promise you." He kissed her forehead. "For now, I want you to get some sleep, Mrs. Chappell. I'll be out in one of the seats for the night. All you have to do is call if you need me."

There was still a worried pucker on Emma's forehead as Simon left her to prepare for the night. The last moments passed through her mind and she sighed. No longer did she need to hide her love; Simon loved her too! No longer did she need to pretend about their marriage. She looked down at the simple band on her finger that Simon had placed there on their wedding day. They were married and were going to stay married. Her hands dropped to the padding around her middle. There was that, of course. She frowned. She and "Josh" still had a ways to go before they were done pretending.

As she drifted off to sleep, one more thought came to her. *I wonder what Simon meant about his mother redecorating the east wing?*

Chapter 19

Boston

Their train finally pulled into Boston. Emma groaned audibly as she stood and stretched her aching back. Thelma and Carl had left the train the day before, so there was no one she and Simon had to bid good-bye to now. They were finally here!

Emma was more nervous about meeting Simon's parents than she was when she faced Simon's kidnappers. Simon sensed her fears, and he squeezed her hand before handing her a nearly empty carpet bag. Their plan was simple. She would hold the bag in front of her to shield her protruding figure from as many people as possible.

Simon hailed a carriage and after the driver had loaded their other bags, he reached for Emma's carpetbag. She shook her head and clung to the bag tightly, causing the man to look at her askance. Once inside, Simon chuckled as he put his arm around his bride.

"I think you scared him, Emma. He was only trying to do his job."

"Well this was your idea," she sputtered. "Now turn around!"

"But, Emma dear, we're married!" Simon teasingly protested.

"Turn around!" she commanded, and her tone brooked no argument.

Simon smilingly did as she requested.

Quickly Emma worked on unfastening her baby bundle. She struggled and twisted and turned until Simon's shaking shoulders indicated that he was laughing at her. "Simon Chappell, so help me when I get this thing off, I'm going to whack you with it!" Emma fumed.

As Simon burst out in laughter, Emma finally got her situation under control. She shoved the bundle into the carpetbag and sat back, exhausted. Simon turned back and grinned at her.

"I'm sorry, Emma," he started to say then he looked at her sharply. "Say, have you lost weight? That dress is pretty baggy."

Emma kicked him with the side of her foot and glared at him until he pulled her into his arms to hide his laughter. She couldn't help but finally join him.

"Oh, Simon, I'm so nervous about meeting your family!" She tried smoothing the dress and her hair. "I look so awful after that long ride; what will they think of me?"

"They'll love you, and believe me; you will make a much better impression in that baggy dress than you would have before you removed Baby Gertrude. We haven't been married *that* long! My mother will want to know every detail about our wedding, but you already know that we can't say anything about our situation. The less they know about my business, the better off they are."

Simon looked out the window to take stock of their whereabouts. "My family isn't saved. I'm the only one who has accepted the Lord, and though I've witnessed to my folks, they just don't see what I'm saying. They feel that they are good people and do good things, so that should be enough. They don't think they need Christ in their lives. I'm hoping you and I together can show them the way of salvation. Will you pray with me before we get there?"

Their prayer together was short, simple, and direct. Simon also remembered to pray for Charles. Before Charles and Tyler had left them, Simon had informed Tyler of his recent discussion with Charles concerning salvation. Simon wanted Tyler and Jade to be ready to help Charles should he have more questions.

The carriage pulled up before a brick house. As Emma stepped down and looked at it, she realized it was the largest house she had ever seen. Her head tilted back to see the roof, and she looked from side to side to see the width. So that's what Simon meant about an east wing!

She turned to Simon to express her awe and found him hiding a smile as he looked at her feet. She looked down and saw that her dress was dragging on the ground. Jade was a bit taller than Emma in the first place, but without her added girth, the dress was now even longer on Emma. Emma noticed their driver had paused to stare at her as well. She lifted her chin and gathered her dress front as calmly as possible and said, "I'm ready, Simon. Shall we go?" She took the arm he held out to her and ascended the steps to the door, only tripping over the skirt once.

Simon lifted the knocker, and while they waited, he bent his head and whispered in Emma's ear until her cheeks turned pink. She knew he was trying to help her take her mind off her nervousness.

A butler opened the door, and Emma watched Simon greet him like an old friend with a handshake and a clasp to his arm. The action made her think of Charles, and she wondered what the family would think of Simon appearing without his man.

"How are you, Samuel? Are my folks in the front parlor? No, don't bother; we'll show ourselves in." After handing the butler the carpetbag, Simon led Emma forward.

Emma clutched at the handful of skirt she held in front of her as Simon tugged her other arm to keep her in pace with him. She saw the anticipation shine in his eyes. Emma barely had time to take in the marble floors, mirrors, paintings, and flower arrangements before they reached a door that the butler hastened to open for them. Then suddenly they were facing the curious eyes of Simon's family.

Simon dropped her arm and held his arms wide for the young girl who ran to him. Emma stepped aside and watched in shy fascination as the other occupants of the room gathered around to greet Simon. After the young girl's exuberance, the rest seemed subdued, yet Emma could see the sincere joy in their greetings. It was the young girl who first noticed Emma.

"Simon, who's this girl with you? Did you bring home another beggar for us to put into service? Honestly, Simon, we can't employ all the poor people in Boston!"

Emma's nervousness slipped away momentarily and was replaced with astonishment. She took a step backward and nearly tripped over her long skirt.

"Vicky! Where are your manners?" Simon pulled Emma forward and proudly placed both hands on her shoulders as they faced his family. "This is my wife, Emma. Didn't you receive my telegram?"

"Your wife? Gracious, Simon, you can't—!"

"That will do, Victoria!" Simon's mother moved to stand before Emma. Her appraisal of her son's choice of a wife took only a few seconds; then she spoke again. "Naturally we assumed the telegram to be a mistake. It would be inconceivable that you would marry before you had our approval." She turned back to her son. "That beard is ghastly, Simon!"

"Nonsense, Katherine! He's not a boy anymore. He's old enough to know what he wants. Simon, congratulations! And, Emma, welcome to our family." Simon's father took her hand gently in his, and his eyes begged hers for forgiveness for his wife's rudeness.

Emma saw the resemblance of Simon in his father. Her chin lifted slightly. "Thank you, sir."

Gordon Chappell caught her eye and nodded his approval. "Let me introduce you to the rest of your new family. This is Simon's older brother, Anson. Anson, meet your new sister-in-law Emma, and don't bore her with shipping talk. Anson has gone into the shipping end of our business, Emma, and that's all we hear from him these days."

Emma smiled faintly at her father-in-law's effort to lighten the mood, but her pride was still pricked at Mrs. Chappell's remark, not to mention Victoria's outburst. She held out her free hand to Anson while she continued to clutch at her long skirt with the other. "I'm pleased to meet you."

Anson smiled absently at Emma then slapped his brother on the shoulder. "When you have some time, Simon, I'd like to discuss some ideas I have with you about—"

Simon bent his head to hear his brother's words.

"Oh, don't mind him, Emma. He's always business. I'm Darlene, Simon's sister." A pretty, brown-haired woman about Emma's age stepped between Emma and Gordon. "I'm very pleased to meet you and I know how tired you must be after your journey. We'll get you to your rooms as soon as possible. The east wing, Mother?"

Emma looked from the pleasant girl back to Mrs. Chappell's stern expression. The girl Victoria stood beside her mother, mimicking her look exactly.

"The east wing? Don't be silly, Darlene. We're expecting the Corneliuses next week. Samuel, take Simon's things to the third floor, please. If you'll excuse me now, I think I will rest until dinner."

Darlene waited until her mother and Victoria left the room before she reached for Emma's arm. She glanced briefly at her father and saw him shake his head sadly. "I'm sorry, Emma. Please don't mind her. Mother thinks everything must be done properly or we'll end up as social outcasts. The news that Simon suddenly got married has thrown her into a tizzy. I'll take you up to your rooms."

"I'm coming now too, Dar. The third floor, huh?" Simon's questioning look was answered with an expressive shrug by his sister.

Simon winked at Emma. "We'll be all alone way up there, Emma. Do you think we'll get lonesome?"

Emma took her cue from Simon. "Sounds like heaven to me!" she said, but an uneasy feeling crept over her at the strange reception she had just received. She slipped her free hand into his arm again while she pulled up the front of her dress to ascend the stairs. Suddenly the material was yanked from her hand.

"Why are you wearing a dress that's too big for you?"

"Vicky! Leave Emma alone! What do you think you're doing?" Darlene was outraged at her sister's behavior.

"Look at her, Dar! Her dress fits like a sack and looks like one too."

Simon took hold of his younger sister's arm and swung her around to face him. His eyes were angry and his voice tight as he spoke. "You will never insult my wife again, Victoria. Emma is the woman I love, and she is now a part of this family. I expect her to be treated with respect; do you understand me?"

"Crikers, Simon! I was only—"

Simon's grip tightened. "Victoria!"

"All right!"

Relentlessly Simon stared at his sister. Her eyes darted from Emma back to her angry brother before she looked down at the floor.

"Really, Simon? You're really married?"

Simon's nod seemed to remove all animosity from the young girl.

"Okay, then." She faced Emma. "I'm sorry I was rude to you, Emma. If Simon loves you, you must be all right no matter what you're wearing. Please forgive me." And with that, Vicky flung her arms around the startled woman.

Emma received the embrace somewhat hesitantly after being embarrassed so badly by the girl, but her school teacher instinct to scold was miraculously replaced with amusement and even affection as she looked down into Vicky's eyes, which were so much like Simon's.

"Thank you, Vicky, and you're right, you know. This dress is awfully big on me, but I have others. I promise you next time you see me I'll look better, okay?"

Vicky grinned. "Okay, Emma. I have to go now to dress for dinner. Can I sit by you and Simon?"

"*May* I."

Vicky shot Emma a surprised look. "Right. *May* I sit by you and Simon?"

"Yes. I think that would be very nice."

Simon scowled after his little sister as she ran off. "I don't understand why she acted like that, Em. I'm really sorry."

Darlene had remained quiet during the encounter, but now she spoke up. "She's gotten to be quite snob-bish, Simon. Mother has taken up with a family who has a daughter Vicky's age, and they have done nothing but try to outdo each other in snobbery. I'm so glad you're here, and you too, Emma. Maybe Vicky will return to sensibility with you around."

They reached the third floor, and Darlene showed them their rooms. She led them through an attractive sitting room and pointed out the bath closet and changing rooms before moving on to the bedroom. A huge, somewhat masculine four-poster bed dominated the main room of their quarters, and Emma avoided looking at it or Simon while Darlene moved about, pointing out details about some of the furnishings.

"You've got a little over an hour until dinner, so go ahead and nap or order a bath, Emma. We dress up for the evening—oh, Simon knows all that!" Darlene shyly looked at Emma. "I'm really glad you're a part of our family, Emma. I hope we become friends."

The door closed behind her, and Simon and Emma were left alone. They stood silent, awkwardly aware of their surroundings. Finally Simon spoke.

"They're really nice once you get to know them, Em, even Mother." He hesitated. "She sometimes overdoes things, especially if she's trying to impress someone socially, but usually she's very sensible and pleasant." He glanced at the silent woman, and Emma knew her embarrassment was still evident on her face. "I'll order you a bath and then you can rest for a while." He stepped toward her and placed his arm around her.

Emma turned into his embrace. A smile appeared on her face.

"It's all right, Simon. Really. I suppose I do look pretty bad in this outfit, and it must have been quite a shock to all of them to learn that you had married me before they even got to meet me." She stepped back. "I like them. I'm sure things will work out." She looked past Simon to their surroundings. She was a bit overwhelmed by the elegance around her, but a shy smile now played on her lips. "Well, we're finally alone."

Simon grinned and pulled her back in his arms. He bent his head to hers then pulled back again. Emma's eyes had begun to close in expectation of his kiss, but they flew open when she felt Simon pull away.

"What's wrong?"

Simon continued to slowly back away from her. "I better order the bath for you now," he said in an odd voice. "Dinner will be here before we know it. Uh…" He cleared his throat. "Uh—I have a few things to do. I'll meet you downstairs later." And he turned and left.

Emma stared at the closed door for a long moment. Now what had she done? She felt hurt, but at the same time she knew that Simon truly loved her. Or did he? Was his family's reaction to her causing him to see her in a different light? Did he think he had made a mistake after all?

Emma felt the emotions churn within her, but she quelled them. *Lord, only you know what Simon is thinking,* she prayed. *Help me not to disappoint him.* Her prayer continued until a knock on the door gained her attention.

"Come in."

A maid entered. "We've brought the hot water, madam."

Chapter 20

Boston

Emma descended the stairway with anticipation and dread. She longed to be with Simon, yet she was fearful of what she might see in his eyes. She was refreshed from her bath, and it felt good to be in one of her own dresses again. She smoothed the skirt nervously. The maid had pressed the dress for her and offered to do her hair, but Emma had politely refused. She was not used to having servants wait on her.

She had brushed and coiled her hair in a becoming style, and she fervently hoped that her best dress would be suitable for the evening. If not, there was nothing she could do about it anyway. She felt herself shiver a little as she reached the first-floor landing.

"Emma, you look much more rested. I must say, Simon picked a beauty to be his wife."

Emma smiled genuinely at her father-in-law. "Thank you, sir."

"Sir? No, that won't do. Why don't you try calling me Gordon? Maybe in time you'll even be comfortable with 'Father'." He took her arm and grinned happily at her. "Now we have to get Anson to find a woman as charming as you!"

Emma felt herself relax. Gordon Chappell was a likable man, and as he escorted her down the remaining stairs she found herself comparing him to her own father. She smiled to herself. What wonderful grandfathers they would both be! Then the thought of having children with Simon caused her step to falter, and she looked down right into Simon's eyes where he waited for her at the bottom of the staircase.

Nothing but love shone from his eyes as he took her from his father. "You look radiant. I love you," he whispered into her ear.

Suddenly everything was wonderful again! Her doubts vanished and were replaced by a loving confidence in her husband and in their marriage. It didn't matter to Simon who she was or what she wore. He loved her.

What she wore. Emma looked again at Simon and realized that his face was freshly shaved. How handsome he was! Then she noticed his suit, and she turned back to Gordon and saw that he too was elegantly dressed. "You're all dressed up," she murmured.

Simon squeezed her hand. "Mother likes us to be refined at dinnertime. Don't worry, Em, you look fine."

Fine! Emma groaned inwardly. Men had no idea of what was suitable, and even though she was not accustomed to the city way of life, she knew she was out of place again. Even her best was not going to be good enough for their family dinners. What would she do if they really did something formal? For now, she'd just have to make the best of it.

Unconsciously she lifted her head slightly and prepared to meet the rest of the family. Out of the corner of her eye, she saw Gordon's nod of approval.

They entered the dining room with Emma holding on to the arms of both men. She quickly took note of the elegant gowns on Mrs. Chappell and Darlene then smiled an answer to Anson's greeting. She saw Mrs. Chappell raise her eyebrows as she examined Emma from head to foot, but she ignored the look and spoke pleasantly to Darlene.

It was Victoria, again, who was almost her undoing.

"Emma, I thought you said you had better dresses. Even my play clothes are nicer than that one!"

"Vicky!"

"Victoria, your manners!"

"It's fine." Emma interceded as Vicky's puzzled expression proclaimed that she did not know what she had done *this* time. "Victoria is right. I haven't many things with me, and I need to do some shopping. Vicky, would you and Darlene"—Emma looked around at her mother-in-law to include her—"and your mother like to help me pick out some new clothes? I could really use some good advice."

"Oh goody, Emma! Dar and I love to pick out new dresses. We can help Emma, can't we, Mother?"

Katherine Chappell inclined her head slightly. "Under the circumstances, I think it would be an appropriate thing to do. We'll get started first thing tomorrow. Gordon, you'll set up an account for Emma, please."

Anson's eyebrows twitched. "Right, Simon! The expensive part of marriage comes up. Now maybe you'll see why I have no interest in it. I have no desire to see all my inheritance frittered away on women's frills."

"Anson, you're as rude as your little sister. Those comments were uncalled for." Gordon chastised his oldest child as he glanced at Emma's whitened face.

Simon, too, realized how uncomfortable Emma had become. "Well, big brother, it is easy to see that you've never fallen in love. If I could, I'd buy Emma anything in the world to please her. I intend to spend my life trying to please her."

Emma heard a sigh from Darlene, and she thanked Simon with her eyes, but then she surprised all of them with her next words.

"I know I didn't come prepared with the right clothes, but I did come prepared to purchase them myself. It is not my intention to be a burden on Simon or his family."

There were small gasps and exclamations from the female members of the Chappell family. Anson looked at Emma with interest as if calculating her worth, and Gordon tried to hide a smile behind his hand. Simon frowned. The *look* was once again on Emma's face, and it was obvious her pride was deeply hurt

"Well, is dinner ready? I'm starved!" Simon tried changing the subject.

Emma knew Simon didn't believe she understood how expensive things were, but she suddenly had a desire to let him and his family know that she wasn't just a poor country girl.

"Simon, I'm serious." She looked directly at him. "I have my inheritance from my mother's uncle, brother to the baron from England."

"England?" Katherine turned her full attention on Emma.

Simon's eyebrows drew together. "What's this, Emma?"

At once Emma felt embarrassed at trying to impress Simon's family, but they really had stung her pride. "My mother was raised in England, stepdaughter to a baron. He never fully accepted her as a daughter, but his brother cared for her and when he died, he left everything he had to my mother. My parents put together an inheritance for each of us children from that. I can assure you that I will not be a financial burden to any of you." She smiled slightly even as her face betrayed her embarrassment. She desperately needed to feel that she could hold her own in this affluent family.

Gordon's smile was genuine, albeit sympathetic. Anson was clearly interested, while Darlene and Victoria were amazed; finances were always left to the men. Katherine's revealing comment, "You mean you are related to a titled Englishman?" indicated to Emma how foolish she was being in trying to win their approval and acceptance.

"It is only through marriage, Mrs. Chappell," she said demurely.

Simon shook his head slightly and smiled at his bride. "You are full of surprises, Emma. I have a suggestion for you. How about if we put your inheritance away for our children as your parents did?" His eyes glinted as he looked into hers. "And you let me take care of my wife as a husband should."

Emma understood Simon completely. He wanted and needed to be her provider. She decided then to give herself fully into his care. "Whatever you say, Simon."

The dinner would have been much more awkward had it not been for Vicky. The young girl quickly forgot the previous tension and chattered on about many things. Without meaning to, she gave everyone an opportunity to know Emma better, for she plied her with questions throughout the meal. Soon everyone was aware of Emma's school teaching job, her close family, including nieces and nephews, and her love of her home.

Simon remained silent, willing to let his little sister continue to pry. The sooner his family knew more about Emma, the sooner they would love her like he did. Finally the questions he had been waiting for arrived.

"Where did you and Simon get married, Emma? Was it a big wedding?"

Before Emma could answer, Simon took over. "We had a small wedding, half-pint, in a little town called Norris. Emma's family couldn't make it either, just like you, but they sent us their best wishes. Later, we'll go back and visit them and together we can celebrate our marriage."

"A celebration? You mean a party? Mother! We should have a party for Simon and Emma too!"

Mrs. Chappell appeared startled, and Darlene joined in with Vicky.

"Of course, Mother, a wedding reception! We can introduce Emma to all of our friends, and it would be the perfect excuse to entertain. You've been wanting to ever since the Logans put on that charming anniversary party for their parents."

"Charming?" Katherine said scornfully. "I could teach Elvira Logan a thing or two about giving a party." She remained thoughtful for a moment, and Simon saw Emma, whose pride was still in shatters at her mother-in-law's treatment of her, about to protest, so his fingers on her hand tightened and he sent her a quick wink. She remained silent, and he could see that she was confused.

"Of course the Bradfords put on a wedding reception a few months ago," Katherine continued almost to herself. "But it was disgraceful. The servants were poorly trained and the musicians they hired for entertainment were a bore!"

The group at the table waited patiently while the monarch of the family made up her mind. Even Anson appeared interested in his mother's decision.

"We'll do it! Of course it will take a lot of time to prepare. Everything must be perfect, you understand. Flowers, music, food, entertainment, and new gowns! We'll all need something special, especially you, Emma, my dear."

They all were startled by the "my dear."

"We'll start looking tomorrow when we go shopping. I really must go put some ideas down on paper. Will you excuse me?"

Katherine left the room with her husband at her side while the others waited with smiles on their faces. When she was gone, Darlene turned excitedly to Simon and Emma.

"What a wonderful idea, Simon! Mother will be so involved in this party that she'll forgive you for not letting her plan your wedding. Really, Emma, it's not you that Mother is upset about; it's the fact that everything was done without her help that irritates her. She's always dreamed of putting on grand parties like this." Darlene's eyes sparkled; then she sobered as she saw Emma's pensive face. "She's really a dear, Emma. Don't let her high-handed ways get to you."

"Dar's right, Emma," Anson injected. "Mother will be happy as a clam now that she has this to plan. Let her have her fun and try not to mind when she bosses you around." He grinned sheepishly. "And try not to mind an old bachelor who doesn't know when to keep his mouth shut."

The smile Emma sent to her new brother and sisters at the table was radiant. "I only hope you'll forgive me for my ignorance."

"And now, my loving family, if you will excuse us, Emma and I are going for a drive."

Emma was as surprised at Simon's words as were the others.

"A drive? Simon, you and Emma have been traveling for days. Emma looks exhausted. Why on earth would you go for a drive?"

"He means they want to be alone," Anson informed his nosey sister. "So I'll say my good nights now." He took Emma's hand. "You're a good sport, Emma Chappell. My brother chose well."

They bade good night to Darlene and Vicky; then they entered the carriage that Simon had waiting at the front of the house and started out on their drive.

Emma lost no time in questioning Simon. "I suppose this has something to do with our job? Is there someone we have to contact tonight?"

Simon put his arm around Emma in the dark carriage and pulled her close. "No, Em, this has something to do with us." He put a finger along her cheek and turned her to face him. "Will you marry me, Emma Newly? I mean, will you marry me again?"

Emma pulled away to look carefully at her husband. "What are you talking about, Simon? We are married."

Simon nodded as he cupped Emma's face with his hand. "Yes, we are. But, Emma, I won't feel that we're really and truly married in God's sight until we make our vows and mean every word of them. No pretending. No acting for the benefit of others. Just you and me and the Lord."

Emma turned her head to kiss Simon's hand. "I'd like that too, Simon." She snuggled up to him. "Is that where we're going? To get married again?"

Simon nodded. "While you were preparing for dinner, I contacted an old pastor friend of mine, Pastor Rill. After I explained the details to him, he gladly agreed to perform the ceremony tonight, and I can trust him to keep it confidential."

It was a quiet ceremony—simple, unembellished, bare of frills, yet more beautiful than Emma could ever have imagined. And this time, Simon slipped an exquisite diamond ring on her finger. Although she would never forget their first wedding ceremony with all the secrecy and pretending, as she and Simon said their vows for a second time, she knew the words would remain with her forever.

It was without hesitancy now that Simon escorted her back to his home and up to their room on the third floor. A sigh of contentment escaped her as he swung her into his arms and carried her through the doorway.

Chapter 21

Freesburg

"*Josh*, you say?" And what was the woman's name? *Sally?*"
The man's brow creased, and thoughtfully he reached into
the breast pocket of his coat and pulled out a torn scrap
of paper.

"Josh...*Joshua*...Hmmm. It could be. And '*P sal*' could
be for Sally. Did you get names of anyone else?"

"They were talkin' to an older couple. Wife's name
was..." The man consulted some scribbled notes. "Thelma;
and the man was Carl."

Again the man looked at the scrap of paper in his hands
while a woman leaned over his shoulder to study it also.
They both puzzled over it for a moment then shrugged.

The man rubbed his forehead. "The point is, we lost
them. Those idiots we hired to grab Chase messed up,
and now Chase and that Newly girl have disappeared."
He slammed a fist down on the desk before him. "These

names are the only clues we have to go by." He turned to the woman. "At least you did something right by finding this paper in the coach."

She scowled briefly at his criticism. "What if Chase and Emma Newly are who they really say they are? Your man Brady was convinced, remember? What if Chase isn't even the man?"

"He's the one; I know it!" The man waved the scrap of paper in her face. "And Emma Newly is in on it too, I'll bet my life! Why else would she carry a coded message in her handbag?"

He got up and began pacing the room. "These names have to be people they need to contact." He turned back to the man. "You know where they got off?"

The man reluctantly shook his head.

"Then send someone to find out. Somehow we'll get a lead back to Chase."

"What about the Barnes Gang?" questioned the woman. "They still want their pay, and if they don't get it soon, I'm worried that they'll interfere with our plans somehow."

"I'm done with them. Sophia Barlow was useful to a point, but her brothers are so stupid they couldn't pour water out of a boot if the directions were printed on the heel. A tip to the local sheriff should get them off our backs."

"Are you sure? They might give us away."

The man scowled. "No, they've never seen us, and I doubt Sophia will allow herself to get caught." He turned back to the man. "See to it."

Chapter 22

Boston

Life in the Chappell house was never dull, Emma found. Preparations for the upcoming party consumed Katherine's days, and Emma was commanded to attend dress fittings and help with decisions on a multitude of things from flowers to the color of the invitation paper. Not that her opinion meant that much to her mother-in-law, who made the final decisions anyway, but Katherine was beginning to acknowledge that Emma, though simplistic in her tastes, had a good eye for design, and she included her more and more in the planning.

Emma didn't mind so much. Simon was away most of the day with his father or Anson, working on the shipping business, she was told. It seemed the only time they had alone was at night in their room on the third floor where they would share the highlights of their days with each other.

One night lying in their bed, Emma asked Simon a question that had been on her mind.

"Where do you live when you're in Washington, D.C., Simon? I mean, do you have a house, or should I say do *we* have a house? After this trial is over, will we move there to live?" She yawned deeply and snuggled closer to him.

Simon hesitated. Now would be the time to tell Emma the truth. He didn't know how she was going to take it. He had debated over and over again when and how to explain. Here was his opportunity. He opened his mouth to reply, but Emma spoke again.

"I suppose that's where Charles works for you? I mentioned him the other day to Darlene, but she didn't know who I was talking about."

"You mentioned Charles?"

Emma yawned again. "Mmmhmm. Darlene was giving the...servants some orders...and I mentioned...that...I.... wasn't used to servants...and Charles..."

Simon felt Emma's even breathing and realized she had fallen asleep. She seemed to be so tired lately, he hoped nothing was wrong.

He eased his arm out from under her and watched her face as she slept. *How beautiful she is!* Her brow puckered, and he wondered if she was dreaming.

She mentioned Charles. He pondered that. For her own safety it might be better to continue to allow Emma to believe *he* was the government official, but he would caution her not to discuss his business with his family. She would agree to that without question. He reminded himself that though he knew he could trust her, she was not a trained agent and the less she knew until the case was over the better. A man had already been murdered because of what he knew, and Simon was not about to let anything happen to this woman he loved.

Emma twirled in front of the mirror admiring her new gown. It had taken nearly two months to make all the necessary preparations, but the night of their reception had finally arrived. Anticipation glowed in Emma's sparkling blue eyes. It was not the party she was anticipating. If any word could be used to describe her emotions about that, it would be dread. She dreaded all the people, the introductions, the scrutiny of her behavior. No, it was definitely not the party.

The glow emanating from Emma was due to the news she had to tell Simon. She wasn't positive, not yet, but she was fairly sure that she and Simon were going to be parents. She patted her still flat abdomen in the stunning dress. It would be awhile before she showed, so she and Simon could keep the wonderful news just to themselves for now. There wasn't much that they were able to keep to themselves living in his parents' home like they were.

It bothered Simon too, Emma knew, so she did her best to make light of the situation. At night when they were alone in their rooms on the third floor, Simon would hold her close and they would talk about their own home, the one they would share when all the hiding was over.

A rap on the door made Emma aware that she had been staring in the mirror far too long.

"Yes?"

The maid came in with a friendly smile. "Mrs. Chappell asked me to bring you this, madam. She requests that you wear it this evening, and may I say you look especially beautiful." Admiration shone in the young girl's eyes.

"Thank you, Tracy." Emma was a favorite among all the servants. "I think the dress may have a lot to do with it."

"No, madam, if you don't mind my saying, it's you. You look just radiant."

Emma smiled her thanks while she reached for the box the maid was holding. A pearl necklace lay gleaming and white against the dark velvet lining of the box. Both Emma and the maid gasped with admiration.

"Isn't it wonderful?" Emma exclaimed. Carefully she took it and held it against her neck. "How perfectly it goes with this dress!"

"Allow me." They both turned as Simon, elegantly attired, appeared in the doorway. Tracy curtsied then scurried out. Simon carefully fastened the pearls for Emma.

"I think you have impressed my mother, Em. These are Grandma Gertrude's famous pearls, worn only for the most special occasions."

A smile played on Emma's lips. "Grandma Gertrude?"

Simon grinned. "You know, our baby's namesake."

Emma's hand fluttered over her stomach. "Ah, yes." She smiled secretly.

Simon's arms encircled her from behind as he teased, "Someday our own little Gertrude will wear this necklace."

Emma's nose wrinkled. "Gertrude…Gertie? No? How about…Trudy?"

Simon laughed, and Emma turned in his arms to face him, ready to share her news, but a knock at the door stopped her.

"Mom says to get down here before the guests arrive!" yelled Vicky through the door.

Simon sighed. "That girl!"

Emma's disappointment at being interrupted lasted but a moment. "Come on, Simon. Your mother doesn't want anything to upset her carefully planned evening."

Simon hugged her close. "You've been such a good sport through all this, Emma. I don't know how you put up with all the fussing."

"I mostly just stayed out of the way." Emma laughed. "Really, Simon, your mother and I have gotten along very well." Silently, she added, *as long as there's been a party to plan.* She wondered what life in the Chappell household would be like after tonight.

"C'mon! Are you kissin' in there or what?" Vicky's voice broke through the door again.

"We're coming!" Simon called back. He held his arm out to Emma. "Have I told you how beautiful you are tonight, Mrs. Chappell?"

Emma answered him with a quick kiss just as the door flung open, revealing Vicky in a charming pink satin dress and matching hair ribbons, with her arms crossed and a scowl on her face.

"Will you two stop that and come on before *I* get yelled at?"

Emma's squeeze on Simon's arm stopped him from scolding his little sister. "We're ready now, Vicky. Thank you for coming to get us. Doesn't she look pretty, Simon?"

The disapproving frown melted as Simon looked carefully at Vicky. At a nudge from Emma, he replied, "You look great, half-pint. Is Mom really worked up?"

"Oh, boy! You should see her! If you two don't hurry, she'll probably come up here after you herself."

"Well, we can't have that, can we? Ready, Emma?"

Sand Creek

"I'm worried about her, Russ."

Sky clung to her husband's arm as the wagon's wheel lumbered over a rock embedded in the road. They were traveling home from town with a load of supplies, but since there was no need to rush, Russ Newly pulled the wagon off the road a ways and stopped it under the shade of a group of maple trees.

He wiped his brow with his sleeve; the summer days were heating up and there were no breezes to help cool him down. Riding in the wagon wasn't so bad, but getting up and down on it still caused his injured leg some pain, so he stayed put on the wagon seat and turned to look at Sky. A tiny line furrowed its way between her lovely blue eyes, and he gently touched the spot while he smiled at her.

"I know you trust this Simon Chase implicitly, and I know we've discussed this many times, but Emma is my little girl and she's been gone so long and...and... I'm worried."

Russ nodded while he studied the face of the woman he had loved now for over twenty years. He felt a twinge of guilt for being the cause of her worries. If it hadn't been for his decision, Emma would not be away from them now, yet as an agent for the Pinkertons, he knew he had made the right choice; as a father, however, he had his moments of doubt.

"I know I can't take your worries away by simply telling you that she's safe in Simon's keeping, but I want us both to remember that she's in *God's* care, and he is going to be with her and Simon in whatever circumstance they find themselves. Simon is a good man, Sky. He's in love with our Emma, and when he asked for her hand, I couldn't have been happier. I think the fact that they are together has taken all interest away from Charles, if there ever was any, and that's important for the case."

He paused as Sky laid her head on his shoulder. "And I know the case means nothing to you; it's Emma you're concerned about."

Sky sniffed.

"From the few messages we've been able to get, you know she's doing fine, honey."

A moment of silence, then a muffled, "I know."

He waited, feeling the heat from her head on his shoulder cause his shirt to stick to him. She moved then and gave him a wobbly smile and a nod. Russ started the horses moving forward again and felt the welcome flow of air fan him.

They rode in silence for a short time before Sky spoke again.

"I missed her wedding."

Ah! Russ grinned to himself. *So that was the real trouble.* "Maybe we should plan a party for when they come home," he suggested.

He felt the squeeze on his arm as Sky gripped him in excitement. "Oh yes, Russ! A party for when they're home!"

Boston

To Emma the evening was a blur of names and faces. Katherine Chappell was definitely in her element and had outdone herself to make it the most lavish party Boston had ever seen. The food, the music, the decorations, and the gowns were in perfect harmony. The guests were entertained by accomplished singers and there was no lapse in witty conversation.

Emma was passed from person to person, group to group, exclaimed over, admired, and congratulated all while a beaming mother-in-law hovered nearby and accepted the compliments of the well-wishers. Occasionally Emma caught glimpses of Simon being passed around in much the same way.

It wasn't until they sat down to dinner that the couple was finally back together again. Etiquette would have demanded that they not be seated by each other, but Simon had been adamant with his mother that he would be at his bride's side for the meal. Emma's face ached from smiling and her feet hurt from standing. With relief she took her place beside Simon at the table.

"Do you really know all these people?"

Simon chuckled at her expression. "Actually, no. Most of them are my parents' friends and I know them only slightly. Many I can't even put a name to, like that gentleman over there." He pointed to a black-haired man dressed in the formal attire typical to most of the men present, yet the man seemed ill at ease in his fancy clothes. "He looks familiar to me, but I can't for the life of me think of his name."

Emma gripped Simon's arm. "The man from the train, Simon! He's the man from the train! Remember? When we were Josh and Sally and I was—" She waved her arms in front of her.

Simon's jaw tightened. *How did he find us?* His thoughts raced while he covertly watched the man. The dinner went on, and Simon and Emma continued to converse with their guests, albeit in a slightly detached manner. Possible options occurred to Simon, and he dismissed them one by one until he came to a decision.

Emma was politely answering a question posed her by the man on her left when she felt Simon's urgent nudge. She turned to him at once.

"Emma." Simon's voice was low, but Emma heard the distress in it. "I'm going to have to leave for a time."

"No!"

"Em." Simon's arm went around her. "I don't see another way, and believe me; I've tried to come up with one. I know a place, but"—he hesitated—"I can't take you with me this time."

"No, Simon."

"Please listen, Emma! My family will understand; I've had to disappear before, and my father will know how to provide protection for you. But I've got to go and get this man to follow me—to get him away from here. It's dangerous for you and my family."

"Simon, please, I can help you. You know I can."

"I know, Emma, and I need your help now. You have to stay right here and convincingly entertain these people until this party is over. I don't know who else is watching. I'll contact you as soon as I can. I love you."

Emma nearly cried out as Simon rose and left the room, but she bit her lip and willed herself to calm down. Slowly she turned to her companion, and with a slightly stiff smile she said, "I'm sorry, you were saying?"

The remainder of the evening passed with unbelievable slowness. She quietly explained to Simon's parents that he had to leave on urgent business, which they accepted with a mixture of irritation and reluctance, causing her to wonder how often this happened to him. Then Emma continued to smile and visit and entertain the guests as best she could. Later, she stood at the door and said her good-byes and apologies for Simon to each of the guests as they left. The man she and Simon had seen stayed and mingled with the crowd for quite some time, but Emma noticed that he left without approaching her or the Chappells as the other guests had done.

Much later, alone in her room, Emma let silent tears slip down her cheeks as she prayed, *Lord, protect Simon. He means so much to me.*

Chapter 23

Boston

Six weeks passed, and with each day, each hour, each minute Emma's anxiety grew. Daily she read and reread the few messages she had received from Simon. They told her little about his whereabouts but volumes about his love for her and assurance of his safety. The few coded messages exchanged between herself and her family in Sand Creek helped allay her homesickness, but it was Simon she missed the most.

Simon's family had become very dear to Emma. Not long after the party it became obvious to all that Emma was expecting. Her frequent bouts of morning sickness, her extreme tiredness, and her rapid gain in weight gave her away, but Emma found that she was glad they knew. Attention on the baby took their thoughts away from worry about Simon and made the days pass by a little more quickly.

Surprisingly, it was Katherine who really kept Emma going. Almost every day she insisted that they take the carriage and go shopping for something for her new grandchild. Gordon always provided a man to accompany them if he was unable to do so himself. Apparently he felt responsible for Emma's safety in Simon's absence.

"We must look for some bonnets today," Katherine commented as they entered the carriage. Emma smiled absently while she noticed Frederick was riding on top with the driver. Frederick was one of the more frequent protectors for them.

"Bonnets, Mother? But what if it's a boy?" Darlene asked.

"We can buy some boy bonnets and some girl bonnets just to be sure."

"Boy bonnets!" Vicky giggled. "Baby boys don't wear bonnets, do they, Mother?"

Katherine Chappell allowed herself a faint smile. "He will if he's going to be my grandson," she replied.

The girls repressed a desire to giggle at their mother's words, and even Emma had to hide a smile.

"How are you feeling today, Emma?" Darlene asked. Darlene's concern for Emma was genuine. The two had become close friends.

"I feel fairly well this morning. In fact, I've been better for about a week now."

"The first three months are over, that's why," commented Katherine. "You should feel well through most of the rest of it, although I still can't understand why you have gotten big so quickly. My babies never showed until my sixth month as least." She frowned as she looked appraisingly at her daughter-in-law. "It must be because you are so small yourself."

"Emma's nearly as tall as you, Mother," Vicky spoke up. "I know! Maybe you've got twins!"

Emma shook her head at Vicky's words, but Katherine slowly nodded. "It could be, Emma dear."

Emma patted her enlarged front. "Or maybe just one very big baby." She laughed.

They shopped for a while, or actually the girls watched while Katherine shopped. Occasionally she would ask Emma's opinion on something, but usually she would make the choices herself. Emma didn't mind. She knew her mother-in-law was having a good time. All Emma wanted was for Simon to come back to her so that she could feel alive again. Only then could she really take an interest in anything else.

They finished making their purchases and left the shop. As usual, Frederick was waiting, and he moved to open the door of the carriage for them. Katherine got in first, followed by Vicky, and Emma was about to enter when a lady passing by caught her attention. Emma turned away from the carriage for a closer look.

"Philippa?"

The woman swung around at the name and gasped when she saw Emma.

"Emma Newly?"

The women sat in the parlor at the Chappell home waiting for Tracy to serve them tea. Emma sat on the sofa next to

Philippa Tunelle, who nervously kept looking at the grandeur around her and then back to Emma and her in-laws.

Emma studied the woman beside her closely. Philippa had dark circles under her eyes, she was thin, and though her dress was fashionable enough, it was starting to wear as if it had seen too many washings. Katherine and Darlene politely conversed with their new guest, and even Vicky thankfully refrained from any embarrassing questions. After a short time they excused themselves to leave Emma alone with Philippa.

Philippa had agreed to ride back with them in the carriage for tea. On the way she had explained that she was renting a small house in Boston for a time because she had grown tired of Chicago. Emma wondered where she was getting the money to live anywhere at all. Ralph certainly didn't have that kind of money, and neither did Philippa's parents. Emma had explained her marriage to Simon and introduced her new family. She told Philippa that Simon was away on business at the time, and their conversation had been pretty general while the others were still with them.

Now Emma leaned forward and placed a hand on Philippa's arm. Silently she prayed for the right words to say.

"Philippa, Ralph's looking for you."

Emma was unprepared for the tears that sprang in Philippa's eyes as she clasped Emma's hand with her own.

"He is? Oh, Emma, I was so cruel to him and he didn't deserve it!"

For the next several minutes Emma related to the tearful woman her news of Grandville and Ralph. She left nothing out, not even Ralph's drunken kiss and apology. Philippa stared at her in shock.

"Oh, Emma! I drove him to that! I'm so ashamed; he must hate me!"

"No, Philippa, he loves you. We had a long talk about how he drifted away from the Lord and allowed bitterness to ruin him. He does love you, Philippa, but he loves the Lord more. He wants you back, Philippa. He wants to rebuild your marriage, but don't you see that mostly he wants you to know and love the Lord too."

Philippa sighed. "I've fought it so long, Emma. I told myself I was not going to be like the other people in Grandville or in Sand Creek, for that matter. All of you— you made me sick with your talk about God and your boring lives. I wanted adventure in my life; I wanted to live, to see things, to be reckless and wild and free of dos and don'ts. Have you ever felt like that, Emma?"

Emma smiled. "Believe it or not, yes, I have."

"So you know what I'm saying. But, Emma, don't try what I've tried. I've seen enough wild living to last me a lifetime. You may not believe this, but when I was just a little girl I accepted the Lord Jesus as my Savior one Sunday after church. You'd think that I would have turned out like the rest of you from Sand Creek, but you don't know what it was like to grow up in my home, Emma. My mother hates your family and so many others in town. Even though at first I wanted to learn more about God, I was kept away from it by my own mother and I grew up not caring what God thought of me or my actions. Oh, Emma, how wrong I was!"

Tears continued to slip down Philippa's cheeks. "I've tried everything, Emma. I kept thinking maybe the next thing I try will make me happy. But it didn't. You know what else I've found?" Philippa dabbed at her eyes. "Even though I turned away from God, I found that God never turned away from me. Always in the back of my mind I knew that he was waiting for me to respond to him."

Emma waited in astonishment as Philippa collected herself to continue.

"I don't know if Ralph will ever be able to forgive me and take me back, but I have to face him and find out. Finding you today is an answer to prayer, Emma. I knew what I needed to do, but I didn't know how I could do it."

Emma lay in bed that night praising God for Philippa's decision to live for the Lord. Tomorrow Philippa would be on her way back to Grandville and Ralph. It was a truly repentant Philippa who swallowed her pride and asked Emma for train fare, admitting that she was barely able to pay the last of her rent, not on a house as she had originally said, but on a small room above a shoe shop.

"I'll pay you back, Emma. I promise. It may take a while, but somehow I'll pay you back."

"Consider it a gift, Philippa," Emma had insisted. "You and Ralph will be starting a new marriage together, and this time Christ will be a part of it."

"I only hope Ralph will still want me back."

"I can assure you he does. I just hope he's not still out looking for you. Why don't you send a telegram?"

"I couldn't!" Philippa wrung her hands. "I need to talk to him myself, Emma. You can understand that, can't you?"

Emma had reluctantly agreed, although she still thought Ralph should be found before Philippa headed back to Grandville.

Emma's thoughts turned to Simon. It was almost October. Simon should be able to go to Washington and finish with the business he had to do. She frowned. There was so much about Simon that she still didn't know. She hoped their future wouldn't always be so uncertain.

The next morning Emma knocked on the study door. She wished to speak to Gordon about Simon.

"Come in. Oh, good morning, Emma dear. How are you feeling today? And how's my grandson doing?" Gordon stood and helped Emma to a chair before returning to his desk.

"We're both fine, Gordon, and how are you this morning?"

"Knee-deep in paperwork already. The shipping business keeps one very busy. I just wish I could have convinced Simon to work with Anson and me, but no, he insisted on a different vocation, much to his mother's horror, I might add."

Emma was surprised. "Isn't Katherine proud of Simon?"

"Proud? No, I'm afraid detective work to Katherine is synonymous with street cleaning. But Simon was determined to be a detective despite her complaining. He seems to thrive on it, but of course, you would know that, dear, since your own father trained him."

Emma became very still. "My father—"

"Excellent man! I met him once. I must say he takes his job seriously and I have full confidence in him. Made it much easier to see Simon committed to the profession with a man like your father to work with."

Emma's tumultuous thoughts prevented her from hearing Gordon's words. *Simon—a detective?*

Ignoring her silence, Gordon stood to pace the room as he continued. "Simon has always been an independent sort, making his own way in the world, you know. He was never one to depend on his family's money, but he's done enough with the shipping business to get a good start for himself and now for you and his child too. Simon is independent in a lot of ways, but I'm sure you've noticed that about him, my dear."

Emma struggled to concentrate on her father-in-law's words. Her silence was in part due to her shock in hearing the truth about her husband, but also due to the anger she felt building in her as she realized that she had been duped. Duped by the man she had put her full faith and trust in, the man whose name she bore and whose baby she carried. Emma stood uncertainly to her feet. How could he do this to her? Why couldn't he trust her as she had trusted him?

Gordon was still talking and she tried to overcome her anger to hear what he was saying. "Simon takes his work so seriously. For instance, this case he's on now. I know only the basics; he refuses to give out any information that might cause harm to come to this family and for that I'm grateful. His mother carries on about his job, but I think deep down she might be proud of the man he's become."

Emma's anger started to lessen as her father-in-law's words began to sink in. Simon was only doing his job, she reasoned. *But why can't he trust me? I'm his wife!* She knew part of her anger was embarrassment at not figuring the truth out herself. She put a hand to her mouth as she recalled how foolish she must have sounded to him, saying she was there to protect him.

But, no, Simon never laughed at her. And their love, their marriage, all that was real, she had no doubts there. Little things started coming back to her, clues she should have caught on to but didn't.

Gordon stopped his pacing when he saw his daughter-in-law's face. "Emma, dear, you wanted to see me?" he asked.

Emma made up her mind. "Yes, Father. I was hoping you would take care of a few things for me while I'm gone."

Gordon grinned with pleasure that she had called him Father, but then he scowled as he realized what she said. "While you're gone? Where are you going, Emma? You know Simon wants me to watch out for you."

Emma's heart was pounding excitedly. "I'm going to Grandville with my friend Philippa Tunelle. Simon will be there to escort the government man back to Washington, won't he?"

"You mean Charles Preston? Yes, that was his plan, but he didn't say anything about you meeting him in Grandville."

So it is Charles! "We were going to finish the job together, Father. Don't worry; Simon will be glad to see me."

"But—" Emma cut off Gordon's protest with a kiss on his cheek then she hurried from the room.

Chapter 24

Train

As the train rattled its way westward, Emma shifted her position in a futile effort to make herself more comfortable. She glanced at her traveling companions to see how they were faring. Philippa was staring absently out the window, apparently deep in thought, and Frederick was passing the time by taking a nap.

Emma sighed and moved in her seat again. The Chappells had been very upset by Emma's declaration that she was leaving, but when they saw she was determined, they had insisted on Frederick accompanying her and Philippa. Katherine had been especially vocal in her disapproval, but Gordon, bless him, had quietly calmed her, saying that Emma knew what she was doing.

"But what about the baby, Gordon? Emma can't be traveling in her condition! She belongs here where we can properly care for her."

But Gordon Chappell put his foot down—an action that greatly surprised his family. Then he further shocked them by adding, "Emma is one of those rare women who know how to take care of themselves. I have every confidence in her as does Simon, I'm sure."

Emma smiled as she recalled Katherine's stunned expression. Gordon may be in trouble with his wife for a few days for speaking up, but she wasn't going to worry about that. For now she was going to concentrate on Simon.

A detective. How had she been so easily fooled? She felt hurt and betrayed, yet she knew that was being unfair to Simon. He had a job to do too, and he did it very well. But couldn't he have told her even after they had married? Didn't he trust her at all? Her questions would have to wait until she was face-to-face with her husband.

Freesburg

When Freesburg finally rolled into view, Philippa grasped Emma's hand tightly with her own. Emma squeezed her friend's hand in return.

"Please send a telegram to Grandville now, Philippa. Ralph should know where you are. He's worried long enough, don't you think?"

Philippa gave a quick nod of her head. "Okay, Emma, I will. And I'm going to try to quit worrying and instead trust the Lord like you've said. I'm so glad you've been with me these last days of traveling. I don't think I could have done it without your encouragement."

Emma hugged Philippa warmly. "I'll get a room for us and book passage on the stage for tomorrow morning. You send that telegram."

After Philippa departed, Emma turned to Frederick, who was gathering their bags. "Thank you, Frederick, for all you've done to help us. Mrs. Tunelle and I will be all right from here, so I want you to head back to the Chappell's tomorrow when the train leaves."

"But, madam, I was told—"

"I know, Frederick, and you've done exactly what you were told to do and I appreciate it, but I'm home now. I have family and friends everywhere around here, and I'll be well taken care of. I insist you go back."

"As you wish, Mrs. Chappell. I'll see you on your way tomorrow; then I'll return to Boston." He tipped his hat and headed to the hotel with their bags.

Emma sighed with relief. Getting rid of Frederick had worried her. Thankfully, that was over. She pressed a hand to her enlarged form as she felt the baby kick; then she moved on to take care of her errands. She was unaware of the eyes that studied her with interest.

The man standing on the end of the train platform looked quite different in his rugged clothing than he had in the formal evening attire he sported at the Chappells' party. He could have reached out and touched Emma as she passed by him, but he only allowed himself a quick glance. Startled, he looked again then quickly away as Emma paused briefly before stepping off the boardwalk.

The man carrying the bags had called her "Mrs. Chappell" and indeed, she was the woman beside Simon Chase at the Boston party. But the man on the platform now recognized her as "Sally Bailey," the expectant woman who had ridden the train before. So that's why the names Sally and Josh were important to his boss. They had been phony names for these two.

Following at a discreet distance, he heard her purchase a fare on the coach to Grandville. As Emma headed for the hotel, the man strode to the livery for his horse.

Chapter 25

Freesburg

Emma's small shoes barely stirred the dust of the hard-packed street as she crossed to the hotel. She smiled as she admired the fall colors in the surrounding woods. A deep breath of fresh air lifted her spirits somewhat, but she was exhausted from travel and in need of rest. She was optimistic that soon she would be reunited with her husband. What a reunion it would be! Their secrets would have to be revealed; hers about the baby and his about his real job.

She still hurt a bit from her disappointment about Simon not revealing his detective work to her. The fact that her own father had trained Simon and he still hadn't told her hurt even more, but she would wait until they could talk, until he could explain. She started up the steps to the hotel and found it an effort to climb them. Maybe a nap would be in order before she considered taking her supper. She pushed open the door to the hotel.

"Emma! He's here!"

Emma snapped to alertness as Philippa rushed toward her and urgently whispered the words.

"Simon's here?"

"Not Simon! Ralph!" Philippa drew Emma into a corner of the lobby and practically hid herself behind Emma's expanded form.

"Ralph's here? In Freesburg?" Emma was delighted with the news but still unaware of Philippa's reaction.

"Not just in Freesburg. Here, in this hotel!" Philippa peeked over Emma's shoulder.

"For goodness' sake, Philippa! Are you hiding behind me?" Emma laughed. She grabbed Philippa by the arms and gave her a little shake. "Ralph's here! Where?"

"He was ordering a room when I walked in here to look for you," Philippa whispered. "I hid behind the wall there until I heard him go upstairs."

"You hid? But, Philippa, why? This is what you came for."

Philippa's face was flushed, and Emma could see that she was trembling. "I'm scared, Emma! He looked so…so tired and so…wonderful!" She hid her face in her hands. "What am I supposed to do, walk up to him and say, 'Hi Ralph, remember me?' Oh, Emma!"

Emma chuckled to herself, but there was true sympathy in her voice when she spoke. "You're at a turning point in your life right here, Philippa. You have to decide what you're going to do, but you're not on your own any longer, are you? You've got the Lord to lean on now, and I think it's truly a miracle from him that you've found Ralph so quickly when he's been looking for you so long. I'm sure it's the Lord's timing. Now let me look at you."

Emma straightened Philippa's hat and brushed some travel dust from her skirt. She fussed and primped awhile; then, without looking directly at Philippa, she asked, "Well, have you decided?"

"Emma Newly Chappell! You dear, stubborn friend—you!" Philippa gave a shaky laugh. "You won't let me give up, will you?" She straightened and stopped Emma's hands from their imaginary fussing. "I'm going to ask one more favor from you, Emma."

"Anything."

"Please come with me. Just speak to him first, okay?"

Emma frowned. "Are you sure?"

At Philippa's urgent nod, Emma sighed. "Okay. I'll get you started; then it's up to you." She moved away from her friend's side and inquired at the desk about a room for herself. Frederick had already secured one for her and Philippa, she found, so she next asked for Ralph's room number and tried to ignore the clerk's inquisitive eyes.

Turning back to the lobby, Emma saw Philippa standing where she had left her. A closer look revealed Philippa's tight features and fearful eyes. When Emma drew near, Philippa spoke to her in a subdued voice.

"How do you approach someone you've been cruel to and ask forgiveness?"

Emma's heart went out to her friend, and she hugged her as closely as her figure would allow. "By God's grace, Philippa," she answered. "I think you're forgetting that

Ralph has already forgiven you. I know he'll be overjoyed that you've returned."

"Well, even if he doesn't want me…"

Emma gently nudged her forward. "Let's just go see, shall we?"

It was slow progress, but finally Emma managed to get Philippa past the curious clerk and up the stairs to the second floor. She prayed silently as they walked along the faded carpeted hall to the door of Ralph's room that Ralph hadn't become discouraged and gone back to his old ways when he couldn't find Philippa. Philippa moved to one side of the door where she couldn't be seen, so Emma gave her one more encouraging smile and quietly knocked on the door.

There was a squeak of the bed then silence. Philippa clutched her hands together and bit her lip.

The door opened part way, and Ralph's head appeared around it.

"Emma!" His hair was tousled a bit, but he was clean shaven and fully clothed except for his stocking feet.

"Hello, Ralph."

His eyebrows rose when he noticed her rounded figure, and he looked past her but did not see Philippa. "Is Simon with you? What are you doing in Freesburg? You taking the train?"

She was aware of the things he did not say, his polite way of not mentioning her condition, and the obvious despair still in his eyes.

"There's someone here who would like to see you, Ralph." Emma spoke the words carefully and knew Ralph understood immediately. His hand gripped the door.

"Philippa?"

At Emma's quick nod, he reached for her arm. "Is she here in town? Does she really want to see me?" He took a step back and began looking for his boots. "Take me to her right away, Emma. Please! I need to talk to her; I need to tell her I'm sorry before she leaves again. Oh, Lord, help me! Do you think she'll even see me? I was just on my way back east again tomorrow to look for her some more."

He had been talking while he pulled on his boots, and now he looked up and stopped short, for Philippa had come within view in the doorway.

"*You've* done nothing to be sorry for," she exclaimed tearfully. "*I'm* the one who needs to ask forgiveness from you." Her voice shook as she spoke.

"Philippa! Oh, Philippa!" The words were torn from Ralph as he opened his arms to the woman who flew into them.

Smilingly broadly, Emma quietly drew the door shut and moved down the hall to her own room. She wiped away a happy tear as she lay down on her bed fully clothed and drifted off to a much-needed sleep.

Chapter 26

Freesburg

Emma met the Tunelles for breakfast the next morning and was delighted over the happy couple. Philippa positively sparkled, and Ralph looked years younger with the worry and tension erased from his face.

"Emma, once again I can't thank you enough for all the praying you've done for me," he told her sincerely. "And you brought Philippa back to me."

"No, Ralph, actually the Lord did that," Emma answered truthfully.

They laughed together, and Philippa wiped a tear from her cheek. "The Lord's been amazing me with his goodness to me after all my willfulness," she admitted. "I feel like I'm starting everything brand new again, including our marriage." She spoke shyly to Ralph.

"We are starting new, Philippa. We finally have the right foundation under us on which to begin building."

Emma smiled at both of them. "Are you headed back to Grandville today?"

"Yes." Ralph leaned forward. "I told Philippa we could go see her parents first if she wanted, but she's as anxious as I am to get home." He put his arm around his wife and smiled lovingly at her. "Home sounds pretty good to both of us right now." He turned back to Emma. "You're coming on the stage to Grandville too, right?"

But Emma was already shaking her head. "No, I was going to go there with Philippa to find you, Ralph, but now that that's been settled, I think I'll go to my parents' home first. It's been a while since I've seen them." Emma was very anxious to have a long talk with her father. She was sure he would know where Simon was.

After seeing Ralph and Philippa on the coach to Grandville, Emma made preparations for her trip to Sand Creek and home. She wired her family to meet her and boarded the coach that would make it possible. A day later she was arriving in the familiar dusty little town, and she wondered what her family was thinking about her sudden arrival. As she looked lovingly around, the baby within her seemed to share her anticipation by choosing that moment to kick her. Emma placed her hand over the spot and felt the baby continue to push against her. She smiled in delight.

Suddenly the coach doors opened and she saw the wonderfully familiar faces of her mom and dad, Rex and Abel searching for her. Moments later she was in their arms and everyone was laughing and talking at once.

"Oh Emma, it's so good to finally see you!" Sky couldn't help the burst of tears that fell as she held her daughter closely. "Have you any idea the nights I've stayed up praying for you, little one?" she whispered into Emma's ear. "Now look at you! All married and soon to be a mother! Where did my little Emma go?"

Emma blinked back her own tears as she returned her mother's embrace. "I've so much to tell you all," she said breathlessly. "But first…" She put a hand to her enlarged abdomen. "I think Baby Gertrude would like to say hello." She laughed at their expressions.

"Baby *Gertrude*?" Abel wrinkled his nose.

Emma laughed again. "It's just a nickname I use," she explained. "My goodness, she's kicking me today."

Sky smiled as she led Emma to a nearby bench. "Too much excitement and travel for both of you, I'll wager. Think you can handle one more ride to get you home?"

Emma reveled in the attention and concern. She felt the love and warmth of her family surround her as if she were cocooned in a soft blanket. "I'll do anything to be home with all of you for a while," she said sincerely. "I've missed you all so much."

Russ patted his daughter's shoulder affectionately. "I never thought when I sent you on that assignment last spring that I wouldn't see you again for nearly half a year." He smiled. "I wonder now if I would have done it had I known."

"I'm so glad you did, Dad." Emma squeezed his hand. "We have a lot to talk about, starting with—do you know where Simon is right now?" Her imploring expression was not lost on her father.

"We'll talk as soon as we get you home and settled, Em," he said. Emma nearly protested, but she saw his quick look around and knew that this was not the time or place for their discussion. But she wouldn't wait much longer.

The trip home went quickly with lots of family catching up to do. Emma learned that her sister Dorcas had a baby boy and named him Leon, Lucy's baby was due at any time, and that Jade and Tyler's little Pamela was healthy and growing quickly. Emma's cousin Gabriel from the way station and his wife Leigh had their baby too, and little Adele was fascinated with her baby sister Irene.

"What about Mallory?" Emma asked. Mallory was married to Michael Trent, Emma's other cousin and Gabriel's brother.

"Mike and Mallory had another boy," her mother replied. "In fact, Hank and Randi are visiting in Grandville now to see their newest grandson, and Evan and Ella plan to go as soon as they can. I believe the baby is named Millard in honor of Mallory's great grandfather; you know, the one who raised Randi. Randi told me so much about him when we came here so long ago on our bride train." Sky's eyes grew thoughtful then brightened. "Just think, Randi's daughter and my nephew married, and my daughter and Randi's son married! Who would have known?"

"Many matches have been made from that venture," put in Russ. "I suspect half of Sand Creek is made up of relatives by now. And most have been good marriages too. Too bad about Ralph and Philippa's, though."

Emma's squeal of joy startled her father, but he grinned from ear to ear as she related the latest events leading up to her arrival in Sand Creek.

"So that's how you came to be here. I've been anxious to ask but wanted to wait until we were away from listening ears. You say Philippa got saved years ago but never grew in the Lord! How amazing that she wants to live for him now! Maybe our prayers for her folks will be answered as well."

"Violet has been bitter for so many years, and she's kept Taylor from forming friendships with any of us," commented Sky about Philippa's parents. "What a lonely life they must have."

The Newlys arrived home, and soon had Emma settled comfortably at the kitchen table while Sky made preparations for their meal.

"I'm certainly capable of helping, Mother," protested Emma.

"And you will." Sky laughed. "But for now, I *need* to take care of you. You have no idea how these past five months have been for me, not knowing where you were most of the time and not knowing if you were truly happy in your marriage or not. Why, when Simon wired your father for permission, we both stayed up all night praying for the two of you. If your father hadn't had so much respect for Simon— you know your dad was the one who led him to the Lord? Of course you did. I'm sure Simon has told you about how your dad trained him when he joined the Pinkertons. I heard of nothing but Simon Chase for months, or I guess I should say Simon Chappell, so I really felt like I knew him too. When Simon told your father he loved you and wanted to marry you, I was unsure, but he promised your father that he would continue to take care of you and that it would be a perfect cover for you to be together in protecting Mr. Preston. Well, let me tell you, I was relieved to know that you weren't alone, but I was so anxious to know if you were really—"

Sky turned from the stove and broke off talking when she caught a glimpse of Emma's face. "What is it, Emma? What did I say? Is it the baby?"

Russ came in from the barn and heard the last words his wife had been saying. He, too, turned to Emma with worried eyes, but Emma held them both off with her hand and a rueful smile.

"It seems I still have much to learn about my husband," she informed them.

At Sky's concerned look, she continued, "Please don't be worried, Mother. I love Simon and I'm very happy to be married to him. It's just that, well, truthfully, until very recently I didn't even know Simon was a detective. I thought *he* was the man from the government."

Russ and Sky both sat down at the table with their daughter. Sky's astonished face told Emma she was dumbfounded, but Russ's understanding smile caught her attention.

"What has Simon told you, Dad? And where is he right now?"

Russ took Emma's trembling hand in his large rough one and patted it gently. "He's safe, Emmie, and he's doing his job. He hates being away from you, but he figures this is the only way to keep you from being involved. He doesn't want you to get hurt, child." Russ smiled gently. "I see him about every two weeks or so, so I know he's really okay."

Emma's father cleared his throat and looked directly at his daughter. "Simon told me that you still didn't know about his work and about his knowing me. I have to admit, I doubted his wisdom in keeping you in the dark, but he said he felt that if you truly didn't know, you wouldn't be in danger. I know he was and is terribly bothered that you will think him deceptive."

Emma silently digested her father's words. "Mother said that Simon wired to ask your permission to marry me. Did you know then that I didn't know who Simon was?"

Russ stroked his chin thoughtfully while he recalled the events of the past months. "I guess I *assumed* then that you knew, Emma. Simon's wire was clear that he loved you and was asking permission to marry you." He chuckled softly. "I was so surprised yet so happy to accept Simon as a son-in-law that I just assumed you knew everything too. Am I correct, then, that you weren't in love with Simon and only agreed to a wedding as a cover?"

Sky's exclamation of protest caused a blush to creep up Emma's cheeks.

"I—I guess I agreed because I wanted to do everything possible to make good on the job you'd given me," Emma struggled to explain to her astonished parents. "Simon brought me the coded telegram from you, Dad, which said I should go along with the marriage. When Simon and I were married in Norris, it was with the understanding that the marriage would be annulled when the case was over."

Emma knew she had shocked her parents, so she gave them a few moments to think on her words.

"So while you lived at the cabin, you weren't *really* husband and wife?" Sky asked slowly.

"We were, but we weren't." Emma tried to explain. "Charles was there the whole time as our chaperone and I had my own room and…" Emma's voice faltered. "It seems impossibly complicated to explain what seemed so clear to us at the time." She let out a deep breath. "Anyway, it didn't take us long to discover that we were in love, or should I say for *me* to discover it. It appears Simon was a little ahead of me." Emma paused for a moment. "As soon as we arrived in Boston, Simon brought me to his pastor and we were married again, privately, but honestly before God."

Sky rose slowly and moved to the stove to attend to the dinner. Emma watched the emotions flit over her mother's face and suspected she knew the cause. She stood and moved to her side.

"I've done nothing to be ashamed of, Mom." Emma spoke carefully. "You do believe that, don't you?"

Sky turned swiftly and embraced her daughter. "Oh Emma! Of course I believe you. I don't doubt your word at all, but what about other people? What will they think? What will they say? I can't bear to think—"

"Actually, no one else needs to know," interrupted Emma. "Simon's family doesn't even know about our private ceremony. I wanted both of you to know and maybe someone should explain to Tyler, I think he deserves to know, but other than that, to the rest of the world, Simon and I have been married since the beginning."

Russ nodded his agreement. "Emma's right, Sky. We'll leave this situation with the Lord."

Having that settled, Emma turned to her father. "It's nearly November, Dad. Has Charles Preston been taken back to Washington? Why is Simon still needed here? When can I see him?"

Russ motioned for Emma to return to her chair before he spoke. "Another agent has taken Charles on and we've had word that he arrived and is safe."

"Then what—?"

"Simon is on the trail of the people suspected of following the two of you," Russ continued to explain. "We need to find out how many are working together and who they are working for." He pulled a folded paper from inside his vest. "Do you recognize these men?"

Emma peered at the sketches of two men on the paper her father handed to her. They looked familiar, but where—? Suddenly, she exclaimed, "Those are the two men who took Simon that night! What were their names again? Uh…Herman…Herbert…no! It was Horace! And the other one was…Fergus! Yes, that's it!"

"You're right. They're two brothers, part of a gang they call the Barnes Gang." He pulled another paper out and unfolded it for her to see.

Emma reached for it eagerly and when she saw Sophia Barlow's face sketched on the Wanted Poster she gasped. "Sophia? What does this mean, Dad?"

"She's part of the Barnes Gang. She's their sister, Sophie Barnes," he explained. "All three of them were caught trying to rob a bank south of here, and they've been telling all they know about the people who were after Simon, hoping to get leniency from the judge for their help."

"She was part of an outlaw gang?" Emma was stunned.

"The interesting part is that she knew that the Newlys and Trents had inheritance money, and she and her brothers were trying to get their hands on it."

"But how? I mean, how did she know and how did she think she could get it?"

"I guess people talk about the inheritance, and if you're part of a gang thinking of robbing a bank, it would pay to know which bank had the most money in it. When Sophia learned of the inheritance money, she thought she could woo one of the men, like Gabe or Tyler, away from their wives and wrangle the money out of them somehow. That obviously didn't work for her, so when you appeared, she thought she could kidnap you and hold you for ransom."

"What?" Emma's mouth dropped open. "I've never heard of anything so ridiculous!"

"Don't think she wasn't capable, Em. She and her brothers have done pretty well for themselves with their thieving and schemes. When she was offered money for help in getting Simon, she went after it. Now that they've been caught, she's the one we've been getting the most information out of. That information has been passed on to Simon, and he's pretty close to rounding up the rest of the people involved."

Emma sank back in her chair, trying to digest all her father had told her. She found it difficult to imagine Sophia Barlow as an outlaw. Her thoughts turned to Simon again.

"So where is he?" Emma persisted.

"He's been in several areas, actually," her father continued. "But right now he's working near Grandville."

"When can we go?" Emma was on her feet questioning her parents. It was clear she was willing to leave immediately.

"Wait, not so fast, sweetheart!" Her father stood. "I'm not so sure that having you appear now will be good for this case. I mean, it's okay that you're here, but you better not be seen near Grandville or Norris. Do you think anyone in Freesburg recognized you?"

Emma sank back in her seat. "No one but Ralph, I'm sure," she said. "You mean that if I'm recognized as Simon's wife, he could be in danger? Ralph and Philippa will tell everyone that I'm home!"

Russ sat down again. "He could be in danger although no one knows *he's* there."

"You mean he's in hiding?" Emma wanted to continue her questioning, but her brothers Rex and Abel were on their way in for supper and Russ motioned for her to stop.

The family had an enjoyable meal together and the conversation was kept light. Emma especially enjoyed watching her father take his Bible and read to them at the end of their meal as he had always done. A deep longing for Simon came over her, and she blinked back tears. At least she was getting closer to him.

Seeing her daughter's face reminded Sky of the long travels Emma had just been through. "You're off for bed now, dear," she said despite Emma's protests. It was clear Emma wished to learn more from her father.

"We can continue this tomorrow, Em," Russ said as he kissed her forehead. "The Lord's brought you this far; he'll get you the rest of the way."

Emma smiled as she readied for bed in her old room. How long ago it seemed that she had left on her search of adventure to work in Lucy and Buck's hotel. As she pulled the thick quilts up around her shoulders, she sleepily wondered who had opened the boxes of schoolbooks she packed away just that last May. She was no longer the school ma'rm. She was now Mrs. Simon Chappell and a soon-to-be mother. She smiled into her pillow as she thought of the news she still needed to share with her husband.

Chapter 27

Sand Creek

"But I really truly want to go to church with you this morning," Emma mumbled to her mother. "Why can't I seem to wake up?"

Sky laughed as she stood by her daughter's bed. "Oh, I imagine several days of train and stage coach travel plus carrying a baby may have something to do with it." She smiled and patted Emma's shoulder. "You just stay there and get the rest your body is telling you that you need. We'll all be back in no time, and we'll have plenty of time to see each other. You need to take care of Baby Gertrude first."

Emma groaned softly as the aches and pains of travel became more evident to her awakening body. "Ohhh! I feel like an old lady," she complained.

Sky laughed again and bent to kiss Emma's cheek. "Just take it easy. You know how long the service is, so you know when to expect us. Rest. And later we'll talk about the wedding party we've been planning for you and Simon."

Sleepily, Emma smiled at her mother while inwardly she groaned. *Another party?*

Emma listened to the familiar household sounds as her family prepared to leave for church. Although she felt guilty at still lying in bed, she knew her mother was right. She was tired! She allowed herself to doze off again.

It wasn't long, however, until Baby Gertrude started pushing and moving and Emma knew her sleeping time was over. That and the need to visit the privy out back. Ruefully, Emma grinned. The Chappells' lavish home with bath closets and servants had spoiled her. Now it was time to face the realities of northern living again.

Quickly she dressed and brushed and braided her blonde hair so like her mother's. She grabbed one of her mother's old shawls hanging on a peg by the door and stepped out into the nippy fall air.

On her way back to the house, Emma paused and let her eyes roam over her parents' ranch. Her mother's garden was almost completely harvested. Only a couple rows of carrots waited to be pulled. She looked beyond the barn to the horse corral and noticed with admiration the fine stock grazing there. Now in her twentieth year she realized that this was not her home any longer.

She expected to feel a sense of loss at that thought, but strangely she didn't. She and Simon would have their own place—not here, not his parents' home in Boston, their own. This would always be a wonderful place to come and visit and to bring their children, she thought as her hand rested on her baby. She could imagine letting her sons come here for extended visits to learn about ranching while they helped their grandfather. She could also imagine her daughters being sent off to school in Boston and being taken shopping with their grandmother Chappell. There was such a wonderful future awaiting her and Simon and their child. If only she could be with Simon again soon.

So deep in thought was she that she wasn't aware of the man until he stepped from beside the house right in front of her. She gasped. This was the man who had been at the Chappells' home the night of their party, the man from the train!

"I thought you might be trying to throw me off the track by buying that stage ticket to Grandville." He took her by the arm and started to pull her along with him. Emma jerked her arm from his grasp, but he grabbed her again by both arms.

"I don't want to hurt you, ma'am," he spoke softly but with a firmness that was unmistakable. "I've got me a job to do and I intend to do it." He pulled her along with him toward the barn.

Emma's thoughts were frantic. She wanted to resist, but to do so meant a struggle, and she did not want the man to harm her baby. "What do you want with me?" She managed to ask as she twisted under the pressure of his hands.

"We're going to take a little ride. There're some people who need to ask you a few questions." They reached the barn, but instead of going inside, he led her alongside the outside wall to the back of the building. Emma began to scrape the side of her shoe into the ground with each step, thinking she could leave a trail for her father to find, but the man was aware of her actions. He picked her up in his arms for the rest of the walk to the two horses she now saw saddled and waiting behind the barn. He then set her down beside one of the horses and looked down at her with a masked expression on his face.

"You was dressed up like this once before a few months back." He indicated her condition.

Emma stared back at her captor without saying a word.

The man shifted his feet and looked down at her again. "I need to know, ma'am, if this is for real or if you're still pretendin'."

Emma's eyes widened.

"Cuz this here ride we're gonna take can either be rough or easy. I don't want no part in hurtin' no baby, so if you're not pretendin', you need to let me know that now."

His voice brooked no argument, so Emma barely inclined her head and said, "It's real."

"It wasn't before, though, was it?"

"No."

"So how do I know you're telling me the truth just so as not to slow me down?" He stared stone-faced at her again.

"I…" Emma started to speak, but just then the baby kicked and the movement was noticeable even to the hard-faced man in front of her.

"Good enough for me," he said. "Stand right there and don't try to run." He glanced down at her protruding abdomen again as if to remind her of how foolish that would be; then he walked back to where she had scraped the ground and began to erase their tracks.

Emma looked frantically around, searching for a way to escape from the man. She knew, as he did, that she couldn't outrun him in her condition and even though he claimed to not want to harm her, she saw his determination to do the job he was sent to do.

Her mind petitioned the Lord while her eyes continued to seek for help, but there was nothing. Her parents and brothers wouldn't return for at least another hour, she knew. She wondered where the man was planning to take her and to whom.

He came back then and boosted her up into the saddle.

"Sorry I didn't bring a buggy, ma'am, but I didn't know for sure about you. We'll just take it easy, as long as you cooperate." He climbed on his horse's back, took the lead rope on her horse, and headed off.

Emma gripped the shawl more tightly around her and hoped that the fall day would warm up soon. She was frightened but thankful for the consideration the man was showing her. She was also concerned that somehow her coming home had put Simon in greater danger. Who were these people who wanted to see her? Were they the ones who sent Horace and Fergus to kidnap Simon from their little cabin several months earlier? Did they still think he was the man from Washington instead of Charles?

Emma knew that as soon as her father found her missing, he would begin tracking them. She knew he'd send a telegram to Hank Riley in Grandville and get her brothers and her cousins all looking for her. Amazingly, though she still felt fearful, she knew the Lord was with her and was going to stay right beside her.

The man was good at hiding his tracks. He certainly seemed to know what he was doing. When he caught Emma breaking a twig as a marker for her father, he just looked at her and said, "Ma'am, I don't want to have to tie your hands. Do *you* want me to?"

She silently shook her head. She knew he would do as he said.

They stayed off the main roads and trails, but Emma realized that they were headed toward Grandville. When they stopped for a rest, she thought they would actually stop for the night, but the man started them off again after a cold meal and rest for the horses.

"We're traveling at night?" she asked, speaking for the first time since they started.

"The people that will be trailing us won't stop, so we can't," was all he replied.

Weariness was rapidly overtaking Emma, and she feared she would fall asleep and fall off the horse. Her already aching muscles screamed out at her for attention, but she could only grit her teeth and carry on. They finally stopped, and the man told her to rest for a couple of hours. She was asleep before he finished unsaddling the horses.

The few hours' rest was enough to revive her and keep her going for most of the next day. She was faltering again by evening when the man turned the horses into a farmyard.

Emma sat up straighter and looked around her. She had never been to this place before, and she wasn't exactly sure where Grandville was anymore since they had twisted and turned while she dozed off and on. She had tried to keep her bearings so she could find her way back, but her weariness prevented her from it.

The man reached up to help her off the horse, and she nearly fell when he set her on her feet. There was real concern in his eyes and almost a look of apology as he steadied her. He helped her up the steps to the farmhouse.

Emma shut her eyes against the lamplight and squinted at its brightness as the door opened and the light shone full on her face. She couldn't see the person holding the lamp; she could only make out the form of a man, but she thought she recognized the voice that exclaimed, "Finally! Now that we've got the girl we should be able to flush Chase out of hiding!"

No, I must be dreaming, she thought as she stumbled into the kitchen. *Why would Giles Findley want Simon?*

Chapter 28

Grandville

Emma woke to sunshine streaming into a strange bedroom. She lifted her head and groaned at the sore muscles that came alive with the movement.

Where was she?

She was still wearing her clothes, and her mother's shawl lay on a chair in the corner of the room. Slowly she recalled her two-day-and-night ride to this farmhouse and the memory of finding the Findleys waiting for her.

Giles and Agatha? How could they possibly be involved in this? Her tired mind searched for answers, but all she came up with were more questions and the main one being, where was Simon?

Emma pushed herself up and tried to straighten her clothing. She knew a trip to the privy was her first concern as she rapidly re-braided her hair.

She stepped out of the room and followed the sound of voices to the farmhouse kitchen. Giles and Agatha

Findley were seated at the table talking with the man who had brought her there. Their conversation ceased when she entered the room. At first no one spoke; they only looked at each other. Then Giles Findley motioned Emma to a chair.

"Did you sleep well, Miss Newly?" he asked. "Or should I say Mrs. Chase? Or perhaps Sally Bailey? Or is it Mrs. Chappell? Hmm? Which is it to be today, Emma dear?"

Emma remained standing and studied the couple before her. Giles and Agatha Findley had seemed like a nice, ordinary grandparent-type couple to her a few months back. Even now their physical appearance looked much the same, but their expressions were their true marks of change. Where kindness and friendliness had once been now hate, malice, and, yes, evil appeared. She glanced at the stone-faced man who had brought her there and oddly felt comforted that he was still present.

"I need to step out back," she stated quietly.

Giles Findley laughed, and Agatha sneered at her. "You can stop the motherhood act now, Emma. That never fooled us the first time either."

The man at the table flicked a look in Emma's direction before turning to watch Giles. "I'll take her," was all he said.

"You do that, Rod, and Emma dear, be prepared to answer some questions when you get back and you might get out of this alive." He laughed under his breath.

Emma followed the man called Rod out the door of the house and turned as he started toward the outhouse.

"What's going on here?" she whispered.

He glanced at her then stared off into the distance as he stopped a short way from the building and motioned for her to go around him. He was still staring afar off when she returned.

As they started back to the house, she heard him say under his breath, "I won't let them hurt you."

She glanced at him and nodded briefly before washing up in the basin on the porch. Stepping back into the kitchen, she took a deep breath then said, "Suppose you tell me what this is all about, Mr. Findley."

Agatha pushed a cup of coffee across the table to her, and Giles motioned to a chair. Rod leaned against the doorjamb.

"It's not that hard to figure out, Emma," he began as she stiffly sat down. "We want Simon Chase, and you're the bait to get him. We knew as soon as he left Boston that he was back here, but we haven't been able to find him. He's hiding, and our time's running out."

"Why do you want Simon?"

Agatha's head jerked up. "You don't know?"

Giles sneered. "Of course she knows. She's just protecting him still." He shook his head. "No reason why you can't know the rest, though. Simon Chase is the main witness in a counterfeiting trial next week in Washington. Without his testimony, there can be no trial and no conviction. If he testifies, some very important people are going to prison, and we can't allow that. So we can't allow your Simon to go to Washington and we certainly can't allow him to testify. We thought we had lost him when you both went to Boston, but fortunately, thanks to this, we picked up the trail again."

Emma looked curiously at the wrinkled scrap of paper Giles Findley laid out on the table. *What?*

She put her finger on the corner and rotated the torn note so that she could read the words written there.

Joshua
Psal

This was part of the list of verses that her cousin Michael had written for her several months ago in Grandville. Her mind raced as she tried to figure out what the Findleys were doing with it and even more why they thought it important.

"I picked it up in the stagecoach when you dropped your handbag," Agatha gloated.

"We were watching for Joshua and Sal not Josh and Sally, but we picked up on those names right away." Giles continued. "You were careless with your employer's instructions, Emma, and it cost you."

He crossed his legs and leaned back in his chair watching her with interest as he continued. "I never expected Russ Newly to survive that fall; it was intended to break his neck, not his leg." He seemed satisfied with the horrified look that crossed Emma's face. "Then I never expected him to send his daughter to finish his job for him. We thought maybe it was the coach driver, but Agatha was the one who said we should watch you, my dear."

"And I suspected Sophia," Emma muttered.

Giles tilted his head back and laughed, enjoying Emma's comment. "She was definitely an asset to us with her snoopy ways, but no, Sophia wasn't part of our plans originally. She was useful to a point, but her bumbling brothers couldn't follow orders, so we cut them all out of the deal," he added disdainfully.

"Well, she helped us a lot because she was so interested in the Newly and Trent families anyway," put in Agatha. "We just tagged along with her while she did her snooping. Everyone was so irritated with her that they never paid attention to us."

Giles sat forward and the chair scraped the floor as he moved. "Enough about her. I must say, Emma, that I can't believe the elaborate methods Simon went to trying to fool us. Marrying you, for example. Did you really think we fell for that? And this ridiculous baby charade." He pointed at Emma's figure. "Why do you persist in continuing with that?

"At first we thought the other man with Simon was the one we were after, that Charles fellow, but we discovered it had to be Chase. He was the one who was hiding. He married you and he disguised himself as Josh; he was the one, all right." Giles slapped his fist into the palm of his other hand.

"His masquerades with you gave it away, for one thing, and then when we picked him up at the cabin by Norris, we knew it had to be him by the way you followed him and got him back. So you see, Emma, you were really the one to convince us he was the right man. You can pretend all you want, but we know."

Emma sat silently digesting this information. If what her father told her was true, then Charles was already in Washington ready to testify. That meant that Simon was here still acting as a decoy to continue to distract the

Findleys from the real witness. And because she hadn't known the truth, she had helped convince them that person was Simon.

The Findleys watched Emma with interest.

"So where is Simon, Emma?" Giles leaned toward her.

Emma glanced across the table at the man but said nothing.

"We're running out of time, girl, and we're not very patient people." Agatha smacked the table with a soup ladle, causing Emma to jump. Baby Gertrude took that moment to do a flip-flop, and Agatha's shocked expression revealed that she had seen the movement.

"Say, what's going on here?" she exclaimed. Without warning she pressed her hand to Emma's side. Emma gasped, and Rod stood up straight from his post by the door.

"What's wrong?" Giles stood to his feet also, looking at his wife and Emma.

"She's really having a baby!" Agatha shrieked. "This isn't an act!"

"What?" shouted Giles. His eyes darted from Emma's face to her abdomen and back as thoughts raced through his mind.

Emma remained perfectly still. The expressions on the Findleys' faces frightened her, but she didn't understand why.

"He really did marry her," Giles was saying to Agatha. "He wasn't acting." He paused, thinking furiously. "But it was enough to throw us off track and keep us from looking for the real person. *Who is it, Emma?*" He grabbed her by the throat, his eyes blazing into hers.

Emma clawed at the hands around her throat, struggling to breathe, and her chair slid backward, banging her head into the wall. Suddenly she was free, and she saw Giles crash into the wall by the stove as Rod shoved him away from her. She gasped for air as she watched the two men face off. Giles was livid.

"Get out of my way, Rod. You're on my payroll and you'll do what I say!"

"Not if it means hurting mothers and children," Rod hissed back. "That's not what I signed on for."

"Stop it both of you! There's someone in the yard headed toward the house." Agatha stilled them with her words.

Giles checked the window, and Rod returned by the door. "It's just that old hermit again," he whispered. "Probably just wants to trade some venison for some more coffee."

Emma's head swirled as she tried to control her racing emotions. Could Rod mean Hermit Jack?

"You keep your mouth shut while he's here, girl, or you'll never see that baby be born." Rod shot Agatha an icy look as she spat the words at Emma. "You get rid of him, Rod, you hear?" she commanded him.

There was a rap on the door, and Hermit Jack ambled into the room. Emma thought she had never been so glad to see anyone in all her life, but the grizzled old woodsman didn't even look at her.

"Need some more coffee iffen you be willin' to do some tradin'." He spoke gruffly to Rod, who nodded. Then the old man turned to look at the other occupants of the room.

"Whooee! Where did all these folks come from? Thought you lived alone. 'Eh, don't I know you?" He took a step toward Emma, and she quickly nodded but stopped when she saw Giles Findley's hand go into his pocket. *A gun?* She couldn't put the old man in danger because of her. She let her eyes drop to the table.

"Sure, I know you! You's the school ma'rm who shot my buck! Ain't you married now? Where's your man? Never did figger out which one you was married to." He chuckled as though he found his words quite amusing. "Yep, you was huggin' one fellar and sayin' you was married to another." He noticed her enlarged form. "Guess you figger'd it out!" He slapped his knee and roared with laughter at his own wit. Then he picked at Emma's sleeve, causing her head to shoot up in alarm.

"You come see this buck *I* shot; he's a beauty, better than that one you got. I got him right out there in the yard. I pulled him here on a travois like the Injuns do."

Emma felt like a lifeline had been thrown to her and she started to rise to follow the old man, but Giles grasped her arm.

"I'll just come along and have a look too," he said.

Hermit Jack didn't even turn around as he headed back to the door. "You can all come; I don't care. Biggest buck I ever shot."

They followed the strange old man into the farmyard. Rod stayed close behind Giles and Emma, and Agatha muttered something unintelligible as she came after him. The woodsman led them to the shady side of the barn where, indeed, there lay a trussed-up deer on a makeshift log sled. It wasn't that big of an animal, Emma thought, so why was Hermit Jack so keen on having her see it?

As they got closer to the animal, the old man turned and pulled Emma by the sleeve again. "Here's where I shot him." He pulled her along, pointing to a spot on the other side of the deer.

Giles reluctantly let go of Emma's arm while he listened impatiently to the grizzled old man's retelling of his hunting exploits. All the while Hermit Jack was talking, he was pulling Emma to the end of the travois away from the others. Suddenly he pushed her against the barn, he bent down, and his rifle appeared in his hands pointed at the three people a few feet away from them.

"Get down, Emma!" he commanded her in a voice that was much different from the old man's raspy one. One that was very familiar to her, familiar and dear. She stared at him in shock.

"Get your weapons out on the ground! Now! And put your hands out where I can see them." The rifle was held steady in the old man's hands, but the voice coming from behind the gray, ragged beard was not the voice of an old man at all.

Emma knew that voice was Simon's, but try as she might, she could find nothing in the woodsman's appearance to prove to her that her husband was really standing before her. She could not have recognized him and would not have if he hadn't spoken normally.

Rod dropped his gun on the ground and held his hands up. Agatha stood with her hands on her hips and an angry scowl on her face, but it was Giles who caught Emma's attention. One hand was raised away from his body, but the other was in his pocket.

"Simon! His pocket!" she shouted.

Giles fired through his coat, but his shot was wild, hitting nothing. Simon's was much more accurate, and the man clutched at his shoulder as blood seeped through his fingers. Simon re-cocked his rifle and swung the aim to Rod, but he hadn't moved. He gave Simon a slight nod as if he approved of him.

They heard horses thundering into the yard, and Emma saw her father and Rex and Hank Riley ride up with their guns drawn and ready. They quickly assessed the situation and jumped down to help Simon. Russ rushed to his daughter and embraced her.

"Emma, darling, are you all right?"

Emma laughed somewhat shakily as she got to her feet and returned his hug. "I am now." Her eyes searched for Simon and her father's followed hers.

"You'd never know that was Simon under that beard and fur, would you?" he chuckled. "He's the best undercover agent I've seen, but, of course, I trained him." As Simon strode to them, Russ released his daughter with a smile and moved away. "Good job, son." He patted Simon's back and went to help the others.

Emma flung herself into her husband's arms while tears poured down her cheeks. Simon held her close without speaking until they pulled apart and looked at each other. Emma made a face at the old man who still held his arms loosely around her. Simon grinned back with his yellow-stained teeth, and Emma had to laugh.

"I never knew it was you!" She spoke with admiration. "I still can't believe it, even up close."

"Emma." Simon hugged her to him again. "I was so frightened for you! Once I was sure that the Findleys were the kidnappers, I kept track of their movements. When I saw Rod bring you here last night, I was frantic with fear for you. All I could think about was how to get you away from them. Only by the grace of God was I able to wait until this morning and pull off my act one more time." He hugged her again.

When he pulled back, he looked at her curiously. "Now, why are you here instead of safe in Boston where you are supposed to be and why the Baby Gertrude act?" he asked.

Emma smiled sweetly into her husband's questioning eyes, the only part of him other than his voice that was familiar to her, and gently informed him, "Baby Gertrude is not an act, my love."

Simon blinked, stared hard into her eyes, and blinked again. Emma saw understanding hit him, and she laughed as his bushy eyebrows lifted and his eyes grew bigger. "It seems we have a lot to talk about," he began, but she interrupted him.

"Starting with what my husband really does for a living."

"Look, Em, I should have told you. I wanted to. In fact, I tried to, but—"

They were interrupted by the men.

"Simon," Russ spoke; then he laughed. "Or Hermit Jack, I should say, we'll take these three back to Sand Creek and the sheriff. Why don't you and Emma rest up in Grandville for a few days then come back to the ranch and we'll talk then."

"Dad." Emma pulled her father and Simon aside, away from the others. "That man named Rod. He's not like the Findleys. He was good to me and even promised to protect me from them."

Her father seemed surprised, but he nodded. "I'll see to it that the judge knows that, honey. Thanks."

They watched as the men got their prisoners ready.

"We'll catch the Grandville stage with these folks and be on our way. See you two in a few days."

Emma waited for Simon to change out of his hermit outfit. When he came out of the farmhouse, she was amazed at the transformation and gladly went into his arms, feeling like she was really hugging her husband for the first time.

On the short ride to Grandville, Emma related to Simon the happenings in Boston since he had been away. He was especially pleased to hear about Philippa and Ralph, but when she came to the part about his father revealing to her who he really was, he stopped her.

"That must have been quite a shock for you. I'm sorry."

Emma nodded, her eyes radiant. "It was, and I'm ashamed to say that my old temper took over before I could stop it, Simon. I felt betrayed by you, but at the same time I felt embarrassed that I didn't know the truth, that I hadn't guessed it all along. Here I was thinking I was doing such an important job by protecting you, and I really wasn't doing anything at all." She explained about her hasty retreat to come and find him after that.

Simon silently thanked the Lord for this wonderful woman. "I have no doubt that you have been the biggest asset in keeping Charles safe through all this, Emma. I don't blame you for being angry when you heard the truth about me, and I'm very thankful that you're not angry now." He smiled.

"I'm so glad Charles got through it safely too and can now testify."

"Speaking of Charles, I have some good news for you too. I managed to meet Tyler occasionally to check up on how Charles, or should I say 'Uncle Vern' was doing, and he told me that Charles had finally accepted the Lord."

Before Emma could open her mouth to speak her delight, Simon continued, "It was Eddie who finally got through to him!"

"Eddie? But he's only three!"

"I know. It seems Tyler and Jade and the other believers in Grandville all wanted to talk to Charles, but they didn't want to bombard him with the Bible; they wanted to let him come to them when he was ready. You know how some people can feel like they're being ganged up on if too many people witness to them too often? Well, it seems that they were being overly cautious because Charles told them later that he was afraid to bring up the subject since they wouldn't."

"One day he was sitting in Jade and Tyler's parlor reading from the Bible and Eddie happened by. He had become quite fond of his Great-uncle Vern, so he just climbed up on Charles's lap and asked him,

"What are you reading, Uncle Vern?"

"I'm reading the Bible, Eddie. Would you like me to read to you?"

"Yes, please. Read the part about Paul and the 'Flipping Jailer'."

"Who?"

"It's in Acts. I know because I can say the verse in Acts 16:31. Want to hear it?"

"Eddie quoted the verse to Charles, word-perfect. Charles was able to find the reference and read the entire chapter. Jade found the two of them later when she was hunting for Eddie and was able to finish leading Charles to the Lord right there when he told her he wanted to know more. He said when he realized a child like Eddie could understand the Gospel and believe it, that certainly he could place his faith in it as well."

Emma smiled in delight. "And is Charles really safe now in Washington?"

"Yes and the best part is that after he's done there, he wants to return to Grandville. He's become quite fond of the people as well as Pastor Malcolm's preaching at the church. Oh, and by the way, he wants to see you again too."

Emma tilted her head to question her husband.

"I guess he wants to thank you for all you've done."

"Thank me?" Emma shook her head. "He had me fooled as well."

They reached Grandville and went directly to the hotel. It was some time later, after catching up with Buck and Lucy and Tyler and Jade and all the family news, as well as a retelling of their own adventures before Emma and Simon were alone once again in one of the hotel rooms.

Simon had to only mention once that Emma needed rest after her ordeal and all the others willingly agreed and let them go.

Emma lay back on the bed feeling exhaustion creep over her. She was unwilling to give in to it, however, for Simon was finally by her side once again and they had so much to discuss.

"It was really Charles, then, wasn't it?" she began. "I feel like a fool, Simon."

Simon stretched out on the bed beside Emma and put his arms around her. "You are not a fool, sweetheart. You did everything you were supposed to do and you did it very well. I owe you an apology." He paused, searching for the right words.

"As my wife, you had the right to know everything there was to know about my life and my work, but I let you believe a lie. Believe me, Emma, I didn't want to deceive you and I didn't mean to. I just thought it might be safer for Charles if you continued to think that *I* was the target instead of him. I know now that that was wrong. I knew I could trust you, but somehow I couldn't tell you. Then when we went to Boston there seemed to be no need to bring it up."

He brushed her hair back so he could see her face better. "I never expected to have to leave and to be gone for so long. I couldn't tell you by wire what I was doing." He sighed deeply. "There were times that I wondered if you would ever be able to love me or trust me again."

Emma knew Simon was waiting for her reply. She turned to face him.

"Simon, I *was* angry. I can't deny that. I felt like you and my father and anyone else who knew didn't trust me at all. Me—your wife! I was angry at all of you. Then when I was with the Findleys, they said something that made me stop and think. They said that *my* actions were what convinced them that you were their man, not Charles."

Emma searched Simon's expression. "If you had told me everything, Simon, I might have given Charles away without even knowing it. I think not telling me was probably the best thing you could have done."

Simon's features relaxed, and he pulled his wife closer to him. "What happened to that terrible temper? I was expecting an all-out argument, not forgiveness."

Emma laughed. "I've learned to depend more on the Lord, Simon. There I was in Boston, a strange city with a new family and no husband and only a lot of questions. I found myself turning to the Lord more and more, and letting go of my anger seemed a natural, or maybe I should say 'a supernatural' result. However…"

Simon raised his head.

Emma laughed again at the expectant look on his face. "However, my dear husband, I think we may have to discuss the future." She patted her rounded front.

Simon's features softened, and he placed his hand over hers. "Those months I was away got me thinking too, Emma. I never want to be away from you like that again. Never!"

She smiled at the vehemence in his voice while she nodded her head in agreement. "It was much too long."

"I don't want you to have to raise our children alone, Em. I believe both the mother and father need to be involved, so I've given some thought to changing my vocation."

Emma was surprised. "Don't you love what you're doing, Simon?"

"I love *you*, Emma. And I think the Lord has brought me to you and to this place all for a reason. The detective work was what I wanted in the past. Now that I have you, I see a different future ahead for us."

Emma pulled away and sat up on the bed. She was confused and looked it. "Simon, I don't want you to have to change everything in your life for me. I want you to be happy and—"

Simon stilled her words with his fingers over her lips. "I've never had an interest in my father's shipping business; it always seemed boring and too much paperwork for my liking. But I can see now how we could send products from the northwest out east by rail and then my father's company could ship them anywhere in the world. He's always looking for new goods, and with the lumber and fur and cattle and wheat and mining there are more than enough things to keep me busy here part of the year and in Boston part of the year.

"How about it, Emma? Could you live near my family part of the time in Boston? We could show our children what life in the East is like. We could teach them about our history and expose them to culture and my mother's spoiling."

Emma smiled thoughtfully.

"And the other part of the time we can raise them here in Norris, Grandville, and Sand Creek. We can let them run free on the ranch and teach them how to work hard, how to hunt and track, and let them grow up with their cousins and know the love of family and the love of God."

Simon gazed at his wife. "Emma, you've followed me wherever I've led you so far. Will you walk beside me and follow wherever the Lord leads us next?"

Emma swallowed and blinked back the happy tears that were forming in her eyes. "Yes Simon." Then she smiled. "I think I know of a little place near Norris that would be perfect for starters."

Simon grinned back. "We'll probably have to clean the cabin all over again, and this time Charles won't be there to help."

Suddenly Simon drew back, a startled expression on his face. "Emma! Baby Gertrude just moved!"

Chapter 29

North of Norris

Emma moved about the small cabin preparing supper and humming happily to herself. She glanced out the window occasionally, watching for Simon to return from town. The winter days darkened early, and she hoped he would return before he found himself traveling dark roads. Her enlarged form made her movements clumsy, but Emma didn't mind. She patted her rounded front that housed the baby inside her, smiling that soon she would know whether it was a girl or boy.

The little bedroom where Charles slept was now prepared for the nursery. Simon had hand crafted a small cradle, and Emma had been busy fashioning baby clothes and making blankets. Life was so good! She felt a push on her rib cage and paused in her movements a few seconds until the pressure passed.

"I know, little one. I'm impatient for you to arrive too."

She heard the bells on the sleigh before she saw it come into the yard, and she waited with anticipation for Simon to unharness the horse and take care of things in the barn before coming in for his supper. The venison roast, potatoes, and carrots were simmering nicely, sending off a tantalizing aroma throughout the room. A pumpkin pie sat cooling nearby. How thankful she was now for the garden she had put in months earlier! She and Simon had been reaping the benefits ever since they moved back into the small cabin, this time truly as man and wife.

Emma bent to put another log on the fire. Simon would be cold from his trip.

She heard him stomp his feet as he came up the porch steps, and she turned, eager to greet him. She would never tire of seeing him come home, and she knew from the look on his face as he entered the cabin that he felt the same about greeting her.

Simon held Emma close and kissed her before shrugging out of his coat. Emma could see that he had news but she waited, happy just to see him and take care of him. She hung his coat on a peg in the wall.

"Hungry?" she asked.

"Starving! But let me warm up a bit first. That wind has a bite to it tonight." He sniffed the air. "Sure smells good in here. Glad I married a woman who can cook," he teased. He rubbed his hands together near the fire then sat down. "Have we time before supper to talk?"

"Of course." Emma slid the pot to the back of the stove and joined Simon. She sat down awkwardly because of the baby. Her knitting was nearby, but she didn't pick it up as she normally did when they were visiting. She watched Simon intently, anxious to hear his news.

"I have letters," he announced.

Emma smiled in delight. "Who are they from?"

"I have one from your parents." He pulled an envelope from a vest pocket. "I have one from my parents." He pulled out another.

Emma could see more mail peeking out of his vest. "Simon, stop teasing me! Who else?"

"Well, there's one here from Tyler and Jade." He slowly pulled out another envelope, but Emma couldn't wait any longer. She snatched the other mail from inside Simon's vest and held it out of his reach when he tried to grab for it.

"Not fair, Emma!" He laughed.

Quickly Emma scanned the remaining mail. "Oh, there's one from Charles!" she exclaimed. "But who is this?" She paused as she examined the official-looking missive. She looked at Simon in astonishment. "It's from Mr. Pinkerton, and it's addressed to *me*."

"I know." Simon was enjoying his wife's surprise.

"What is it about?"

"You'll have to open it, dear. I can't tell you what it's about until it's opened." Simon chuckled at her perplexed expression.

"You open it!" She handed it to him.

"It's not mine. You open it." He tossed it back to her.

Emma turned the envelope over and studied it. "I can't imagine what Mr. Pinkerton would write to me." She carefully opened it and slid the single sheet of paper out. She unfolded it and began to read silently while Simon watched.

A smile played on her lips, and when she finished reading she looked up at Simon with a sparkle in her eyes.

"You aren't going to believe this. Mr. Pinkerton has named me an official Pinkerton detective and awarded me a commendation that will be in my record for outstanding service. And guess what else, Simon! There is reward money for the capture of the counterfeiting ring leader, and we get a portion of it!"

"I know." Simon pulled another envelope from the other side of his vest. "I got a letter too."

"Simon! You tricked me!" Emma laughed with her husband. "Mr. Pinkerton also writes that he knows I am officially retired from the agency and that it was an honor to have had me on his staff. Wasn't that sweet?" She folded the letter and set it aside while she reached for the one from Charles.

"Would you like to read this one?" she asked.

"No, please, go ahead. I like watching you." Simon grinned as Emma eagerly opened the next letter. She read the entire letter out loud as Simon listened, a wide smile spreading over his face.

"Say, that's great news! Not only did Charles testify and put the leader in jail, but he also was able to help them ferret out other men in top positions who were defrauding the government. Charles is the real hero in all this. I don't suppose we'll ever realize what he's had to give up in order to see justice served. It will be good to have him living in Grandville after this. When did he say he would be coming? Can we eat now?"

Emma laughed as she rose to her feet. "He's coming in the spring. I'm so happy for him! He didn't mention it, but I believe he also will be receiving some of the reward money."

She began dishing up their meal while Simon helped her put the food on the table. "I've been wondering…I know all the people involved in the counterfeiting have been caught, but did they ever recover the gold that was swindled?"

Simon seated her before sitting down himself. "Let's pray," he said. They gave thanks then Simon answered, "No. They were able to get some of the gold back, but a lot of it had already disappeared, whether they hid it or spent it, I don't know. It's a shame, but by capturing those involved, they've sent a message to future criminals that crimes will not go unpunished."

Emma nodded in agreement. "And to think that by God's grace we were a part of it!" She laughed. "I never thought I would have so many adventures when I set out for Grandville last spring to work in Buck and Lucy's hotel. I remember telling my brother Abel that I wanted to go places and see things before I settled down. Well, I certainly got my wish!" She looked lovingly at Simon. "I think being married to you is the best adventure of all, and only the Lord knows what will be in store for us in the future."

Then an odd look came over her face and she set her fork down and gripped the edge of the table. "Simon! I think it's time!"

The twins were born on a cold day in February. Simon was delighted that Trudy would have her mother's blue eyes and blonde hair. As for Troy, Emma laughingly proclaimed that his fuzzy head and red face kind of reminded her of Hermit Jack.

For more information about
A Newly Weds Series or
author Margo Hansen, visit her at
www.margohansen.com.

Margo would enjoy hearing
from her readers. Send your
comments or questions to
margo@margohansen.com.

Other books by Margo Hansen

Sky's Bridal Train   *Jade's Courting Danger*

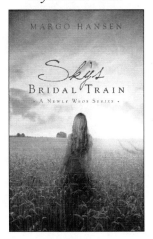